The Left-Hand Path: Apostate

T.S. Barnett

The Left-Hand Path: Apostate

T.S. Barnett

Pensacola, FL

Cover Art by Jake Clark
jcalebdesign.com

Corvid House Publishing
Dark Urban Fantasy and Science Fiction Novels

Pensacola, FL
www.corvidhousepub.com

ACKNOWLEDGMENTS

I hope everyone who reached the end with me can take a little bit of Nathan with them.

1

Bloodied hands gripped the steering wheel, squeezing tight to keep the car between the lines. Every cough swerved the tires toward the edge of the road, and Nikita's ribs heaved as he fought to take in air through clenched teeth.

Moore had gotten the drop on him. Poisoned him. And Nikita's wards had been useless. Broken and stepped over. He needed to be smarter. Better. He needed to be better.

When another racking cough ran the wheels of his rental into the grass, he slammed to a stop along the side of the highway. He threw the car into park and crawled over the passenger seat to fling open the door. His palms and knees hit the ground as he fell from the car, his lungs burning and fresh blood warm on his lips. Nikita wiped at his chin and pulled to his feet, stumbling toward the trees and patting the pockets of his jacket.

Stupid. Should have been more prepared. Left too many things behind.

His wet fingertips found the chunk of hematite in his breast pocket, and he pushed the rough stone into his mouth and laid his hands flat against the trunk of the first tree he could reach. With his jaw set, he took slow breaths, shoulders shaking as he bit back another round of coughs. The bark beneath his hands softened and darkened, black stains creeping from his skin and up the body of the tree. The trunk blackened in even flows with each exhale, bark creaking and cracking as the poison seeped upward. Dark, shriveled leaves began to drop from the branches above him, taking with them the bitter fluid filling his lungs. A chirping birdsong cut short, and the pair of black bodies fell into the brush at his feet.

Nikita took a deep breath with clear lungs and let his hands drop from the withered tree, then spit the black stone back into his palm. He wiped the sleeve of his jacket over his mouth to clean away the remaining blood and started back through the grass toward the car.

He couldn't keep making the same mistakes. He'd let his guard down after waiting for so many days in that motel—and he'd allowed Moore to sneak up on him. This was the last time Nikita would underestimate him.

He needed sleep—but before that, he needed a svyato mesto. A place of power. The Magister hadn't stopped calling to ask about Nikita's progress with Willis. And he and Moore together were a threat Nikita wouldn't face again. They needed to be separated—and that meant giving the former Chaser something more important to do.

Nikita shut the driver's side door behind him and flexed his fingers on the steering wheel, allowing his head to fall back against the seat. He breathed slowly, listening past the rise and fall of the engines that rushed by him on the road. The pull was always faint, and it was easy to lose focus. But the prickling in Nikita's skin was unmistakable. He lurched the car back onto the highway and drove.

The trees were thick even close to the edge of the river. Nikita had abandoned his car along the side of the road and walked the quarter mile or so toward the bank, drawn deeper by the trembling sensation in his bones. Across the river, cars idled by, and people went in and out of the grocery store or the gas station visible in the distance. Across the river, people lived—but here, under Nikita's feet, there had been death. He could see it just as clearly as if the blood still stained the rocks. This was the place.

He stripped his suit jacket from his shoulders and left it in the grass, sparing a moment to pick his damp shirt away from the sweat on his back and roll up his long sleeves. Pale eyes scanned the brush between the trees as his fingers worked the knot of his tie loose. There was enough space.

His body was still weak from Moore's curse, but he didn't have time to spare. So he moved to the center of the largest nearby clearing and slid the tie from his collar, instead drawing the black silk across his eyes and knotting it at the back of his head. He took one more breath, and then he moved—two steps forward, then a turn, and two steps backward, hands held lightly out at his sides—slow progress drawing the outline of a circle in the earth. Beneath his feet, the ground changed—soft grass wilted and hardened, leaves withered, and a ring of black formed his path as he traced the circle once, twice, thrice. Heat filtered up his legs and into his chest, waking up his aching limbs and weary heart. The static in the air grew into painful needles on his bare arms, and he slowed to a stop facing the center of the ring he'd made.

"Иди ко мне," he said, fingers spread wide over the blackened grass. "Посетите своего нового мастера. Бес," Nikita finished, and he dug his heels into the ground, bracing against the drag that threatened to haul him into the center. The hot summer air rushed over him, but he stood firm, fighting the pull with teeth clenched and shoulders hunched. When the force let him loose, he almost stumbled, swaying on his feet until he found his balance at the edge of the circle. Ahead of him, something breathed, and light footsteps moved the brush below.

Nikita stood up straighter and extended his hand, reaching forward until he touched the smooth snout of the creature he'd called. He heard its low, deep nicker, and he traced its narrow jaw with his fingertips, following the line of its hard skull and down into the rough fur at its neck. The creature twisted its head, sharp teeth biting into Nikita's wrist in protest, but he clenched his hand and pulled, grasping the thick straps of binding cloth that lashed around the animal's face at his gesture. The lead burned into his hand, seeming to sink beneath the skin to better fasten his grip, but he didn't flinch.

"Повинуйся," he said simply, holding tight against the creature's thrash. "You belong to me now, and you will fulfill your use." He tugged the animal closer to him, allowing its damp breath to touch his cheek. "I have someone for you to find."

By the time Elton approached the parking lot of the motel, it had already been blocked off by police cars and ambulances. A number of people stood at the perimeter of the scene, assisting what appeared to be a collection of tourists all seated on the curb or lying on gurneys and struggling to breathe.

"Well," Cora sighed beside him, "I guess he's been here." She leaned across Elton to get a better look out the driver's side window. "But where is he now? I don't see Korshunov."

"We must have missed them. I don't see any structural damage; that's something."

"Yeah, great." She dropped back into her seat and checked her cell phone again, but there were still no new messages on the screen—only the ones she'd sent to Nathan without answer for the past three hours. "Any suggestions, Mr. Chaser? If we keep just seeking him like this, we'll always be behind."

"It's been a while since he hasn't been chasing me back," Elton admitted. He took his phone from the cupholder and turned on the screen, giving it a few taps with a growing frown on his face. He let out a small snort and dropped it again in favor of scowling out the windshield toward the parking lot.

"He hasn't texted you either?"

"No. His phone isn't even on." He gestured vaguely toward his own sitting in the console between them. "He's still not showing up."

"Showing up? What do you mean, showing up?"

"A couple of months ago, we had to get new phones, remember? Because he dropped his and then mine out the RV window trying to take a picture of a dog in a truck bed to send you."

She snorted. "I never heard the why, but yeah, I remember."

"When I was setting them up, I added him to my account as a child, so that I could track his phone."

Cora stared at him. "You put parental controls on Nathan's phone?"

"No," he said sharply. "I just made it so that I could see where he was. For just this sort of situation, in fact," he pointed out. "But he must have let it die again. I told mine to notify me when it turns on again, but until then—" He shrugged. "At least he's still not covering his tracks. And we know what he's after."

"But I can't find Korshunov, either!" She pushed at the bag at her feet with her toe, glaring at her mirror through the canvas. "What good is this crap if I can't see things that matter?"

"Don't start," Elton warned. "You see plenty, and you know it. This is Nathan we're talking about. And Korshunov isn't someone to take lightly, either," he finished grimly.

"So we just follow the bodies and hope we catch up?" Cora frowned down at her phone and squeezed it tight against her chest as if willing it to make a sound. "I don't want him to be alone right now."

"I know." Elton pulled the car away from the parking lot entrance and started down the road back toward the highway. "Nathan is...capricious. Korshunov might be easier to predict, and if we find one, we'll find the other. He's laid traps for Nathan before. So he's probably planning to hole up somewhere else until he thinks he can get the upper hand again. If we keep moving every time they stop, then we'll get to them."

"Well, I've never tried divination on the go before, but I'll give it a shot."

While Elton drove, turning his willow token almost idly in his fingers—he doubted the chances of finding Nathan this way were great—Cora sat cross-legged in the back seat with her mirror in her lap. She huffed in frustration a few times but was mostly silent, until almost an hour had gone by. Then she stuffed the black stone back into her bag and slumped over the passenger seat as Elton pulled off the road into a gas station.

"There's no way," she muttered. "With the car moving, and stuff going by outside...it's no good. And I can't exactly light a candle in here. I'm useless."

"If you need to be somewhere quiet, we'll find you somewhere quiet," Elton promised. He opened the door and climbed out, but she rolled down the back window to keep talking to him.

"And what about staying moving whenever they stop? We can't stay moving if my dumb ass has to sit still to do anything."

Elton pushed the nozzle into the gas tank and stared flatly at her. "Are you done putting yourself down yet? What would Nathan say?"

She paused with her elbows on the door and let her chin rest on her folded arms. "He'd tell me to quit it," she answered in a reluctant grumble.

"You're perfect and powerful, my love, and you mustn't ever doubt it," Elton said in a poor mockery of Nathan's lilting voice, but when he realized Cora was watching him with barely-restrained mirth, he turned his face pointedly back to the gas pump and gave a small cough. "Something like that."

"Well, anyway," she went on with a smile, "if I need peace and quiet to do this, it's not the most helpful thing right now. So what do we do?"

"We have to change the way we're thinking," the blond murmured. "Chasers only ever caught up to Nathan when he let them. So, clearly, chasing is the wrong approach."

"Except you *did* find him," Cora pointed out.

"After he was on an oxygen tank," Elton scoffed. "Also, worth noting that it took me ten years and cost me my marriage."

"Even so!" she went on, undeterred. "You said you tracked down someone he knew, right? That's, like, detective work. So can we...you know, detect?"

Elton didn't answer; when the nozzle clicked off, he slid it back into place and sat behind the wheel again. He sat for a moment or two, looking down somewhere past the dashboard, and then reached forward to turn the key in the ignition. "Maybe."

Under Cora's guidance, Elton found his way to a small, teal-painted building on a quiet street near the outskirts of Utica. He pulled off into the alley driveway, the only parking available, and tilted his head toward the door. The shopfront had a single, dark window shielded by bars, and the bright orange door was missing a lot of paint. Even the sign above the window was barely legible. "This is the place?"

"I mean..." Cora trailed off, leaning forward to peer out the windshield at the broken shingles making up the shop's dilapidated awning. "Does this *not* look like a place Nathan would shop?"

"Point taken," Elton agreed. He pushed open the car door and stepped out, waiting for Cora to circle the car and join him before approaching to turn the store's rusty doorknob. He poked his head inside first, as if expecting something to drop on him, but the inside of the shop was as expected—a glass counter containing piles of bead jewelry, racks of candles and incense, a crowded bookshelf, and a sign by the register advertising psychic readings.

A man in his twenties looked over from where he was arranging some bundles of sage in a basket and offered them a welcoming smile with pierced lips. He didn't look like the usual kitschy new age shop owner—his jeans were torn at the knees, his Misfits shirt had lost its sleeves, and his dark hair fell messily into his face until he raked it back with fingers bearing a number of silver rings. It was a good sign they were in the right place, at least.

"Morning!" he called. "You two looking for anything particular?"

"Sort of," Elton answered. Cora lingered behind him as he approached, leaning around his shoulder to peer at the young man. The blond paused to glance around the shop, taking in the assortment of goods before he spoke again. "Do you carry ingredients for rootwork? Specialized ingredients, I mean. Not just herbs."

"Specialized?" the owner answered. He chewed one of the rings in the corner of his lip as his dark eyes flicked up and down Elton's frame as though sizing him up. Elton resisted the urge to sigh—this was what Nathan called his "cop face" working against him, he was sure. "Depends on what you're looking for."

"Anything gross, really," Cora piped up. "We're looking for a friend of ours, and we're just trying to find out if he passed through here or not. And he usually needs...pretty unusual stuff."

The man paused, frowning. He glanced between the pair, but before he could open his mouth again, Elton cut him off.

"Is this shop registered?" he asked, and the owner hesitated, then nodded when Elton folded his arms, subtly showing his hand to be lacking any silver rings.

"Sorry," he said. "It's hard to tell sometimes who's here on real business and who's not, you know? I mean, I might have guessed *you* didn't want a zodiac necklace, but..."

"Are you trying to say I look like a basic witch?" Cora interrupted, and the owner laughed as he stepped aside to make way for a younger man carrying a box.

"Sorry." He leaned over to wave a hand at the teenager, who had crouched by one of the shelves to restock a pile of white candles. "Hey," he called. "Didn't a guy come in late last night looking for sulfur?"

The boy looked up with his elbows on his knees and a wrinkle in his pierced brow. "Yeah," he said. "We didn't have it, so I sent him to Catherine."

"This guy," Cora cut in, "was he a white brunette, kind of flirty and dramatic?"

The teen snorted. "Yeah; he was about like that."

"Catherine owns a...more private shop down in Schenectady," the owner spoke up, drawing Elton's attention back to him. "I can give you the address."

Elton followed him to the counter and accepted the slip of paper he scribbled on with a nod of thanks.

"I hope you find him," the young man offered along with a kind smile.

"Thank you!" Cora called as they exited, returning the owner's brief wave. She took the paper from Elton and began to type the address into her phone on the short walk back to the car. "Dang; do I just have a thing for dudes who own witchy shops, or was he super cute?"

"I'm not a good judge," Elton admitted as he dropped back into the driver's seat.

"Anyway, Schenectady is a little over an hour away, this says, so I'm gonna need you to hook me up with some drive-through breakfast."

The blond chuckled softly. "That I can do."

2

Cora kept the window down during their drive—partly to feel the wind in her hair and partly to help blow out the smoke from Elton's cigarette. She hung one arm out of the car and leaned her head against her shoulder, but there was no chance of dozing off. Her stomach was too tight with worry. Nathan was out there on his own—grieving and angry. Why wouldn't he answer her? Didn't he trust them to help?

She puffed out a sigh and let her cheek smush a little harder into her arm. The scenery was nice, at least, since Elton had taken back roads through the country. He didn't have to tell her that it was smarter for them to keep laying low. She didn't mind—even if it was just farmland, it was at least a different view from the creepy woods she'd been staring at in Thomas's backyard for the last few months. If she let her mind wander, she could almost pretend it was a normal road trip. Elton had forsaken his usual suit jacket and tie, instead leaving a couple of collar buttons scandalously undone, and he had his pinstripe shirtsleeves rolled up to his elbows. The radio was on, and now and then they chatted and exchanged stories about the time they'd spent apart. Cora pulled one knee up under her in the seat and settled a little more comfortably. They'd find Nathan. They'd get all this sorted out. It would work out fine in the end. She had to believe that.

A small smile touched her lips as she spotted a rooster standing on a wooden fencepost ahead of them, but as they drew close, it reared back its head to crow—and let out a series of vicious barks.

Cora lifted her head and turned to watch the animal as they passed it, both hands on the car door and a frown on her lips. When she lost sight of the bird, she looked back at Elton.

"You heard that, right?"

The blond had his eyes on the rearview mirror. "Yeah."

"Is that...something we should worry about?"

He didn't answer. Cora tried to spot the rooster out the back window, but they were too far away now. A jerk of the car whipped her attention back to the road ahead, and she braced herself as Elton slammed on the brakes and narrowly avoided burying the front of the car in a ditch. Just a few feet in front of them, something stood in the center of the crossroads made by a dirt road passing between the fields. It stood on four clawed feet, like a dog, but its skinless head rose higher than the hood of the car—and its pair of curling antlers made it even taller. A long tail twitched on the ground near its feet, a tuft of grey fur brushing the dusty road and a line of sharp, visible vertebrae running all the way up to the creature's haunches. Thick, coarse fur gave it a dark mane, but the hair stopped where the skull began. Too many teeth overlapped in its long snout, and where it should have had eyes, there were only black holes. A red cloth had been fastened tight around its head like a bridle, straps tangling in the base of its antlers and hanging down from its jaw in tattered bits that dripped some dark, unidentifiable fluid.

Cora unfastened her seatbelt without taking her eyes off of the monster. This thing wasn't lost. It belonged to Korshunov—it had to. She'd been up close with enough of his pets to guess.

"We're going to have to handle that," she murmured, but when she flicked her eyes over to Elton, he hadn't moved. He sat stock still, cigarette burning between his fingers where they rested loosely on the steering wheel and gaze locked onto the animal ahead of them. She hissed at him, but got no response. He just looked straight ahead, seeming mesmerized by the empty stare of the creature. When she snapped his name, he finally turned to look at her—but his eyes were strange. Cora inched away as Elton unbuckled himself, his cigarette dropping to the floor of the car at his movement, and before she could get a good grip on the door handle, the blond had jerked forward, hands fixed around Cora's neck.

In a panic, she shoved at him and hit him, but Elton was much larger than her. She had no chance of moving him gently, and not much air to call out to him with, so she did the best thing she could think of— snapped her knee up as hard as she could into his crotch, threw open the car door, and fell backward onto the side of the road in the moment's reprieve his cringe gave.

"Sorry!" she said as she scrambled back and onto her feet. Elton didn't give her much time. He climbed out of the car with mechanical determination and reached for her again, taking hold of her arm and dragging her forward, but this time, Cora let herself be drawn close. She slapped her hand flat against his chest and shouted out, "Boule!"

Her palm grew hot against her friend's skin, burning a singing mark in the shape of her fingers through his shirt and into his flesh. Elton made a startled, choking sound, and his grip faltered.

"Wake the hell up!" she snapped at him, giving him a violent shove that sent him back against the side of the car. She risked turning her attention to the creature, which still stood silent and staring, its only movement in the faint drifting of the cloth hanging from its skull. Cora called out a spell to force the monster back, and it shifted on its feet as though she'd barely nudged it.

She jerked away on instinct when she felt Elton grab her hand, but he held firm and tugged her back toward the open car door.

"Get in, Cora!"

She did as she was told, following the blond as he slid back over the center console and into the driver's seat. She slammed the door shut behind her and held on when Elton put his foot on the gas.

"My book," he said, and she obeyed, snatching up his wallet of talismans from where it had fallen by her feet and offering it to him. His fingers barely touched the stack of papers before he picked out the one he wanted, and as the car veered around the edge of the dirt road and past the creature, he let the spell loose out Cora's open window. She turned to watch the talisman shoot through the wind in their wake and bury itself in the asphalt, instantly cutting a deep, wide circle around the monster's feet. Only then did it seem to respond—the animal reared back on its hind legs and pounded its front feet back to the ground, but it didn't move forward—the ring dug into the street had made a barrier around it, sealing it within a faintly shining green dome.

Elton sped down the country road so fast that the back tires skidded in gravel the next time he had to make a turn. Cora leaned across him and snapped his seatbelt into its latch for him, then did the same in her own seat. She kept turning to look behind them, and Elton's gaze flicked regularly to his mirrors.

Cora sat murmuring her seeking spell and touching the wood on her bracelet, the force of the creature's magic almost making her sick to her stomach—but it eventually began to fade. She allowed her shoulders to unclench and let out the breath she'd been holding in an attempt to be silent, but she didn't really relax until she saw Elton's grip loosen slightly on the steering wheel. His mouth pulled into a frown as he shifted in his seat without looking at her.

"Sorry I hit you in the dick," she offered as she bent to pick up and put out the still-burning cigarette rolling by her feet. "And burned you."

Elton grunted softly in acceptance. "I hope I didn't hurt you."

"Well, it wasn't the way I hoped you'd hold me down someday," she answered, leaning over onto his armrest with a grin that grew wider at his uncomfortable grimace. "It's fine. But what was that? The thing was just standing there, and you went nuts."

He shook his head. "I don't know," he admitted. "It felt like—being pulled. I was there, watching, but I wasn't moving my own body."

"So like, it was mind-controlling you? That's not okay."

"I guess it was. I've never seen an entity like that before."

"I haven't seen one that *looked* like that, but I've sure seen one that gave me the creeps like that—the spirit Korshunov had in the woods that night at the lake."

"It did seem similar somehow to the one guarding Maduro," Elton agreed. "And the way it looked like it was waiting—that isn't an accident."

Cora slouched in her seat and frowned down at her hands. "Before...at the lake, it seemed like he was controlling the...I don't know if it was a spirit or something more real than that or what. But it stopped holding me when I hurt Korshunov enough."

"But Korshunov wasn't *here*," Elton murmured. "Or he was hidden well enough that I couldn't feel him."

"What a prick, always getting those things to do his dirty work," Cora spat.

Elton gave a small grunt of agreement but didn't comment. "Let's just try to put distance between us and it, and find this shop."

"That's a solid plan. I like that plan."

Catherine's shop was even more of a hole in the wall than the previous place—but the other owner's directions were good. The woman said she had seen Nathan, and that he'd bought his sulfur and a few other ingredients but hadn't lingered. Cora wanted to ask if he'd seemed okay, but how would this person know? Nathan hadn't said anything about where he was going, either.

Cora shut the passenger door with a small, dejected huff, and she sat with her hands in her lap while Elton settled in the car beside her. Both of them were silent for a while, and Cora had to swallow down a small lump that began to form in her throat. They would find him. They would.

"Nathan is going to want somewhere to work, too," Elton finally said in a quiet, pensive voice. "Without his connection to Kalfu, he'll have to rely on his voodoo, and those spells take prep and time." His eyes narrowed faintly in thought as he stared down at the steering wheel. "We can assume he isn't going to go to New York, after all the complaining he did about it. But we are near to Boston." He glanced sidelong at the girl next to him. "Do you think he'd try to stay with Nock?"

Cora sat up a little straighter. "Hey, maybe! See? You're a detective after all."

"Let's see if I'm right before you heap on too much praise."

She leaned over and let her head drop sideways, dramatically close to his shoulder. "You're perfect and powerful, darling, and you mustn't ever doubt it."

"Mhm."

They reached Boston by the middle of the afternoon, and, luckily, Nock's shop was searchable online. Cora swung the glass door open and made for the back without waiting for Elton, and she squeezed her way by a man standing at a shelf full of robotic animals to reach the counter.

"Nock," she called, and the goblin woman disguised as a human looked up from the register. Her eyebrows lifted in surprise as she spotted Cora, but then she frowned and pointedly returned her attention to the woman waiting to pay. Cora waited with her heels bouncing impatiently, and as soon as the customer left, she rushed forward to take her place. "You remember me, right?" she said, even as Nock began to turn away again.

"Yeah, I remember you. What do you want?"

"Has Nathan been here?"

The goblin hesitated. She picked up a box from the counter and placed it on the back shelf before she answered. "No. Why?"

"He left us," Cora said. "And we're worried he's about to do something stupid."

Nock snorted. "That's different from any other day how?"

"Something exceptionally stupid," Elton added from behind Cora. "He's hunting a Chaser."

Nock put her hands on her hips and turned to stare at them. "That's not new, either."

Cora leaned against the counter and lowered her voice. "This Chaser killed his daughter and almost killed him. And he did something to his magic. Nathan's not thinking clearly."

"His—" The goblin stopped short and pressed her lips into a tight frown. She shook her head. "I haven't seen him."

The girl's shoulders slumped, and she leaned back against Elton in defeat. The blond put a steadying hand on her shoulder.

"If I leave my number, will you let us know if he shows up? He's been in the area, and we thought he might come here. We just don't want him to get himself killed."

"Sure," Nock answered curtly. She took the sticky note Elton wrote on and stuffed it into her jeans pocket, then seemed to have no more to say to them.

Elton let Cora pull away from him and lead the way from the shop, holding the door open for her on their way out.

"So much for that lead," she sighed.

"We'll think of something else."

She looked up at him with a furrow in her brow. "Let's find a hotel. I can keep looking if I have somewhere quiet."

Elton agreed, so they parked the car at a place nearby, and Cora registered them for a room paid for with a glamour. Elton didn't bother trying to argue; he had no money of his own to pay with and doubted Cora had much, either. She at least got them a normal room instead of a penthouse suite.

He checked his phone regularly for any notification from Nathan, but mostly sat still and quiet on the far bed, pretending he could focus on his book while Cora stared into her mirror. Occasionally the girl would murmur to herself, or sigh, but every attempt ended in frustration. Still, she didn't give up—she would get a glass of water or shake out her shoulders, then settle in to try again. Elton tried to make her stop to get something to eat, but she pushed him away and pulled a blanket over her head like a barrier.

Finally, Elton noticed her go still on the floor, and he rose from the bed to check on her. She'd laid down at some point, mostly hidden by blanket but with her fingertips still touching the smooth edges of the black obsidian. Even unsuccessful divination attempts must have been exhausting.

He gave a small, quiet sigh, and crouched down to gather the girl in his arms. His bad shoulder complained as he lifted the weight, but he ignored it and settled her on the bed. He pulled off her laced boots, arranged the blanket in a more traditional orientation and tucked it up around her, then left her to sleep.

3

Nikita needed supplies. He needed rest. He'd bought himself some time by summoning the Bies to keep Moore and Willis busy, but he needed to use it wisely. The closest Magistrate office was in Boston, so once he'd found his way back to the car and his hand had stopped shaking, he drove down the highway toward the city, weaving through traffic that traveled too slowly.

The office was easy to find—Nikita checked the marker activated by his ring at the Massachusetts State House and soon stood at the entrance of a seven-story building of pale stone, dark iron, and glass, each corner marked with carvings of stag heads and filigree. The engraved sign at the front named the building as office space for a bank, but when Nikita pushed on the door, the silver ring on his hand burned hot, and he was allowed to see the true interior.

Men and women of the Magistrate moved through the building, some carrying file folders, others escorting civilians to back hallways. The broad front desk sat front and center in the lobby, and the woman at the computer looked up at him with a smile that faltered as she took in the sight of him. Nikita knew what he must look like—dirty and tired with still-healing cuts on his face—but her startled expression didn't bother him. She didn't matter.

"I need a phone," he said simply. "Nikita Korshunov, out of Ottawa, Ontario. Registration number 8957624."

"Oh—of course," the woman said. She paused just long enough to verify his credentials on the computer in front of her, then smiled at him again. "Do you know the number, or do you need me to put you through to someone?"

"I need to talk to Magister Hubbard."

"Sure thing. One second."

Nikita stood to the side of the desk while she dialed, and once the receptionist had someone on the line, she offered him the phone's receiver. She frowned as her eyes focused on his burned hands, but he paid her no mind. He gave Hubbard's secretary his name and was put on hold just long enough for him to turn away from the desk.

A click sounded on the line, and Hubbard's voice came through the receiver. "You'd better have some damn good news for me, Nikita."

"Magister, I—"

"Since I've been keeping you housed and fed for the last *four months*," the Magister cut him off, "and you've given me absolutely nothing to show for it."

Nikita gripped the plastic so tight that it made his injured hand ache. "Sir—"

"So I desperately hope that you're calling me from the morgue where Willis and Moore are lying in a drawer."

"Sir," Nikita managed to get in, "Willis is as good as dead. And Moore is where I want him. It's just a matter of time."

"How *much time*, Nikita? You assured me you were the man for this job, and you haven't even been answering my calls. Did I put my trust in a boy who now finds himself in over his head?"

"No, sir," he ground out through a tight jaw.

Hubbard let out a long-suffering sigh. "Then why have you called me now, if not to tell me that it's finished?"

"I was put in a situation where I had to leave behind the majority of my supplies."

A beat of silence passed, and Nikita heard the soft creak of a chair. The next time the Magister spoke, his voice was lower. "Are you calling to ask for more money, you impertinent disappointment?"

"Sir, everything is under control," Nikita insisted. "I just need to replace—"

"You listen to me," Hubbard said sharply, silencing the young

Chaser. "This is the very last time I'm going to offer you this undeserved aid, do you understand? The next time I hear from you, it *will* be because you've succeeded, and because Moore and Willis are dead. And that call will be soon. Otherwise, I'm going to have you stripped of your license, shipped back to Ottawa in a crate, and locked in a basement under the cuimne until your brain comes out the other side as something *useful.* Am I making myself clear to you, Nikita?"

He swallowed down the rage threatening to bubble up through his teeth. "Yes, sir."

"Good. Now you wait there like a good boy, and I'll make arrangements with the staff where you are. Boston?"

"Yes, sir. Thank you, sir," he forced himself to add, then he passed the receiver back to the receptionist without looking at her. He waited near the desk, his hands balled into painful fists that almost shook with fury. He was better than this. He had to show them. Had to *be* better. Perfect. Show them. Be better. Be perfect. Prove it—

"Korshunov?"

Nikita looked up at the sound of the man's voice and forced his face into a more placid mask. He was handed an envelope and told it contained a small stipend of cash as well as a card he would be permitted to use for any supplies he might need. He gave the man a curt thank you and pushed the envelope into his jacket pocket on his way out the door. He pushed it open so hard that the glass gave a warning shake against the brace of the hinges as he passed through, and he bumped hard into a man on the sidewalk at the first step he took.

Without hesitation, Nikita grabbed the stranger by the shoulder and growled out a curse that snapped the collarbone under his thumb. He shoved the man away from him and didn't stop walking long enough to see him connect with the nearby wall.

He didn't have time to waste. Using the new credit card he'd been given, he bought himself a new cell phone, then a briefcase and a couple changes of clothes, and then he sought out a shop to resupply. He spat out a list of ingredients to the woman behind the counter and waited while she gathered his purchases. His hands ached. The sting of the lash binding the Bies was as sharp as if he still held the creature in front of him—and that wouldn't change until the creature was released from his service. Nikita could bear it. The pain was inconsequential.

Now he needed a place to stay. Close to somewhere sacred. Close to lots of people. Somewhere Moore might feel compelled to restrain himself, in case he found Nikita before he was ready.

He found a room just across from the Old North Church, and once he had the key, he dropped his briefcase and bags inside the door. Wards.

Nikita scratched markings into the walls near the door and windows. He found a sharp knife in the kitchen, stripped off his jacket, tie, and shirt, and cut long wounds into his forearm, letting the blood pool in his palm so that he could smear it at the edges of the doorframe, across the floor, and along the windowsill. He wet his lips between murmured incantations until he grew lightheaded from the blood dripping freely down his arm. It would be enough.

4

Nathan scowled, half-crouched in the narrow gap between buildings. He forced his attention to the vial of oil in his hand, rubbing the slick liquid into his fingertips before pressing them to the skin of the man at his feet. He winced and groaned at the pressure on his broken bone, and Nathan tutted at him.

"Quiet now. You'll still need to get this looked at."

"What the hell—"

"Shh, shh, shh." Nathan pulled another little bottle from his pocket and pressed it into the stranger's hand. "Drink that. And keep your mouth shut."

He straightened, leaning against the side of the building with one hand on the stone. A grim frown pulled at his lips as he watched Korshunov's back disappear down the street and around a corner. This boy deserved even more than Nathan planned to give him.

Leaving the confused reg behind on the sidewalk, Nathan wiped his oily hands on the thighs of his jeans and headed in the opposite direction. When he stood at the steps of Nock's apartment building, he paused to scuff out his cigarette under his boot, then made his way up to her floor. His legs felt heavy as he took the final few steps to her door, but he still had a smile on his face when she answered his knock.

"What the hell are you doing here?" she asked in place of a greeting.

"I need a place to stay, beloved. You wouldn't turn away a man in need."

"I absolutely would." She stood on tiptoe to cast a skeptical peer over his shoulder. "Where are all your friends?"

"Just me," he admitted. "Please. Just tonight, at least."

Nock pursed her lips while she considered, but after a moment's pause, she stepped back to let him in. "I have to go open the shop soon."

"I can manage on my own. I won't set anything on fire; I promise."

She shut the door and watched him drop his heavy bag near the sofa. "What happened to you? You look like shit."

"Hence the necessity for a quiet place to lay my head, beloved," Nathan murmured, already collapsing onto the sofa and letting his head fall back against the cushions with his eyes shut.

Nock crossed her arms and glared at him from the front hallway. "You promised last time you wouldn't bring me any trouble, Nathan."

"It's one I intend to keep. You've nothing to fear; everything is quite in order. I find myself in the city on business, and as soon as it's done, I'll be on my way."

"Business?" she snorted. "What, you've just got a big account coming in? Making a sale? Trading some fucking stocks?"

Nathan shook his head against the couch without opening his eyes, speaking over her as gently as possible. "Beloved, beloved—"

"Don't fucking 'beloved' me."

He sighed lightly and sat up to look at her properly. "Please. There's nothing worth concerning yourself with. I don't want to interfere with your day. I'll be quite fine here; go tend to your livelihood." He did his best to brighten his smile in the face of her scowl. "What time will you be done? I'll make sure there's dinner."

For a while, she stared at him without answering. She sucked one of her sharp bottom teeth and drummed her fingers on her bicep. "You're full of shit," she spat. "Fine. But if I get back here and there's magic shit all over my floor, I'm gonna throw you off the fire escape. Bad enough fucking Proctor ruined my spare room."

"Another debt I've yet to repay." Nathan stood and approached her, gently guiding her hands from their tight fold and running his thumbs over her knuckles. She glared at the floor instead of looking at him, but she allowed his touch. "I swear I'll do everything in my power to avoid provoking your defenestrating urges."

Nock snorted. "Fine, fine. I'll be back at six."

"You've no idea how much I appreciate you, beloved, nor is it within my capacity to satisfactorily convey."

"Oh shut up," she grumbled, shaking her hands free of his grasp. She grabbed her small canvas bag from its hook near the door and called one more warning over her shoulder before leaving him in the apartment.

As soon as the door closed, Nathan set about laying wards at every window and around the front door itself, double- and then triple-checking them until he was satisfied. Then he lifted his bag onto the couch, sat next to it, and began to spread his supplies across the coffee table. He carefully laid the personal concerns he'd gathered from Korshunov to one side, then focused on the small glass vial he'd taken from the boy's suitcase. He twisted off the simple black cap and raised the liquid remnants to his nose to take a slow, deep inhale. Mugwort. He tipped a drop onto his fingertip and touched it to his tongue. Definitely mugwort. And belladonna, and perhaps...amanita?

"Tricky little bird," Nathan murmured. "This is how you've been keeping such a good eye on me, isn't it?"

He gave the little bottle a long, pensive stare. A mixture like this would certainly help with the sort of projection the Chaser had been managing—but to use it so effectively was still a feat Nathan had to give the boy credit for. He looked down at the vial for a minute longer before tipping it to his lips to swallow a mouthful. It was worth a try. You were never too old to learn new tricks.

Nathan settled on the sofa and shut his eyes, waiting for the tonic to seep into his blood. He tried to focus on moving his vision out of his body, the way he'd been told this sort of thing was done—but all at once, his stomach rejected the potion so violently that his mad scramble to the bathroom almost wasn't enough to keep his promise to Nock. Thankfully, all of his vomit ended up in the toilet, but it was a close call. He sat on the bathroom floor a moment or two before crawling up to the sink to rinse his mouth and spit the last of the mixture's taste down the drain. That hadn't exactly gone as planned. Maybe best to give up on divination entirely. Cora was gifted in it, at least—

He stopped, letting water drip from his chin as he reached to turn off the faucet. Cora wasn't here. Only he was here. And he had powders to mix.

The building Korshunov had chosen was old, but well kept; an appropriate companion to the aging church across the street. Nathan stood on the sidewalk near the front door, looking up at the window while he took a long drag from his cigarette. This little bird thought he could hide away. But as long as Nathan had his track—the dirt taken from his footprint outside the motel—there wasn't anywhere he could go that Nathan couldn't follow.

He flicked away the butt of his cigarette and pulled open the door to the entryway, making his way with an easy pace up the stairs and down the hall to the warded door. He reached the apartment Korshunov hid inside and stopped, laying his fingertips lightly against the door. Heavily warded. Strong, but not strong enough.

Nathan took a deep, quiet breath with his eyes on the dark wood. Silent inside. It would be so easy to end it now. To string Korshunov up, pull out his guts, and leave him hanging from the roof like a trophy of war. He stepped closer and let his forehead touch the door, the thrum of magic tingling under his skin.

Not yet. Not quite yet.

He pulled a paper sachet from his pocket and gently shook the powdered contents into his palm. With his lips almost touching the door, Nathan whispered, barely breathing, "Moutre l 'sa li te pran nan men m'." He ran his fingers along the narrow gap near the door's hinges, then lifted his palm and blew the fine powder through the crack. He hesitated a moment more with his eyes on the door, then gave a small snort, tucked his thumbs into the pockets of his jeans, and started back to Nock's apartment.

He cleaned up after himself, as promised, then took a fitful nap on the couch. Sleep hadn't been easy to come by for days. He forced himself back up and into the kitchen to search Nock's cabinets for dinner ingredients, and by the time she came back through the door, he was almost finished cooking a simple curried chicken and rice. Nathan welcomed her home with a smile and a kiss to her green cheek that she grudgingly allowed, but he could feel her eyes on him while he set two full plates on the table and poured two glasses of the wine he'd found open on the counter—an inexpensive red, so not ideal, but not bad. He pulled her chair out for her and took his place across the small dining table, all the while ignoring her pointed stare.

"So are you going to tell me what's up?" she said without touching her spoon, her elbows leaned heavily on the table.

"I thought I already had," Nathan answered easily. "I have a few things I need to do here, but I'll be on my way shortly."

"That's not telling me what's up," Nock shot back. She sucked at one sharp tooth and tilted her head at him. "Your two friends came to the shop asking after you today. The Chaser and the girl."

He hesitated, taking a moment to swallow his mouthful and keeping his eyes on his plate. "And what did you tell them?"

"Nothing. I figured you showed up here alone, so that's how you wanted to be."

Nathan let out a small snort of amusement. "You know me too well, beloved. Thank you." He paused again before looking back up at her. "What did they have to say?"

Nock watched him with a furrow in her brow. "Nothing," she said, more quietly. "Just that they were worried about you. So tell me why."

"I'm not sure how you expect me to say—"

"Don't bullshit me, Nathan," she snapped, dropping her fist heavily onto the undeserving table. "You think you can just show up here and I'm not going to be able to tell there's something wrong with you? Give me a break." She softened, just a little. "Talk to me."

"I'm *fine*, beloved," he assured her. "Ready for a deep sleep, warm under the blanket beside you—"

"Keep dreaming."

Nathan gave a mournful sigh. "So cruel."

"Don't change the subject."

He watched her carefully for a few beats, then set down his spoon. "Nock, please. May I stay the night or may I not?"

"Of course you can, but—"

"Then I'll excuse myself," he cut her off, already standing. "Good night." He grabbed up his bag on his way to the spare room and shut himself inside, ignoring the sharp way the goblin called his name. He took a deep breath once he was alone and set his bag at the bottom of the futon. A pillow still sat on top of a neatly folded blanket at one end, clearly left behind from when Thomas Proctor had been a guest.

Nathan sat at the edge of the worn mattress and laced his fingers between his knees, his unfocused gaze somewhere between them and the floor. He waited, listening distantly to the clearing of dishes and the passing of footsteps that lingered by his door before moving on. Once the apartment was silent, he rose, taking packets and jars from his kit and arranging them on the floor. He ground the star anise, althaea, and acacia to a powder, then mixed them with myrrh resin and formed them into a rough incense, which he lit in its bowl and set aside. He stole silently to the kitchen and borrowed a large bowl, filled it with water, and shut himself back in the spare room, crouching on the floor in front of his fresh basin. After adding a few drops of Florida Water, he carefully unwrapped the fresh acacia branch he'd tucked away in his bag, dipped the long leaves into the basin, and circled the room, leaving drops of water in a large ring around the place where he would sleep.

"Talk to me, kè mwen," he whispered. "Show me you're free. Show me this boy isn't keeping you. Please." He left the leaves free to float on the surface of the water and sat down on the futon again with a soft sigh. He pulled off his boots and curled up on the futon without bothering to lower it down into a bed, his arms wrapped around the pillow only half tucked under his head. He kept his eyes on the faintly drifting leaves for as long as he could, until his eyelids finally drooped closed, and he fell into a less than restful sleep.

The sunlight pouring through the workshop window woke him when it reached his eyes, and he cringed against the intrusion and threw an arm over his face to block out the offensive rays.

Nothing. For the third night in a row, Nathan had cast the spell that should have allowed the dead to visit him in his dreams. For the third night in a row, he'd called to Adelina. Asked her for some sign. And for the third night in a row, he'd been disappointed.

He sat up on the futon, rubbing at his eyes with the balls of his hands, and twisted his back to crack his spine. That was that, then. Korshunov really had trapped her inside his token somehow. That meant it was time to get serious.

5

Nikita barely had the strength to pull himself from his bed the next morning. He'd hardly slept. He made coffee, but the liquid turned rancid in his mouth. The taste made him retch, and he'd spat it out and poured the rest down the drain. Even water tasted sour, and no matter how much he forced down, his throat still felt dry and tight. He sat on the kitchen floor, as still as possible, for hours. Any movement created a lurch of nausea in his stomach. What was this? His wards hadn't been breached, and the door hadn't been broken into.

He looked down at his hands, fingertips trembling lightly. Burst blisters still flaked the reddened skin all the way up to his elbows, the still-unhealed scars left by the oil he'd used to strip Moore of his magic. The mark around his right hand and wrist had darkened, scratched with deep red lines as though squeezed by the invisible binding of the Bies. The burn remained, so the Bies hadn't been destroyed. And it hadn't yet returned to him, which meant it was still on the hunt. But no spirit had ever made him this sick before. This was something else. It had to be Moore. Somehow.

Nikita pushed slowly to his feet, his insides protesting as he steadied himself on the kitchen counter. He couldn't be stopped by something like this. Pain didn't mean anything. He took a gulp of air and forced himself across the room to his briefcase on the coffee table, flipping the latch and throwing open the lid. His hands fumbled with the cap of one of his jars, and he cursed at himself as he twisted it open.

This couldn't stop him. Moore would be dead soon, and it would be Nikita who did it. There was no other way for this story to end. Hubbard thought he was useless. His instructors at the Academy had watched him with wary eyes, and his classmates had whispered and skirted hallways to avoid crossing his path. He would be better than he'd been. Better than them. He would prove he was better.

He spilled barberry oil on the carpet as he tried to lift the stopper to his mouth. The foul droplets that made their way onto the underside of his tongue made his skin crawl, and his fingers struggled to fasten the cap back into place. It didn't have to be easy. None of this was supposed to be easy.

Nikita folded over on the couch with his arms gripped tightly around his legs, fighting to breathe steadily. Somewhere in the back of his mind, a child hiccupped with tears on his face, a stinging handprint swelling the meat of his cheek.

"Living your life is not like crossing a meadow," his grandmother snapped at him. "Life is hard—none of it is easy." Nothing was ever easy. Nothing you wanted was going to come easy. Suffer for it. Push through. Persevere. Don't show weakness. You are koldunya. You are not some hedge witch boiling roots.

He lifted his head and took another slow breath, pale eyes skimming the perimeter of the room. With another push, he rose to his feet, shoving the coffee table to the far wall to clear a space. He would fix this. He had to. No one else was going to do it for him.

Nikita forced his unsteady hands to work, placing a circle of small stones in the place he'd made in the center of the living room. He swallowed down another glassful of putrid water, failing to ease the rough scraping as each breath moved down his throat, and filled a large basin from the cabinet. Careful to avoid bumping his pebbles, he placed the bowl at the center of the circle, stripped off his clothes, and fell to his knees in front of the basin. He held himself up on his hands, watching the soft ripples on the surface of the water. A droplet of sweat rolled down his jaw to his chin, but he reached up a hand to catch it before it could touch the pure water below him.

"Mat Syra Zemlya," he whispered, planting his hand back firmly on the floor to keep himself from falling. The water stilled in its basin, and

Nikita curled his fingers against the carpet. "I submit to the dawn, to the red maiden, to the damp earth. I ask her mercy."

Magic rumbled under his knuckles, sending subtle vibrations up the injured flesh of his arms. The threads of carpet at the far end of the circle he'd made began to split, as though torn at the seams by a knife.

"I arise her servant, and go from door unto door, gate to gate, to the empty fields," he went on, pausing to swallow down a rush of nausea.

The crack in the floor broke wider as bursts of dark soil began to pour through. The black earth spilled like water through the break, building upon itself until it towered over him almost to the ceiling.

His throat constricted in protest at its use, and his voice came out as little more than a rasp, but he continued. "Subdue and wash away from your servant all evil. Engulf the unclean power in your boiling pits, in your burning fires."

Nikita's shoulders tensed as he inched backward to rest his weight on his heels. He didn't raise his eyes to the figure forming above him, but he felt the press of its magic and heard the soft crumbling of the earth rising and building together.

"By your thought be your servant untouched, unpricked in the day or night."

When the mass before him grew still, Nikita lifted his gaze and slowly straightened, clammy palms flattened against the thighs of his pants. The soil had taken on the shape of a woman in a rough canvas apron dress decorated with cross-stitched geometric patterns in tones of brown and orange. She stood straight and tall, her skin the soft black of deep, packed earth. Long, dark rivers of soil ran over her shoulders and down to the floor, flecked with dark leaves and sprigs of birch and subtly flowing in a mimicry of hair. Her blank face was half hidden by a mask formed of the gnarled branches of a tree, and long fingers stretched toward the ceiling from her upturned hands, tangled with threads of flax that ran taut down to the ground like the strings of a marionette.

"A firm lock on my words," Nikita croaked. Every muscle in his body ached, but he remained upright.

The spirit's face didn't move, but he heard its firm, rumbling voice clearly even so. "душегуб."

He froze, just for a moment, and then his hands tightened into fists.

"All I have done has been in the service of the law," he forced out. "Any word I may have overspoken, any word I may have underspoken—"

"душегуб," the spirit said again. "непростительный." She lifted one hand, tightening the pull of the strings, and Nikita fell forward, unable to catch himself on his hands before he hit the bowl, sending an arc of water onto the floor as it tipped and rolled away from him.

"Mat Syra Zemlya," Nikita tried again, but he had no strength left in his arms. By the time he picked himself up enough to focus on the spirit, her form had crumbled and sunk back into the crack in the floorboards, leaving no trace of the black earth. Nikita pulled at the break in the floor so wildly that his fingers bled, but there was nothing there.

The spirit's voice ran through him over and over again. He pulled his knees under him and curled up with his forehead on the damp floor, each breath coming in ragged, furious growls. душегуб. *Murderer.*

"Murderer," he snarled with disdain as he shoved himself back up. "Murderer." He stood and took a few steps toward the coffee table where his briefcase sat, pausing to spit out a sour mouthful of bile that rose in his throat. To catch someone like Moore, there were bound to be sacrifices. Of course there would be damage. He'd done what he had to do. But he was running out of options.

He had to accept that, at least for the moment, Moore had him against a wall. He clearly knew where Nikita was, and Nikita lacked the reciprocal information. There was nothing left but to face him directly. He would have to wait until Moore came to him, just like he'd planned before—but he could choose the killing ground.

6

When Nathan emerged from his host's spare room, he found her in the kitchen, pouring a cup of coffee. Before he could get out his "good morning," Nock turned to face him with a frowning glare.

"Gonna tell me the truth yet?"

He let out a light sigh and moved around her to fetch his own mug from the cabinet. "Beloved, please. It's early."

"And I appreciate you not walking around my house with your dick out for once, but that just makes me even more sure something's wrong with you."

Nathan warmed his hands on the black mug as he lifted it to inhale the dark scent. "Can I convince you, at least, that it's nothing you need to worry about?"

"I worry about *you*, you jackass."

He gave a soft gasp and pressed one hand to his heart. "Beloved, I'm touched."

"I'm about to touch you with the back of my hand if you don't quit trying to feed me bullshit."

"It isn't bullshit," he insisted.

"Well it sure sounds like bullshit. Why won't you talk to me?"

"What is it you want to talk about? Is your shop profitable this quarter? How are the Red Sox doing?"

"You're serious? This is how you're going to be?"

Nathan set his mug back down on the counter. "There isn't anything else I want to talk about."

"What did you even come here for?" When he tried to get by her, she stepped into his way, and he stopped short with a small sigh. "This isn't a hostel; you can't just show up whenever you want. Am I your friend, or am I not?"

"Of course you're—"

"Then stop treating me like someone you can just use!"

"Nock, I would never—"

"If you came here for my help, then let me help you! If you're just here for a couch to surf on, you can get the fuck out."

"Nock—"

"It's your call." She crossed her arms with a grunt and moved aside to get out of his way, her face pointedly turned away from him. Even so, Nathan saw the subtle jut of her lower jaw and the tension in her shoulders. He wasn't being fair.

"I came here to kill someone," he admitted, not quite meeting her gaze as she slowly turned back to look up at him. "Because that someone killed my daughter. My Adelina." Her name tasted like ash in his mouth.

Nock softened and let her arms unfold so that she could reach for his hands, but he pulled back from her.

"I don't intend to bring you any trouble," he went on without letting her speak. "The one I'm after isn't in any position to come after you. I only mean to be here a short time, and then this will be over."

"Nathan, I'm so sorry," Nock said, but he only shook his head.

"I don't want pity. I want recompense."

"You mean revenge." She moved a little closer to him but didn't try to touch him again. "It won't bring her back. You know that."

"I know," he said. "But it *will* make me feel better."

The goblin's brow tightened into a frown. "It won't even do that," she said gently.

"We shall have to see." He skirted her to get through the kitchen door. "Don't let me disturb you. Please. I'll make certain none of this comes back to you. I promise."

"Nathan, come on—" Nock started.

"Thank you again for your hospitality. I appreciate your kindness, and I hope I can someday repay it to your satisfaction. Until then, please allow me to take advantage of you just a little bit longer."

She sighed from the doorway and watched him retreat into the spare room, the click of the lock seeming too loud. "Sure," she said softly to the empty room.

Elton walked the sidewalk alone, periodically checking the map on his phone to make sure he was headed the right way. He'd left Cora sleeping, with a note promising his quick return with breakfast, but he'd bypassed the coffee shop. Instead, he stood outside Nock's Nick-Nacks again, watching the woman at the counter through the broad window. It was still early—no customers yet.

He paused just long enough to check his reflection in the glass and do up one more of his collar buttons, then stepped inside to the soft ring of the bell above the door. Nock turned to look, but instead of the scowling frown Elton expected, the goblin only sighed, shoved the register drawer closed, and waved him over.

"I wanted to talk to you in private," he said as he reached the counter.

"Yeah? How many guesses do I get about what?"

"Just one," Elton answered. "I didn't want to press in front of Cora. She's been taking it hard, Nathan running off again. But I was a Chaser for a long time. I know when someone's lying to me."

"You gonna arrest me?"

"I just want to know where he is. I know what he's doing, and he's in no shape to do it."

"What's wrong with him?"

Elton shook his head and gave a small shrug. "Something happened to his magic. He's not...at full capacity."

Nock picked at one of the buttons on the register. "But he's hunting this Chaser anyway."

"I'm certain he is."

The goblin looked up at him with a skeptical knit in her brow. "What's an ex-Chaser care? Who is he to you? Even if I did know where he is," she added, "I don't know you."

Elton stared flatly at her, unconvinced. "He's a friend," he answered, the word still sounding strange to him in reference to Nathaniel Moore.

"He's the reason I'm an *ex*-Chaser. And he's a pain in the ass—but he's...done a lot for me. Too much for me to let him do something like this alone."

"So you're planning to be co-murderer, is that it?"

"If that's what he wants."

Nock went quiet for a few beats, her shoulders hunching as she leaned the balls of her hands on the counter's edge. "He did come see me," she admitted after a pensive pause. "He's at my apartment. He doesn't want to see anybody—I don't think he even really wants to be around me—but he won't talk to me. Maybe a murder buddy is what he needs right now. So I'll take you to him." She pushed away from the counter and narrowed her eyes up at the blond. "But if he doesn't want to see you, you've gotta go. I don't want any shit-stirring, you got it?"

"I understand. Thank you, Nock."

She grunted at him in response and walked to the front of the store, flipping the sign on the door to closed and locking it up behind them. When they reached her apartment, the human glamour hiding her true form melted away, and she took long strides across the living room to knock on the workshop door.

"Nathan, get out here," she called gruffly. She waited a moment, then tried again but still got no answer. She turned the knob and pushed open the door, and inside, the sheet and pillow on the futon had been neatly folded again, and there was no sign of Nathan's bag. "Fuck," she sighed, and she stepped aside to gesture into the empty room for Elton to look.

The blond sighed through his nose with his hands in his pockets. "Of course."

The fire wasn't so large that it was uncontrollable—though it was a shame to damage such a quaint old building. People had begun to gather on the far sidewalk, pointing and chattering, and residents were piling out of the building. Someone would call. The sirens would start soon—but Nathan would be long gone by the time they arrived.

He waited patiently across the street from the blaze he'd started, casually breathing in smoke from the cigarette between his fingers. He'd give Korshunov enough time to get well and truly smoked-in before he fetched him. He imagined the boy must be miserable already after spending the last day with Nathan's powders in his lungs, but a little extra wouldn't hurt. Wouldn't hurt Nathan, anyway.

He was about to snuff his cigarette when something seemed to burst inside the building, shattering one of the upper windows and raining glass down on the concrete below. Nathan leaned to one side to get a better look and paused at the creaking sound coming from deep within. A dull roar filtered through the windows, and then through the entry. The glass cracked as the door bent outwards, then snapped from its hinges and hit the front steps. Within the flames licking around the edges of the now open space, something moved—and as the freed smoke spilled upward from the doorframe, Nathan saw Korshunov, hands splayed close to his sides. The fire raged around him, but didn't touch; it beat wildly against the young Chaser's barrier, the flames surrounding him blocked by the sphere of clear air around his body.

Nathan watched with his cigarette burning between his fingers as the boy took his last unsteady step onto the sidewalk and let the barrier fall. His shoulders heaved as he took heavy breaths, and the hem of his untucked, half-buttoned shirt was singed. His narrow face was pale, and dark circles seemed to sink his bright eyes deeper into his cheeks. His hands shook, still held as though maintaining the spell—but his gaze was on Nathan, his jaw tight and his eyes full of so much rage that the older man smiled.

Not bad. But not good enough.

"I told you you'd have to fly faster than this, little bird," Nathan said as he flicked his cigarette butt away.

Korshunov scowled across the narrow street at him. "I didn't want to go so fast that you lost me." His voice sounded scratchy and dry, but it still carried an impressive amount of venom. The boy took off down the street with surprising energy, bashing his way through a patch of onlookers attempting to help him.

Nathan followed, but the binding spell he called out only made the Chaser stumble—something tore around his body like a living wind and picked him back up onto his feet. Nathan kept running, past a fenced-off alley and onto the broader cross street, where Korshunov drew a number of curious looks as he raced half-dressed past a cramped convenience store. At Nathan's sneering murmur, the front window cracked, then burst, firing shards of glass toward the boy. He ducked and swerved away from the missiles, and the same wash of air batted them away from him as he ran. The mundanes passing in the street shouted in alarm and backed away to give Nathan a wide berth as he rushed by them.

Korshunov shoved pedestrians lingering outside the Old North Church's little grey ticket booth to clear himself a path and slid on the pavement as he swung around the corner to take the next street. Nathan was being led somewhere—and he'd had enough of this Chaser's games.

He stopped running and dropped low to slap his hands against the asphalt, his fingertips digging into the rough surface as he growled, "Fann." Ahead of Korshunov, the street split apart into a deep, sharp crevasse, forcing him to skid to a stop at the intersection. The boy threw a vicious, wild look over his shoulder at Nathan, but then, with a heavy rise and fall of his shoulders as he breathed, Korshunov turned back to the broken street and leapt. He seemed carried by something over the break in the ground, and in the brief moment he was in the air, Nathan saw a flicker of a tall, spindly shape above him. He hit the ground so hard that he had to catch himself on one hand, but he kept going.

Nathan hissed out another spell that brought him across the broken street in a sudden jolt. The effort put a jab of pain into his chest, and he cursed to himself as he pushed into a run again. He needed to remember that he wasn't at his best—but with Korshunov right in front of him, it was difficult to keep things like his own health in mind. Along the narrow street, blocked in on both sides by tall, red brick buildings, Nathan flung a parked car from its place on the curb, narrowly missing the fleeing Chaser. Windows broke into spiderwebs and spilled glass like rain from above them as Nathan passed—but when he slowed and spread his hands, ready to pull down the wall of the next building to block Korshunov's path, his arms were instead pulled downward, his back arching forward and his knees bending him to the ground against his will.

He pulled, shoulders straining as he spit out countercurses. A binding. But Korshunov was still—

"Nathan!" Cora's voice carried over the rush of his own blood in his ears, and as Nathan turned his head to look back down the street behind him, he saw Elton approaching with slow steps, holding a paper talisman with burning edges between two fingers. Cora edged around him and started to hurry forward, but the blond put a guarding hand around her arm to keep her close.

"When did you learn this new trick?" Nathan sneered as the other man stopped a good distance from him.

"Somewhere around month two of living with you. Seemed like a skill I was guaranteed to need eventually."

"Let me loose! He's going to get away!" Nathan shifted his head enough to follow Korshunov's path down the street just in time to see the Chaser jumping an ivy-covered brick fence and dropping out of sight.

"Stop this," Elton countered. "Look how much damage you've caused. This is insane."

"He's getting. Away." Nathan's body tensed, and with one more growling incantation, the spell fell away.

Elton's paper crumbled to ash, and Nathan rushed to his feet to carry on the chase. But before he could get more than a few feet, something wound painfully tight around his ankles, lashing them together and sending him face first into the ground. He flattened his hands against the pavement and pushed himself slowly up to stare back at the blond.

"You don't want to interfere here, Elton."

"I'm not going to let you destroy a whole city block."

Nathan stopped, and he let his head drop with a low, humorless laugh. "You aren't going...to *let* me."

"Nathan, please," Cora called as he tore the talismans around his feet with a word.

"No." He rose to standing again and turned to face Elton, matching the other man's steady gaze. "I want Elton to try to show me what he plans to *let* me do."

The former Chaser watched him without answering.

"Go on, Elton," he pressed. "Put a stop to me. And be quick about it—I have another appointment to keep."

The flare of irritation in the blond's nostrils was unmistakable. He would fight now. And, just as Nathan suspected, Elton didn't let another beat pass before he flung a spell from his fingertips. The paper split and spun around Nathan's wrists and ankles like spiderweb, drawing him down to his knees as the talisman fastened itself into the concrete. Nathan hefted himself upright, pulling against his tethers.

"Rale," he growled with a jerk of his head, and a loose brick from one of the buildings making up the alley scraped free and flung itself across the gap, cracking into the side of Elton's face with a satisfying, hollow thunk.

The blond's head snapped to the side, and blood spilled from his lip, but he kept his footing. His eyes ran over his opponent, checking his wrists and focusing briefly on the new string of groundings around Nathan's neck. Nothing got past this one. Elton knew Nathan's capacities were currently limited—must have hoped he only had a few spells at his disposal. Nathan could almost see the gears spinning in the other man's head, counting the new tokens, trying to guess their carvings. An almost imperceptible line of worry crossed Elton's brow.

Good.

As Nathan tore himself free of the binding, he laid a hand on the ground and split it open with a word, forcing Elton to retreat to one side of the alley while Cora shouted scoldings at them both. This shouldn't take long. He intended to teach Elton a lesson. They weren't equals. They weren't partners. They never had been. They had only met because Elton wanted him dragged to the Magistrate and hanged. He needed to be put in his place. But the former Chaser had his own arsenal of tricks Nathan didn't know—more than once, he had no defense against being hurled against the wall or burned by a paper slithering up the skin of his arm.

Cora put up a barrier around the ends of the alley, blocking them from the view of curious mundanes and keeping the growing debris from reaching any passers-by, but she never gave up yelling at the two men. Neither of them had enough spare focus to listen. Nathan noticed in passing that the sky above them had begun to darken, but he was too busy pulling his leg free of a talisman that tore into the meat of his calf to pay the sky any mind.

With blood filling his shoe, Nathan scowled down the narrow alley at the blond, who looked just as bruised and out of breath as Nathan felt. Cora strained under the effort of holding such a large barrier on her own, battered as it was by bits of stone and brick flung free by the men's spells. It was time to put an end to this. The next time Elton took a step, the heavy stone pendant at the center of Nathan's new necklace burned against his chest.

"Ou se pa'm."

Elton grit his teeth and pulled against the spell, but at a turn of Nathan's wrist, the former Chaser's knees hit the ground—then his back, and then his arms, as he was flattened against the broken asphalt. Above them, thunder cracked, and Nathan distantly heard Cora calling his name in a panicked voice. He ignored her. The rain was hitting his shoulders now. Her barrier was broken. It didn't matter.

Elton was at his feet at last—the perfectly-put-together Magistrate dog who had appeared in his doorway and given him hope of a hunt for the first time in years. So stern, so straight-laced. Unwavering and single-minded. Always pressed and polished. He didn't look so poised now. The sleeves of his shirt were torn and dusty, his hair mussed and stuck to his face with sweat. Blood ran from cuts at his temple and lip that Nathan had put there. This was the end Nathan had imagined back in Yuma—the Chaser, panting and broken, bleeding into the dirt.

But it wasn't what he saw now.

He saw Elton, collapsed on a hotel sofa they were both bleeding on, watching him with wary eyes unused to trust. *You were a real friend to me today.*

He saw him leaned against a pool table in a smoky hall, lifting a glass of beer to his lips as though he could hide the soft, private smile there. *Am I your best friend, Elton?*

Nathan's chest hurt. He let the clenched glare fall from his face. He wasn't going to kill this man. Not him. Not Elton.

Impossible.

As the spell's grip loosened on the blond below, and he lifted a hand from the ground, Nathan stood still. Even when he saw the marked yellow paper in Elton's palm, he didn't move. The weight in his gut kept him in place. He knew the truth now, even if he couldn't say it aloud—he would never raise a hand against this man again. Not him.

When Elton threw his spell, Nathan barely felt it graze his cheek— but he heard the shriek as the talisman cut deep into the creature that now flailed on the street behind him. The thing was spindle-thin, with tiny cat's paws at the ends of its elongated limbs and sharp cat's teeth bared by the flattened head held up by a stretched neck. Black blood seeped from the wound Elton's spell had made as the creature twitched, and when Nathan turned back to look at the man on the ground, he saw the same resignation in the blond's green eyes that he felt in himself.

Nathan swallowed. This was why. This was precisely why. There was no way he could stay near him—him or Cora. So Nathan did what he always did.

He ran.

The ache in his body, the blood spilling from his wounds, was meaningless. He had to make it to the cemetery. To Korshunov. Another of the bony, slithering creatures wailed at him from the low cemetery wall, its dapple-grey skin glistening in the rain. When it leapt on him, he had to tear its claws free from his skin with both hands around its slick, narrow body, but his quickly spoken spell split it open, so that its final cry was cut short and its blood stained the puddle Nathan dropped it in.

He lifted himself up and over the wall—and stood in the center of an entire brood of the writhing spirits. He couldn't see the end of them beyond the sheets of rain from the sudden storm. He couldn't see Korshunov, either. He didn't have much time to look. The creatures were swarming him. He pushed them away, broke their bodies, cut open their skin, and even crushed them underfoot—but they kept coming, squirming out from every crevice and shadow in the yard, their shrieks painful and almost deafening even over the sound of the rain.

At some point, Elton and Cora had appeared beside him. They took on their share of the spirits, but the spindly things only had eyes for Nathan. He was beginning to lose a lot of blood. Finally, when he lost his footing and had to catch himself against a tall gravestone, one of the spirits took the opportunity and came screeching toward his face. It was yanked back by the invisible hand of Cora's spell, and then, a moment later, Nathan himself was hauled up by an arm around his middle. He flailed against the hold as he was flung over Elton's shoulder like a sack of flour, but the blood and rain in his eyes made it hard to focus.

Cora did his fighting for him as the creatures chased after them. Flashes of blue appeared in the air around her as she threw up patches of hard barriers, holding them just long enough for one of the spirits to crash headlong into them and be sent crumpled back to the ground. She formed blue spheres around others that got too close, shrinking them down until the monster inside hissed and wailed, its body crushed by the shimmering prison. She was using her barriers as a weapon. Despite everything, Nathan felt a swell of pride for the girl who had once struggled to lift a glass of water.

The last thing he saw before being carried around the next corner was Korshunov, hauling himself up and over the cemetery wall with seething hatred written on his face. He stood on the street across from Cora, fighting for breath, ever more of the spirits slithering over the wall behind him. Nathan didn't see the next spell Cora cast, couldn't hear her shout over the rain—but by the time Elton finally stopped at the end of the block, the rain had slowed to a light patter. Cora approached them at a weary trot and leaned her hands on her knees to catch her breath once she stopped.

"He left," she said between pants.

Nathan struggled against Elton's grip until he was let down, then leaned back against the closest wall and glared at each of them in turn. "I've lost him again because of you two," he muttered, but he didn't have the energy to put much venom in his words.

Cora raised her head with her lips pressed into a hard line. "You're *welcome* for not letting those things fucking *kill* you, Nathan! Jesus Christ," she swore, "why are you both so *god damn stupid?*"

"What did I do?" Elton asked with a frown, but she ignored him.

"Please," she began, pushing herself upright to look Nathan in the face. "Please stop this. You need help. Come back with us—let us help you."

Nathan paused, then gave a great, heavy exhale. "Perhaps you're right. We can talk once we're somewhere a bit less open, hm? Lead on."

"Thank god," the girl sighed with such relief that guilt pricked at Nathan's chest.

Even so, as soon as the pair of them turned their backs to show him the way, he gave a soft whisper that heated one of the bones strung around his wrist and disappeared down the other end of the alley without either of them turning back to notice him.

He still had an appointment to keep.

7

Nathan stood outside the Old North Church and ran a hand through his wet hair and over his face, smoothing some of the blood from his skin. The rain had weakened now, and the clouds were beginning to part—had Korshunov caused the storm? He'd certainly been the one who summoned all of those creatures from the cemetery—Nathan had to admit he was impressed. But now the spirits were gone, and the storm had passed. Police cars had gathered by the cross-streets near the church, keeping tourists and residents at a distance from the damaged street. None of them noticed Nathan. They must not have noticed Korshunov, either—but Nathan could smell him. He was inside.

Nathan crossed through the metal gate and pushed open the red doors to the church, letting himself in without a glance from any of the surrounding officers. His bones were tired, and blood still dripped down his limbs in slow-moving rivers, but he forced his legs to move him down the center aisle's worn red carpet.

"Where are you, little bird?" Nathan murmured to the silent hall. He walked slowly by each numbered white door enclosing the cubicle-pews of the old church, fingertips skimming the gold nameplates of long-dead New Englanders. At each tiny room, he gave a gentle rap with his knuckles before peering over the shoulder-high wall.

Soft, restrained breaths reached Nathan's ears from farther down the hall, but he took his time, checking each pew with the pensive hum of a parent playing hide and seek with a child whose feet were showing from behind a curtain. When he reached the door Korshunov trembled behind, Nathan leaned his elbows on the wooden rail of the cubicle wall and let his chin rest on his folded arms.

The Chaser stared up at him with fierce defiance unequal to the gauntness of his cheeks and the sweat pouring from his skin.

"That's enough now, little bird." Nathan put a finger to his lips, and he whispered, "Enkonsyan."

Korshunov pulled back, feet scraping against the carpet as he tried to put more distance between them, but he clearly didn't have the gas left to block the spell. So he collapsed against the far wall of the pew. Nathan stepped back to click open the door and swing it aside. He bent down and pulled one of the boy's arms over his shoulders to lift him up, then carried him at an easy pace back down the hall and away from the police barricades, humming softly to keep their glamour up while the flashing lights of the parked cars washed over them.

The spot he'd chosen was an old brick building not far from the center of town. Once, it had been some sort of amateur theatre, perhaps; a few heavy drapes and wooden chairs lay scattered around the upper floor, and a slick black stage rose a few inches above the rest at the back of the long room. Now, it was derelict and abandoned. The second-story windows had been blacked out, the metal awnings were only precariously attached, and heavy roll-down doors had been rusted firmly into place at each lower window and entrance. No one would disturb them here—and the wards Nathan had put up would block out the sound.

The chairs were still sturdy enough, with the help of Nathan's agrimony-soaked bindings, to keep an exhausted boy in check. He left Korshunov with his head hanging heavily over the back of the chair where he'd been bound at the chest, arms tied behind him and calves strapped securely to the legs of his seat, while he peered into a small glass vial and swirled its murky contents. It was ready.

Nathan circled around to the front of the Chaser and tilted his head as he looked down at Korshunov's pale, slack face. He really was just a boy. He couldn't have been even twenty-five. In any other situation, Nathan might have felt sorry for him—raised up, groomed, and half brainwashed by the Magistrate at their damned Academy, then sent out on the streets to hunt people like Nathan by the time they were old enough to drink. But as he took in Korshunov's thin collarbones and gaunt cheeks, listened to his shallow, hissing breaths, he couldn't find a scrap of pity inside his own chest. Not for this one. Not for him.

He released the spell that kept the Chaser sleeping and gave him a sharp slap on the cheek when he failed to rouse quickly enough. Korshunov took half a moment for his eyes to focus, then pulled against his bonds with all the strength he had—which didn't seem to be much.

"You've been wanting to meet me," Nathan said evenly. "I think it's time we stopped missing each other; don't you?"

The boy spat out something in Russian that could have been either a curse or a spell. Either way, nothing happened; the oils on the cords tying him would keep him from casting, especially with his Magistrate ring gone and his small collection of stones and tokens emptied from his pockets.

Nathan tutted at him. "You're here for a very specific purpose. I believe you're holding onto something that doesn't belong to you." He turned to his bag and lifted out the delicate twine-wrapped eggshell he'd found among Korshunov's groundings. The Chaser glanced at it, then back to Nathan's face with a sneer on his thin lips.

"You can't open it, can you?"

"I'll admit, this is magic I haven't encountered," Nathan answered. "But I don't need to open it. You're going to open it for me. And you're going to free my daughter from whatever hellish curse you've trapped her under."

"You think so?"

Nathan leaned down close to the boy's face and gripped him firmly by the chin. "I do. And I think that, if you've got a brain in that pretty little head, you'll do it sharpish."

Korshunov stared up at him without flinching, his pale eyes locked onto Nathan's gaze. "I'm not an idiot. You won't kill me while that thing is still sealed. Not without knowing how to release it."

"You poor boy," Nathan murmured, almost sadly. "You really are so young. You still think that death is the worst thing I can give you."

He pulled back and set the egg gently aside, then uncorked his vial and snapped out a hand to fasten on Korshunov's jaw. He forced the boy's mouth open and poured the dark liquid into his throat, then covered his nose and mouth, holding onto his head as he attempted to thrash his body within his bindings. When he could no longer hold his breath, Korshunov relented and swallowed, and Nathan released him, giving his shoulder a light, reassuring pat as he returned to the front of the chair to let the boy take a few gasping breaths.

"Now then," Nathan said, waiting with his hands casually holding onto his folded elbows. "I believe we were discussing your trap."

He watched the Chaser choke, then heave, then drop his head as low as his straps would allow. He let the boy shudder in his seat for a few moments, and smiled faintly with satisfaction as he saw the sweat beading on Korshunov's forehead when he finally lifted his eyes.

"What did you give me?" he asked, slowly, as if his mouth was numb. It probably was.

Nathan stepped closer and rested his hands on his knees so that he could look the boy more directly in the face. "You're going to tell me what you have trapped in that egg."

Korshunov shook his head as it drooped again.

"Yes, you are," Nathan said patiently. The boy's shoulders twitched, his body subtly convulsing. "That's it," he purred. "Good boy."

The Chaser grit his teeth as if that might help keep the words inside, but then he gave another choking retch and fought to take breath. "Rusalka," he murmured.

Nathan's dark eyes narrowed. "And what, precisely, is rusalka?"

"Dead," Korshunov answered. "Drowned, drowned."

"The spirit locked inside that token," Nathan pressed, "is it my daughter? Is it Adelina?"

"Rusalka," the boy said again, with a soft, dark laugh in his throat. "Утоплен, призван и захвачен."

Nathan couldn't help the tight sneer that pulled at his lips. He laid a hand on Korshunov's knee and squeezed it tight, cracking the joint with the simple word, "Frakti."

The boy cried out, but only for a moment; he tightened his jaw again and hissed a breath in through his teeth.

"The spirit you trapped," Nathan said again. "Is it my daughter? Is it the woman you murdered?"

"душегуб," Korshunov growled. He pressed his eyes shut and

Apostate

hunched in on himself as much as his bonds let him. "I choked her. She never saw me coming. Choked her, pushed her under the water. The river. Hands...slapped me, shoved me, so I pushed her deeper. Until the bubbles stopped." He raised his head to look Nathan in the face with drained blue eyes. "It took longer for her to die than it did to get her head off."

Nathan held the boy's gaze, though his insides burned with rage and regret. He forced his voice to remain even. "Did you seal her in your trap?"

"Easy to summon a newborn rusalka," he muttered. "Easy to lock it away. Easy to keep it." He glanced between Nathan's eyes and snorted. "Not so easy for you to free."

Nathan grabbed the seat of the chair and flung it upwards, sending the Chaser onto his back with a heavy, painful crash as his weight landed on his bound arms. He crouched down and took Korshunov's face in one hand, drawing close to him with his voice a low, dangerous whisper.

"You and I have a long night ahead of us. I am going to break every bone in your body, and then I'm going to show you exactly what it feels like to be drowned. Before you stop breathing, I'm going to pull you out, let you taste the air, and put you under again. When you're weeping, bleeding, and broken, and you finally beg me to let you die...I'll consider it," he finished softly. He pushed the boy's face away and stood to turn his attention to his bag.

Elton and Cora were blocked from getting too near any of the buildings they passed by idle police cars with their lights flashing—keeping pedestrians a safe distance from the damage Nathan and Korshunov had done.

"Anything?" Cora asked, looking up at the blond's frowning face as he turned his willow token in his fingers. He looked rough after his scrap with Nathan, but neither he nor Cora had even considered stopping now.

"It's faint," Elton murmured. "He's trying to cover his tracks. But I think I can follow this trail."

The girl sighed. "Why did he leave? What the hell is he thinking?"

"He's not. Come on." Elton led the way down the sidewalk with the

45

smooth wood warm in his hand.

More than once, Elton gave a quiet curse, stopped walking, and turned around to head back in the opposite direction. Cora let him work—she had little to contribute when it came to tracking magic on the street, and she knew it. Her divination hadn't even been any help so far; it had taken a burning building for them to track Nathan down.

Finally, after they'd circled the same neighborhood at least three times, Elton began to slow his pace, his eyes scanning the buildings they passed. They finally stopped in front of a crumbling, abandoned building, and Elton pressed his palm against one of the metal doors rolled down to the sidewalk.

"Is this it?" Cora asked, craning her back to look up at the second floor windows.

"I think so." He stepped back and glanced at each door in turn. "It's been warded."

"Why would Nathan hole up in a place like this when he could still be staying with Nock?"

Elton frowned faintly. "I guess we'll see."

Cora stepped closer to the building and banged her hand against a couple of the drawn-down doors, then walked toward the corner, still eyeing the upstairs windows. "If Nathan got in somehow, there must be a way," she muttered. "Maybe if we go around back, there's a door I can unlock, or—"

She was cut off by a sudden, loud rattle, and she glanced back in time to see Elton crouched in front of one of the metal doors with his fingers slipped underneath. He gave one more jerk upward, and the rusted latch broke, allowing him to scrape the gate up and over his head back into place. He dusted off his hands and reached out to turn the handle of the simple, unlocked door underneath.

"Well," Cora said before she moved, "I forgot why I used to think you were hot for a while there, so, thanks for that reminder."

"Can we not?" Elton sighed, gesturing toward the open door to allow her inside first.

Cora gave the blond's chest a reassuring pat as she passed him and stepped inside the dark building. Once Elton closed the door after them, it was pitch black.

"Sorche," she said easily, lifting her hand to let the ball of pale blue

46

light illuminate the room. It was as empty as she expected an abandoned building to be, she supposed. Just dust and a couple of tipped-over chairs. She raised her hand a little higher to send the light farther, but both she and Elton went still when a choking cough echoed through the room. She looked back at him, then followed his gaze to the far end of the hall.

"Upstairs?" she whispered, and Elton nodded. He took the lead and moved quietly through the room, testing the integrity of the wood at the bottom of the old stairs before glancing back to tell her to follow.

When they reached the top, Cora's spell died in her hand. Nathan was there—and so was Korshunov. The Chaser was on the ground, surrounded by broken wood and rope that still tied his wrists. Blood ran from his mouth, dripping down to the pools that seeped into the wood floor, and one of his legs was twisted into an angle a leg shouldn't have made. The same blood fell from Nathan's hands where he stood over Korshunov. He gave them a careless shake, sending splatters onto the ground.

"Nathan," Cora breathed. Elton put out a protective hand to keep her from rushing forward, but he didn't need to. She didn't want to get any closer.

Nathan didn't turn to look at them; he just kept his eyes on the boy at his feet, who was struggling to breathe. "You aren't meant to be here," he said evenly.

"What the hell is this?" Cora asked, her voice a little louder, though she had to fight to keep a tremble out of it.

"Don't ask silly questions," he answered. "You know what he's done."

"This kid was worth ripping up streets? Burning down a whole apartment building?" Elton cut in, but Nathan still didn't look over.

"A dozen of them," he murmured, and when he lifted his hand, Korshunov's grimacing cry rang out through the room, his body curling in on itself as one of his bound hands was crushed by Nathan's spell.

"Nathan, stop it," Elton said, taking a few cautious steps into the room. "I know what he did. If you want to kill him, kill him, but don't...do this."

"How did you even manage to saddle that high horse, Mr. Willis?" Nathan snorted. "After the things you've done?"

Now he looked, and the bitterness on his face made Cora's stomach hurt. This wasn't Nathan—Nathan was teasing, and laughter, and karaoke in the car. Even when he was violent, he wasn't this. This was monstrous.

"This isn't about me," Elton said. "This serves no purpose. It's just torture."

"If you'd heard the things he—" Nathan stopped himself, but Cora saw his hands tightening into fists. "If you disapprove, you're welcome to go. I didn't ask either of you to come here."

"Please, Nathan," Cora tried. She moved forward to stand beside Elton. "We came because we're your friends. Because you're hurting, and we want to help."

"Then go away and let me finish."

"Are you going to finish it?" Elton pressed. "Or are you going to keep torturing a kid?"

"This is not a *kid*," Nathan insisted. "This is a *Chaser* who murdered my daughter in cold blood. I'll deal with him how I please."

"This isn't what Adelina would want," Cora said softly, but she flinched a little at the look Nathan turned on her, and Elton subtly shifted to stand more fully in front of her.

"Look at what you're doing," he said. "What is this going to fix? If you're feeling guilty about not being there—"

"Careful," Nathan sneered in warning, but Cora saw the hurt in his eyes.

"Stop it!" she shouted, but before she could scold either of them further, slow movement on the floor caught her attention.

Korshunov had drawn himself up onto his elbows, and now he lifted unsteadily onto his knees. The ropes fell free from his broken hands, coiling on the floor as his head fell backwards, like it was too heavy to hold upright any longer. His spine arched, and he began to claw at his own shoulders with bloody hands, tearing the stained shirt from his chest.

Nathan noticed Cora's shifted gaze and turned to follow it, but when he moved to reach for Korshunov again, the Chaser's body jerked so suddenly that he paused. The boy pulled his shirt free and let it fall to soak up the blood on the floor, and he kept scratching at his own skin, bringing up welts that deepened into gashes wider than his fingers should have been able to make. Something dark and matted appeared everywhere he tore, and where his hands couldn't reach, his skin split apart on its own, growing and shifting with each heaving breath.

Cora let herself be pulled back by Elton's hand on her shoulder, too dumbfounded to move on her own, but it only took seconds more for the bleeding Chaser on the floor to break apart entirely—replaced by the blood-soaked body of a massive brown bear.

Even Nathan took a step backward as the thing let out a snarling roar that seemed to vibrate Cora's bones.

"What the *fuck?*" she managed to get out before the animal charged.

It hit Nathan and sent him crashing to the floor. Elton moved toward it, a paper talisman in his fingers, but the bear had already fastened its jaws on Nathan's blocking arm. Elton's spell tore into the animal's fur, spilling blood, but it barely seemed to notice. When a burst of fire erupted from Nathan's captured hand, the bear recoiled with a deep growl and pawed at its charred face. Elton didn't even have time to get Nathan on his feet—the bear lunged again immediately, and Cora saw its massive claws raking across Nathan's body.

Elton sent binding wraps of paper around its legs to hobble it, but it seemed determined to fight regardless; it snarled and pulled against the hold of the spell, dragging Nathan back toward it even as he tried to pull himself away. Cora tried to pin the animal down with a binding spell, and it roared in fury as it was crushed closer to the floor. The next time Elton had a spell in his hand, the bear lashed out a paw and slammed him backward, knocking his head against the wall with an audible thud that tightened Cora's stomach. He didn't get up right away—so Cora put herself in front of him and Nathan, who already seemed to have lost a good portion of his blood, and held out her hands to erect a deep blue barrier between them and the rushing bear.

Bloodied claws scraped wildly at the iridescent wall, and sharp teeth in a singed and stained muzzle ran across the surface in search of weakness, but Cora shifted her feet to brace herself and held the spell firm. The animal dropped onto all fours, its body heaving with labored breath, and its black eyes watched her through the barrier. She looked right back at it, fighting the tremble in her hands, and, after a heavy snort, the bear rushed toward the stairs, limping on one of its back legs and leaving a trail of fresh blood behind it.

"I'll go," Elton said, and Cora glanced over her shoulder to see him finally standing.

"No," she answered. She dropped the barrier and kneeled at Nathan's side. His right arm had been chewed so thoroughly that she thought she saw bone, and deep gouges crisscrossed on his chest and stomach. He was breathing, but he didn't respond when she called his name or touched his face. She looked back up at Elton with a tight throat, but no tears in her eyes—she couldn't afford them. "Help me."

With Elton keeping his eyes on the exit in case Korshunov decided to return, they both set to work on closing Nathan's wounds. Cora used up the oils she had in her bag and even dug through Nathan's kit on the floor to find more ingredients, but even as sweat ran down her temples, her best spells couldn't fix the damage Korshunov had done—not well enough. He still had deep tears in his belly that had only begun to knit back together at the ends, and Cora had no idea how to deal with the amount of flesh Nathan was missing from his arm. There was just too much blood.

"What do we do?" she whispered.

Elton smoothed one of his papers over a cut in Nathan's side they'd been able to mostly close, the oil on his fingertips slicking the talisman onto the wound like a bandage. "He probably needs a real hospital."

"And what do we tell them? There was a bear attack in central Boston?"

The blond sighed, shaking his head as he looked down at his friend. "Not to mention how often he's been on the reg news. It's not an option." He took another slip of paper from his folio and offered it to her. "This is my last one. Do what you can to stop the bleeding at least— I'm going to go get Nock."

Nock had a string of curses coming out of her mouth the entire way to the abandoned building, and they grew even more venomous as she sat on the floor, bent over Nathan with a medical kit and stitching his torn skin back together. Cora helped as she could, passing the goblin clean gauze and wiping blood away where she was directed.

"Every witch thinks magic can solve every problem," Nock grumbled. "Never even think to just put a goddamn Band-Aid on."

Cora wanted to counter that magic was all they'd had, but she didn't think it was wise to argue with the woman currently sewing Nathan up like a ruined teddy bear. Instead, she put Elton on sanitation duty and moved over to Nathan's bag to check what supplies he had left. She carefully avoided jostling the jars of dirt with names on the lids, which she assumed had come from graves. They wouldn't help her now.

He was well equipped; she was able to mix a potion that she hoped would help until his body could replace the blood he'd lost. She returned to him with the newly-mixed tonic and gently lifted his head into her lap, then poured the liquid into his mouth, slowly so that his body would notice and swallow it.

"He's going to need antibiotics," Nock said as she snipped the last thread. "Even a witch shapeshifter bear, or whatever this was, probably had germs in its mouth." She sighed and gingerly turned Nathan's arm with two fingers. His skin was closed up, at least, except for a few wider wounds that she'd slathered in ointment and wrapped with gauze. "I can probably get some. But it's going to be on you guys to get him back to the house without making a scene."

"I can do that," Cora said. Elton frowned at her, and Cora knew she looked a mess—her shirt was glued to her back with sweat, and she had blood on her jeans and hands. "I can," she insisted before Elton could question her. "You carry him, and I'll hide you."

"If you're sure."

"It doesn't matter if I'm sure. It's what we have to do. We can't leave him here."

Nock packed up her kit and stood, wiping her hands on a spare scrap of cloth. "I'll see about the meds and meet you back at the house." Without waiting for their agreement, she tucked her little box under her arm and started down the stairs, picking her way as she went to avoid stepping in the puddles of blood.

Cora packed up Nathan's things, pausing when she spotted what looked like an egg at one side of his bag. She picked it up and ran her fingers over the brown twine wrapped around it in tiny knots, a frown forming on her lips. She didn't recognize it. It was light—an empty shell? What was Nathan doing with an empty eggshell? Carefully, she laid it aside, then slung Nathan's bag over her shoulder and took up the egg again. If Nathan was keeping it, it was useful. She kept it in her hand rather than risk it breaking in the bag and moved back toward the stairs to wait for Elton.

The blond wasn't in great shape himself. He had cuts and bruises all over, and he must have been just as tired as Cora was, if not more. Even so, he picked Nathan up more gently than Cora had ever seen Elton do anything, probably—he slid one arm under the smaller man's knees and the other around his shoulders, then shifted him to get a better grip with the bulk of Nathan's weight against his chest.

They made their way as quickly as they could out of the building and down the street. Cora kept one hand on Elton's arm, hiding all three of them from the sight of the passing mundanes with the whispered incantation of the glamour. She was sure that the spell faltered after about three blocks, but she took another breath and kept going, though she squeezed Elton's shirt a little tighter after that.

He almost had to carry both of them into the apartment. By the time he was tapping Nock's door with his foot, Cora was hanging from his elbow so heavily that he had to lean to the opposite side to keep her upright. Nock graciously helped the girl inside once the door was open, and Elton followed her direction to lay Nathan down on the spare futon, where a towel had been laid out to soak up any remaining blood leaks.

"Don't suppose either of you are good at finding a vein," the goblin said as she scooped up an IV bag and tubes from her coffee table.

"Don't know if there's a spell for that," Cora sighed. She sat down on the floor near Nathan's feet and laid her head on her folded arms against the cushion.

"Then some bruising is the price he'll pay for making me deal with his bullshit." Nock turned Nathan's good arm outward and inspected his inner elbow in the light. It took her a few tries and a few swears to get the needle where she wanted it, but once she'd taped it down, she hung the bag up on the workshop shelf nearby and headed for the door. "I'm going back to work," she said with a pointed huff. "If he dies, get him out of here before he smells."

"How warm," Elton muttered once she'd snapped the front door shut after her.

"I don't think she means it." Cora scooted up a little closer to Nathan's face and settled in again. She shook her head when Elton tried to suggest she get some rest on the couch, so he just pulled a dining chair through the doorway and sat across the room from them both.

8

Nathan didn't wake up until well past nightfall. He opened bleary eyes and struggled to focus on his dim surroundings, and when he lifted one hand to rub his face, he was stopped short by a length of plastic tubing attached to his arm. He wasn't dead—unless corpses got intravenous medication these days. God, his stomach hurt. He winced as he raised his head to look down at himself. He hoped he had skin left at all underneath all of those bandages.

Cora was at his side, asleep with her head on the futon mattress. At the other side of the small room, Elton sat, arms folded and green eyes studying Nathan with a mild frown. Nathan swallowed, then exhaled softly and let his head rest back on the futon.

"I suppose you're waiting for a thank you," he murmured.

"Thank Cora," Elton answered in a low voice. "She and Nock are the reason you're alive."

"My things?"

"They're here. Cora got everything."

Nathan relaxed into the mattress, just slightly. "You shouldn't have interfered."

"Then you *would* be dead."

Nathan snorted. "I had the situation well in hand until you two showed up. Now Korshunov is gone *again*. Twice in one day. I'll have to track him again and catch him again. So thank you for butting in

54

where you were neither needed nor asked for."

"You irresponsible, ungrateful shit," Elton spat, his chair squeaking on the floor as he stood and gestured to the sleeping young woman at Nathan's side. "Do you know how worried she's been? How hard she's been working trying to find you just so you don't grieve alone?"

"How I *grieve* is hardly any business of—"

"Don't give me that. Tell me it's none of *my* business if you want, but you can't brush her aside like this. She looks up to you. Deserve it."

"I feel it's worth repeating that I didn't *ask* either of you to get involved in this. I've been on my own for more than two centuries. I've always been on my own in the end—that's the way it will always be."

Elton scoffed at him. "Don't throw yourself a pity party. How many of the people you've known left *you*, and how many did you walk out on?"

"The ones I didn't walk out on are *dead*!" Nathan snapped back, so harshly that he had to stop to cough.

Elton paused. He didn't answer; he only kept his eyes on Nathan's reddened, frowning face as Cora stirred. She stretched her arms and straightened her legs out across the floor with a soft grunt, then blinked up at Nathan and smiled.

"Are you guys arguing already?"

Elton stepped past her. "I'm getting some sleep." Without looking back, he closed the door and left them alone.

Cora glanced between the door and Nathan's face. "So that's a yes?"

Nathan turned his head to look at her. "Are you all right? Unhurt?"

"I'm fine. Worried and a little freaked out, but fine." She picked at a loose thread on the towel underneath him and didn't meet his gaze. "You scared me."

"Cora, you know that I could never hurt you. You've no cause to be frightened of me."

"I wasn't afraid of being hurt. I was afraid of...*you*. I'm not blind; I know the kinds of things you're capable of. I guess I just thought that...it was too far even for you."

He sighed. "Am I to be scolded by both of you without even room to breathe in between?"

"I'm not trying to scold you. I just—I guess I want you to think about who you want to be. Not who you've been, or even who you are, but..."

She shook her head. "Even after you kill Korshunov, then what? You go back to hunting down strangers on some list?" Cora looked up at him and reached to take a gentle hold of his hand. "I mean...all this killing that you've been doing with Elton, has...has it actually changed anything? Has it made a difference to the awful things the Magistrate does? Has it even made you *feel* better?"

Nathan didn't reply straight away. Cora watched him, a pensive crease in her brow and disquiet in her rich brown eyes. She always wanted him to be better than he was. He seemed destined to disappoint her.

"You think I ought to find a purpose, two hundred and fifty-odd years in?"

"Why not? You hate the Magistrate, right? Me too. Elton too. Let's do something about it. For real. Let's do things that will help people."

"My love," Nathan said softly, "what would you have me do? Storm the Council? Demand higher wages for their secretaries?" He looked up at the ceiling, unable to bear her frowning face. "Would you bring my things where I can reach them, please?"

Cora hesitated, then let out a small, sad exhale and pulled her hand away from him. "It's the middle of the night, and you're hurt. Get some more sleep. Whatever it is you need to do can wait a little while." She rose from the floor and moved quietly to the door. "And I hope you'll let me help this time." She left him then, shutting the door with a soft click.

Nathan frowned at the ceiling tile above him, shifting slightly on the mattress and cringing at the bolt of painful protest his body gave. He did need rest. But he had limited time. Korshunov was in poor shape, as well, but he had access to Magistrate resources. Clinics. Nathan tried to force his jaw to unclench as he reluctantly shut his eyes in an attempt to sleep.

"A fucking *bear*," he muttered to himself. "What sort of witch can turn himself into a *bear*?"

Elton stirred at the mild ruckus Nock made in the morning, but the goblin didn't seem to have any interest in waking up her guests. She poured coffee into her thermos and left the apartment, presumably to open her shop as normal. She must have been even more used to Nathan

than Elton realized, if she was willing to just leave him behind to his own half-dead devices.

He'd fallen asleep on the couch, fully dressed except for his shoes, and expected that Cora would remain with Nathan—instead, she'd nestled herself between his body and the back cushions, so that one of his legs and half his torso had been forced halfway off the sofa. His arm was fully numb and still trapped under her head. He slid it free with ginger slowness as he eased himself away and flexed his fingers through the pins and needles that followed his escape.

Even asleep, she still had a wrinkle in her brow, and she reached for one of the couch pillows and held it close to her as a substitute for Elton's warmth. She cared more about Nathan than he deserved.

A thud and a curse came from behind the spare room door, and when Elton looked inside, he found Nathan on the floor, the IV needle stripped from his arm and now dangling loose from its empty bag. One of the bandages on his chest had begun to seep red.

"I'd ask if you were stupid, but I can see the answer in front of me," Elton said. "What are you doing?"

"I need my things," Nathan answered simply. He leaned his back against the futon and took a breath that very poorly hid the amount of pain he was in, then looked expectantly up at Elton. "There was an egg. In my bag. You said Cora got everything, yes?"

"She did. She has it." When Nathan started to speak again, Elton cut him off. "It's in the living room. If you're well enough to make demands, go get it yourself."

Nathan scowled up at him. "First you insist upon inserting yourself where you aren't wanted, and now you refuse to help at all?"

"I'm not going to help you kill yourself."

He snorted, then flinched at the movement it caused. "Just bring it to me—please," he added as an afterthought. "I need to know it's safe."

Elton stared at him. "An egg."

"It isn't just an egg!" Nathan snapped. He winced and put a hand to the bleeding bandage, hissing through his teeth in frustration. After a moment, he gave a small sigh of defeat. "Elton, it's *her*," he said without looking up again. "It's Adelina. However Korshunov trapped her, she's trapped in *there*."

The blond paused. With a frown, he turned from the room and took the thread-wrapped egg from where Cora had left it tucked safely in the nest she'd made of her flattened purse. He placed it in Nathan's waiting, outstretched hand, and stood by the door as the other man brought it close to his chest.

"You really think that's her in there?"

"I know it is. The way Korshunov talked about her—" He loosened his fingers around the token and frowned down at it. "I only need to work out how to get her free."

Elton didn't voice his apprehensions—that Korshunov might have said whatever he thought would upset Nathan the most, or that trapping an actual human soul inside an egg was magic he'd never even heard of. Neither had Nathan, apparently. It was a long shot, but if it kept Nathan from burning down any more buildings, then it might be worth it to humor him.

"Then let's figure it out," he said, but Nathan's frown only deepened.

"This isn't anything to do with you. Either of you. This is family business."

Elton started slightly as he noticed Cora inching into the doorway beside him. The girl held the door frame tightly with one hand and kept her jaw tight as she swallowed.

"Nathan," she said after a pause, her fingers squeezing the wood tighter as he looked up at her. "I know Adelina was your daughter, and how much you cared about her. And...I know I'm just some kid who happened to live next door."

Nathan's expression softened, just slightly. But when he took a breath, Cora shook her head, so he stayed silent.

"I want to help you. But even if you want to do everything on your own...I hope you know that you guys are the only family I've got. So I'll...whatever you decide to do, just...don't think you're all alone just because you lost someone related to you by blood."

"Cora," Nathan said gently, but she pushed away from the door and didn't look at him.

"I'll call Thomas and see if he can find out anything about a trap spell like that. And I'll...go get some breakfast, I guess."

Elton watched her scoop up her purse and head for the door without looking back at either of them. He put his hands in his pockets and looked over at Nathan, who stared down at the egg in his hands, one

---

thumb running lightly over the rough twine.

"I wonder if you might leave me alone for a while, Elton," he said.

The blond paused, but then he sighed through his nose and left the room, closing the door and dropping down onto the couch. He wasn't even getting paid for this babysitting.

Nathan didn't answer when Cora knocked to ask him if he wanted any of the coffee and bagels she'd brought, so she set some aside for him and settled on the couch beside Elton. She'd come back from her walk with red, puffy eyes and news that Thomas was going to look into the spirit trap, but whatever tears she'd shed during the call, they were wiped away now. Neither of them spoke while she mixed a new poultice and helped him smooth it over his remaining cuts and scrapes, but when she'd finished, she wiped her hands clean on a towel in her lap and looked down at it as she twisted the cloth in her fingers.

"I was worried you guys were going to kill each other," she said softly.

Elton exhaled quietly. "I wondered if he would. He could have. I lost that fight," he admitted with a small shake of his head. "But...I don't have it in me to kill him anymore. If I ever did."

Cora smiled and leaned closer to nudge the blond's arm with her shoulder. "I won't tell him you said so."

They drank their coffee and picked at their breakfast, Cora tilting her ear toward the door at any sound from within. After a while, soft footsteps padded on the wood, and the door gave a quiet click as the knob turned. Both of them turned to look over the back of the couch at Nathan as he leaned heavily against the door frame, keeping himself upright with some difficulty.

"You shouldn't be up," Cora said, but he waved her concern away with a brief gesture.

"I've decided that, perhaps, my attention these past few days has been...misdirected." He looked down at the twine-wrapped egg he held, turning it in his fingers instead of meeting the eyes of the others. "And...now that I have what truly matters in my possession, I might spend this time whilst I recover pursuing the answer to the next most important riddle. *And* that I might do so...in the company of friends."

He peeked up at them with a kind of reticent contrition pulling his mouth into a frown, and after a moment, Cora climbed over the back of the sofa and wrapped her arms around him as tightly as she dared.

"That's a quick turnaround," Elton said flatly from the couch, and Cora turned her head to glare at him.

"My way was...doing no good. As a wise young woman pointed out to me recently," Nathan added in a softer voice. "I made an enemy so dangerous that I lost my dearest flesh and blood. My connection to Kalfu has been severed. He won't answer my prayers or accept my offerings. And for all the blood I've spilled, the Magistrate is no nearer to abolishment or reformation than it was when I was born. Perhaps it's time I gave some thought to...the man I want to be."

A slow smile grew into a beam on Cora's face, and she squeezed him so hard this time that he winced. She grimaced and apologized as she pulled back, but he just raised a hand to gently touch her hair.

"Just like that?" Elton spoke up again, disbelief faintly curling his lip.

"I can't promise that if Korshunov crosses my path again I won't kill him," Nathan admitted. "But, for the time being, I think I ought to take my cues from Cora. If she would be so kind as to provide them."

"I have a *lot* of ideas," she agreed, nodding eagerly.

"I thought you might. And I hope I can count on your help with this?" he added, holding the eggshell up between them.

"Of course. I already talked to Thomas. He said he—"

"Hold on," Elton cut in, and they both looked back at him with raised eyebrows. "This is it? We just spent days hunting after you, watching you tear up three blocks' worth of Boston, torture a kid half to death, and almost get torn apart yourself. You almost *killed* me, and now you've, what? Turned a new leaf? Seen the light?"

"Is that so impossible?" Nathan asked.

"It's fucking unlikely," the blond countered. "What's the game? Is this how you get us to let our guard down so you can leave again? If you go, I'm not coming after you again."

"Yes you would, darling," Nathan tutted with a smile that made the other man scowl. "But I'm telling the truth. I intend to lie here and get well, study this trap, and release my daughter's spirit whatever that takes. And, following that, I intend further to abide by my young guide's direction as pertains to meaningful action for the greater good."

Elton stared at him without speaking for a few beats, then turned around to settle on the couch with his back to them. "You're full of shit," he muttered, but he left it at that.

"I do think I'm due for another lie down now," Nathan said, and Cora helped him back to the futon and settled him in with his coffee and poppy seed bagel.

"So I think first, we should try talking to Councilor Marquez," Cora began, dragging the chair from across the room to sit beside him. "And I want to see if Thomas can track down Magister Calero, to see if he...made it, you know? He seemed like a decent guy. Either of them could probably give us a little more direction. Oh—and I heard about these people down in Georgia who—"

Nathan swallowed his bite of bagel in a lump so he could cut her off. "Cora." He waited until she paused before continuing. "I owe you an apology."

She dropped her head to let out a small chuckle. "Yeah, probably. I won't make you say it." She peeked back up at him with a smile. "I'm just glad you've come around."

He looked down into his paper cup and shook his head. "I feel as though I've only ever been...one sort of way. But looking at you—the woman you've become, I..." He stopped and gave the best shrug he could without hurting himself too badly. "I'll try it your way for now."

"You were about to say something sweet about me," Cora teased, leaning in a little closer to him. "Go on. My heart is ready."

"How can I possibly hope to encapsulate all that you are into such paltry words as my lowly tongue can form, my love?"

"You must be feeling better. Do you want to hear my ideas or not?"

"Of course."

"Then shut up and eat your bagel. I'll tell you what you missed while you were on murder vacation."

Nathan smiled faintly and nodded for her to go on. "I'm all ears, Cora."

Nathan didn't have the energy to listen for long—he was hurt worse than he would admit. Cora was happy to leave him to sleep once she'd used up the last of her poultice on the wounds that bled the worst. She shut the door quietly, made Elton promise not to rile him up, and threw her purse strap over her shoulder on her way out of the apartment.

They needed more supplies—and Nathan had given her a list.

Elton stared at the spare room door for a while after she'd gone, frowning and drumming his fingers on the back of the couch. There was no way Nathan had simply given up on his revenge. Not after everything Korshunov had put them through. There had to be some other angle—some other purpose. Elton was beginning to think that he really ought to just let Nathan go if he tried to go off on his own again. But he knew that, if Cora asked him to, he would put the other man on the floor and sit on him to keep him from leaving.

He let his breath out slowly and ran a hand down his face, letting it rest over his mouth while he leaned his elbow on the sofa and watched the silent door. Nathan's words echoed in his head. *The ones I didn't walk out on are dead.* He'd grimaced and looked away as though he hadn't meant to let them slip. Was that fear? From Nathaniel Moore?

Elton's hand dropped from his chin, and he pushed himself up from the sofa and went to the kitchen for some water, rolling his weak shoulder as he went. He'd hit it against one of the brick walls of the alley when Nathan had thrown him. Nathan wasn't exactly light, either, and Elton had carried him a few blocks back to the apartment. It was going to ache for the rest of the day, for sure.

Before nearly enough quiet had passed, Nathan's voice called out for Cora from the spare room. Elton considered ignoring him, but instead gave a snort and opened the door himself.

"She's shopping," he said, already leaning back out of the room when Nathan tutted at him to wait.

"Actually, I need you as well. This may be a good time."

"For what?"

"My things. If you would be so kind, Elton."

"Aren't you resting?"

"I'm not a complete invalid," Nathan sighed. "I want to talk to Señora Marquez."

"About your new humanitarian calling?"

"Skepticism is a worthy trait only in moderate doses, darling." He gestured toward the door, indicating his bag beyond. "Please."

Elton forced his hand to release its tight grip on the doorknob and turned away from the room, scooping up Nathan's bag and dropping it unceremoniously beside the futon.

"And this pouting doesn't look good on you," Nathan muttered as he reached for the duffel's side pocket. He scooted a little further upright and paused with his hand still inside the pocket, then peeked up at the blond. "Will you allow me to give you a gift, Elton?"

"If you've got any variety of body part in there—"

"A real gift," Nathan assured him. "Give me your hand."

Elton hesitated, but Nathan waved him closer with a tutting gesture, so he took a step forward and offered the other man his hand.

"Now," Nathan began, reaching up to wrap long fingers around Elton's wrist, "I couldn't help noticing, during our too-brief sojourn together, that you've rather limited yourself by abandoning the shackles of your Magistrate employment."

Elton's eyes kept locked on Nathan's gasp, his mouth pulled into an untrusting frown. "What are you talking about?"

"Your groundings, of course; all the potential the Magistrate poured into that ring you refuse to wear again. I thought you could do with having it back—sans the troublesome memories of your government service. So—your gift." He finally lifted his hand from the pocket of his duffel bag and pulled Elton gently closer by the wrist, then showed the gold bracelet in his palm. It was just like the ones Nathan wore himself—a simple bangle with carved, rounded points at each open end. In fact, now that Elton looked, one seemed to be missing. But this one had been engraved around the entirety of the ring with ogham marks that the former Chaser knew even at a glance. Bindings, barriers, tracking spells. Things he hadn't used since he'd given up his own ring.

"Nathan—"

"Hush now. Consider it a peace offering—or an apology." Without waiting for Elton's approval, Nathan slid the bangle over his hand and gave the gold a light squeeze to tighten and secure it. He let Elton's wrist slip from his fingers and sat back against his pillow, allowing the blond to retreat a step.

Elton frowned down at the bracelet in silence. Nathan didn't seem to be waiting for a thank you—he'd already pulled his bag a little closer and was humming tunelessly to himself as he searched for his phone.

He lifted his phone into his lap with a soft, holding down the power button until the screen lit up. A moment later, the phone in Elton's pocket gave a loud chime, and the blond flattened his hand against it as though that might disguise the sound.

Nathan paused and glanced between the phone in his hand and Elton's pants pocket. "That's a guilty look on your face, Elton," he said, lifting his eyes to the other man's frown. "Have you been seeing other people?"

"It's your AMBER Alert," Elton grumbled, taking the phone from his pocket and turning the screen to face Nathan

He stared at the screen for a few seconds, then his eyebrows pulled upward along with his gaze. "Elton—you were *tracking* me?" Before the blond could defend himself, Nathan cut him off with laughter that caused him to wince and hold his injured stomach. "And here you've done nothing but claim you hope to be rid of me for months. How am I to trust a single one of your objections now that I've seen the true feeling in your heart?"

"I should have let Korshunov eat you," Elton sighed, Nathan's wheezing laughter following him out of the room.

"But wait—I'll be so far away! How will you stand it?"

Elton shut the door sharply behind him and let his eyes briefly shut as he exhaled. The unfamiliar bangle was cool against his wrist.

Nathan was still on the phone when Cora returned. She dropped her bags by the door and rushed to sit in with him and listen, though there wasn't much point—Nathan's Spanish was too quick for someone who'd given up learning it in the eleventh grade. She did poke him in the arm once and frowned at his swatting hand.

"Even I know *matar*," she hissed. "You're asking about helpful things, not murder, remember?"

He waved her away, thanked Councilor Marquez, and ended the call. He looked between Cora's eager face and Elton's doubting one in the doorway, then gave as deep a sigh as his injuries would allow him.

"Well, I'm very sorry to say that, if Señora Marquez is to be trusted, there's only one place for us to go next if we intend to follow through with Cora's suggestion of giving real help." He shook his head with a somber frown. "We have to go to Cancún."

"We *have* to," Elton repeated dryly. "We *have to* leave the country and go to a touristy beach town."

"Nothing for it, I'm afraid."

"And what, exactly, is in Cancún?"

"Cancún is," Cora spoke up, turning to look over her shoulder at him. "Last fall there was that bad hurricane, remember? It got damaged really badly."

"What does that have to do with the Magistrate?"

Cora ignored him and returned her attention to Nathan with a slight crease in her brow. "Is that why? Marquez thinks there's something there we can help with?"

"Possibly."

Elton started to protest again, but Cora put up a hand, slowly closed her finger to her thumb, and drew it across her lips, then pointed at the blond to be sure he understood he was being shushed.

"Like what?" Cora pressed instead, but Nathan only gave a pensive hum.

"I wonder."

"And you want to just go," Elton said. "Forget that Korshunov has been after all three of us for months and that he's still out there. Isn't it better to finish this while he's weak, and while we know he's in town? I can do it if you've decided to become a pacifist."

Nathan exhaled softly in amusement. "He's not recovering from what I've done to him anytime soon, darling." He looked up at him with a quiet promise in his black eyes that Elton knew well. "Let him enjoy it."

9

Too heavy. Everything was too heavy. Too thick. Too hard to breathe.

Nikita's massive body lurched unsteadily through the narrow back street, claws scraping asphalt with every heave forward. He needed somewhere to hide. Somewhere to rest. This shape wouldn't hold—he'd barely kept it this long.

The alley was shadowed and empty, leaving just enough dark space to squeeze between a corner and a rusted dumpster. His spell failed before he could even try to fit his body there—fur fell from him in clumps, and his bones cracked as they shifted back into human shape. He let his head rest against the brick in the hidden corner, blood seeping from the cuts on his limbs and each breath seeming to take in half liquid instead of air.

He couldn't stay here. He needed to move, needed to get—somewhere. He just had to stay awake. Just stay awake.

Nikita jolted, fingers gripping tight into the sheets underneath him as his eyes opened. He scanned the ceiling and thick-painted walls around him. Just a single room, with the bed he was in, a sagging sofa and a small television by the wall, and a stove and refrigerator at the far end. Cramped and empty all at once. He didn't know this place.

Something smelled like broth—but even the hollow hunger in his belly couldn't overcome the swelling of nausea at the thought of tasting it. A toilet flushed behind a door by the stove, and a man stepped out. Late twenties, white, brunette, average build. Wire-rim glasses. He smiled. Nikita didn't know him, either.

"Hey, you're up," the stranger said, moving a few steps closer to the side of the bed. "You were touch and go there for a little while. How you feeling?"

"Who are you?" Nikita asked in place of an answer.

"Oh—sorry. I'm Collin. This is my place. You were passed out in the alley, and you looked like you'd been in some shit, so since I live right here, I brought you in." He tilted his head slightly and nodded toward him. "I saw your ring. You're a Chaser, right?"

Nikita shifted and tried to sit up, but his body wouldn't obey. He hid his wince as best he could and settled back against the pillow again. "What's your registry number?"

The man paused, gave an uncertain sound, then seemed to remember his answer. "4597132. Sorry. I don't have to use it much," he admitted with a smile. "Keep to myself, you know? But I still know magic injuries when I see them. That leg looked fucked. I tried putting some stuff on it. Is it any better?"

Nikita swallowed down the rising bile in his throat. His head was swimming, his body ached, and even the scent of the cooking soup put the memory of ashes on his tongue. He distantly heard the stranger speaking to him again, but the voice was muffled. His vision darkened again, and sleep took him.

He woke up periodically, though it was impossible to judge how much time had passed—he couldn't tell if it was a streetlamp or sunlight coming through the yellowed blinds in the brief time he was lucid. Sometimes he was able to sit up enough to drink from the glass of water the man left by the bed, but even that went down by force—the taste was still sour in his mouth.

Once, Nikita opened his eyes and found the stranger sleeping on the sofa, wrapped up in a blanket with frayed edges. Why had he brought him here? They didn't know each other. Why not just report him to the local Magistrate office and let them take care of it? What did it matter to him what happened to some Chaser on the street?

Nikita eased himself out of bed, flexing his fingers slowly through the burn of the spell still wrapped around his hand. The man's t-shirt was too big for him, and the cotton boxer shorts almost slipped down once he was upright. He didn't like the feeling of wearing someone else's clothes. It was inappropriate. Like taking liberties. Too close.

He stumbled on the way to the tiny bathroom and had to brace himself against the wall. His knee still felt crushed, but he managed to make it back to the bed without undoing what good his little rest had done. He took another swallow of the rancid water and laid back down with a furrow in his brow. He didn't have a choice for now. He didn't have the strength to leave.

The stranger—Collin—was talkative when Nikita was awake. Noisy. He didn't seem to notice or care that Nikita wasn't answering any of his questions. He just chatted and offered food and drink, which the Chaser choked down and didn't always keep there.

Collin tried more than once over the next couple of days to touch Nikita's hand, to ask him about the purpling lines there. Nikita didn't allow it. His fingers felt tight and stiff now, but he couldn't afford to release the spell. Not until the Bies returned to him. It would complete its work—separate Willis from Moore, get him out of the way for good. Nikita just had to hold on.

10

Nathan complained about the lack of luxury in the rental car Thomas had provided—of course he did—but he satisfied himself with a spare blanket gifted from Nock and settled across the whole of the backseat, leaving Cora the shotgun seat while Elton drove.

The goblin hadn't wanted him to go. She hadn't said so, exactly— she'd complained loudly about the fuss Nathan had made and told him that the next time he tried to die, he'd better do it somewhere she wouldn't be responsible for his corpse. But even Elton could see the worry in her tight-lipped frown as Nathan kissed her cheek goodbye.

Maybe all of them would have been better off if he'd decided to become a househusband.

Elton was just grateful for some peace as they made their way South. Nathan dropped off to sleep shortly after they started, so it was blissfully quiet. Cancún was a long drive, but even Nathan wasn't keen to try to fly, given the state of the Magistrate's close supervision. He hadn't taken the further step to admit that he was in no shape to maintain their glamours even if they'd wanted to try, though Elton and Cora both knew it.

Cora seemed happy to watch the trees pass by outside the window for a time, but her eyes began to shift back to him with greater frequency the longer they went.

"Is there something you want to talk about, Cora?" Elton finally asked.

"I just thought maybe I should congratulate you," she mused.

"For what?"

She reached across the center console and flicked the gold bangle on his wrist. "On your marriage."

He snorted in distaste. "It's not remotely like that."

"Well it's adorable."

"It's *practical.*"

"When you showed up at Nathan's apartment last year, did you think you'd ever be accepting jewelry from him?"

"It's not—jewelry," Elton argued, refusing to acknowledge the slight heat at his collar. "It's a grounding. That's all."

"Sure sure. Anyway, it's cute on you," she finished with a poorly-restrained smile.

Elton stared ahead at the road and didn't answer her. It wasn't *jewelry.*

When Nathan did wake up, he leaned back against one of the doors so that he could stretch his legs, allowing the smoke from his cigarette to filter out through the cracked window above him. He kept a pile of small, striped wooden tokens in the hammock made by the blanket in his lap and picked one out, holding the cigarette in the corner of his mouth while he carved lines into the wood with a small, sharp knife.

Cora sat sideways, one leg tucked underneath her so that she could watch him over the shoulder of her seat. "What's all that palm for, anyway? I almost cleared out the shop getting what you asked for."

"It's a surprise," Nathan murmured around his cigarette, and Elton saw his teasing smile in the rear-view mirror.

"Haven't we had enough surprises?" he cut in.

"What a life, devoid of surprise," Nathan sighed. "I'd rather have been eaten by the bear, I think."

"What a tragedy that would have been," the blond muttered, ignoring Cora's light thump to his bicep.

"If you must know, I was thinking that it's only polite to arrive with gifts when partaking of a host's hospitality," Nathan went on. "We are going to be guests of Señora Marquez, after all."

"Grounding gifts?" Cora asked, and Nathan paused to tilt his head and blow his next exhale of smoke toward the window.

"Is there a better sort of gift?"

She smiled, absently touching the pair of bracelets on her wrist. "I guess not."

Elton glanced up at the mirror. "Are you planning on telling us what we're doing when we get there? Marquez must have asked you for something."

"A gentleman never kisses and tells, Elton."

He flexed his fingers on the steering wheel and watched the road rather than taking the other man's bait. "I'm just telling you now that if I drive for six days and end up in Cancún just because you want to go to a beach, I'm going to drown you there."

"Always flirting, never following through," Nathan said with a sad sigh.

"Can I help carve?" Cora spoke up, clearly hoping to change the tone of the conversation, but Nathan shook his head.

"Better if I do them myself, I think." He set down the first completed token and took up a fresh one. "But if you would tell me more about the advice you got from Mr. Proctor?"

"Oh—of course!" She turned to dig in the bag at her feet and scooted back to face him once she'd retrieved her phone. "He texted me some stuff. He said if you wanted to bring the egg to him, he could do some tests and try to open it himself, but I...figured that wasn't what you wanted."

"You know me so well, my love."

"He sent me a list of things to try, but some of them use the tools he has at the house, and those are—" She shook her head. "It would be underselling it to say they're complicated to make. Like, go cut a branch from this kind of tree, but not one that's too old, and do it on this day at this time, *then* carve it, and then you can use it for this other thing you have to do at midnight on the third Thursday or whatever the hell."

Nathan's brow creased faintly. "He's a curious one," he said with a soft, pensive hum. "He didn't force you to partake in any dark blood rituals, did he?"

"Well, he didn't *force* me," she teased, and Nathan snorted. "For real though, some of this stuff is doable. I have the ingredients he said to use, so we can try once we stop somewhere for the night."

"You are a greater gift to me than I could ever deserve, Cora."

"Yeah, I know." She smiled and rested her cheek against the side of the seat, satisfied to watch him work.

Elton stopped for gas somewhere just the other side of the Virginia state line. There hadn't been much around for miles except farmland, so he almost drifted into the truck stop on fumes, but they managed to arrive at the pump without having to push. Nathan had fallen asleep again but woke up now at the sound of Elton's door, squinting into the afternoon sun as he pulled himself up from his blanket.

"God, finally," Cora sighed. She climbed out of the car, stretched, and then leaned back in through the open door to look at Nathan. "There's a Dairy Queen in there—I'm going to go get the biggest container of fries they'll give me. Do you want anything?"

"I wouldn't say no to some solid food," Nathan answered. "Pick me something delicious; I trust you."

"You got it." She straightened and leaned her elbows on the top of the car. "What about you?"

Elton shook his head. "I'll find something in the shop. Don't get into trouble," he called after her as she crossed the parking lot, but she only waved over her shoulder at him without looking back.

"She's not a child," Nathan said, his voice coming through the cracked-open back window while Elton pumped the gas. "She's a competent witch, fully-grown and capable of seducing her choice of moth-eaten widowers."

"We just don't need any more heat than we've already got." Elton glanced across the lane as a car pulled up opposite him. A man rose from the driver's seat and stood by the hose, but he didn't reach for it—he just stood, his eyes steadily peering around the side of the pump directly at the blond's face.

Elton gave him a brief nod of acknowledgment, but he still didn't move. He stared, not speaking, barely even seeming to breathe. Elton glanced down at the other man's hand in search of the silver ring that would mark him a Chaser, but it was missing. With a frown, he turned away enough to pull the nozzle from the car and slide it back into place, briefly catching Nathan's eye. He didn't need to say anything for Nathan to move across the seat toward him and follow his gaze back toward the lurking stranger. Elton stepped back from the car and headed for the store, skirting the staring man even as his head turned slowly to follow the blond's path.

As he stepped into the convenience store, he walked by another customer standing near a slowly spinning display of lighters, who raised his eyes to Elton as he passed but did not return his nod. Cora's voice rose over the dull music over the speakers as Elton approached the row of metal coffee servers by the wall.

"Hello? Excuse me?" She stood on tiptoe to lean a little farther over the separating glass, waving a hand to catch the attention of the teen girl behind the counter. The young woman just stared forward from beneath her visor, thin-lipped and focused. Cora twisted her neck to follow the girl's gaze and gave a small huff. "I know, he's cute," she said as she dropped back onto her heels, "but could I just get some food, please?"

Elton paused with his hand on a stack of paper cups, locking eyes with the girl at the counter. She didn't move or speak despite Cora's questions—she was watching him. A quick look over his shoulder told him the man by the door had begun to inch closer to him, and, through the glass front of the store, he could see the man at the pump had turned to stare after him, motionless in the parking lot. A woman at the back beer case had stopped with the door wide open to look across the shop at him.

"Cora," Elton called, and she lifted her hands toward the teen worker in exasperation, but when she saw the state of the rest of the customers, she went still.

"You're not *this* cute," she murmured.

"It's time to go," he said evenly, leaving behind his hopes for coffee as he stepped toward the door.

The man by the lighters turned slowly as Elton passed, following him with steady steps but not crossing the threshold after him. Cora stuck close beside her companion, and her hand fastened tight on his sleeve at the staring, blank-faced gathering that now waited for them in the parking lot. All around the perimeter, strangers stood staring, while others climbed with purposeful, mechanical movements from their parked cars. Too many to simply bind—maybe thirty of them.

Nathan had pulled himself from the backseat and now leaned against the side of the car with a hand pressed to the bandage beneath his shirt. He scanned the men and women around him with a pensive frown on his face, but he didn't call out.

Elton didn't need his willow token to sense the magic in the air. These weren't Chasers; something else was at work here. It was almost the same feeling as—

"Cora," he said, touching a hand to her back that made her jump, "get to the car."

She complied without question. As she approached the man at the pump, he didn't even seem to notice her, though his breath hitched his shoulders up slightly as she passed him by.

Elton moved forward to follow her, and the surrounding strangers closed in tighter in time with his single step. He stopped—and so did they. He barely heard Cora murmur, "What the hell?" across the parking lot as he chanced another step forward. The group shifted with him, pausing as he did, and Elton looked across at Nathan.

"A bit more quickly, perhaps," Nathan suggested, and Cora nodded in eager agreement as she backed toward the car.

When Elton tried to comply, the men and women circling him rushed forward, reaching for him with clawed hands in contrast to their blank, staring faces. The one that reached him first seemed to be jerked backward by strings, hitting the ground with arms flailing. A cut began to bleed at his collarbone, drawing no response from him, but Cora's shout stilled the splitting skin.

"They're just people!" she scolded. "Don't hurt them!"

"That's all very well to *say*, my love," Nathan countered in exasperation.

Elton didn't have much attention to spare. The distance between himself and the car was almost immediately filled with bodies, each grabbing for him, snatching at the sleeves of his shirt. The gifted bangle on his wrist warmed, and at his hasty word, "Sreïd," the attackers nearest him fell back as if pushed by a fast-expanding wall. He moved past this first wave as they fell to the ground and dodged a few of the next as Cora pulled them to the ground and held them there, but a woman from behind him took hold of his arm to stop him short and drag him backward.

As soon as she touched his skin, nausea hit him like a punch in the gut. His vision washed white, and the scene around him shifted—the faces of the men and women blurred, eyes darkening to black pits, and Elton's skin burned from their scratching hands. The red air thickened in his lungs, drowning him, and something loomed at the edge of the lot, black and pulsing and immense.

Cora's fist jerking him by the front of his shirt drew him back to reality. Her dark eyes were focused through their panic as she threw a glance over her shoulder in the direction of the shadow Elton had sensed.

"Keep moving," she commanded, leading him by her grip on his clothes over the top of a pair of men pinned with their faces against the ground.

There were too many of them—though Elton got good use out of the gold bracelet, he could only hold a dozen bindings for so long. The people still free grabbed at him, fighting to keep him from escape, each touch sending a heavy pounding into his skull and a flash of white over his eyes. Cora kept a steady hold on him through the path she made, though he heard her spells more than saw their effects as they moved forward.

Nathan had already situated himself behind the steering wheel by the time Elton and Cora made it to the car, so they both piled into the back seat. Elton had to give a woman a firm kick to the shoulder to get her to release his ankle so that he could shut the door, and even once they were enclosed inside, the strangers outside still pulled at the edges of the doors and windows, some climbing onto the roof and hood to pry at the windshield. Blood smeared the glass as their fingernails tore away from the machinelike relentlessness of their hands.

"I'm just going to go, shall I?" Nathan asked as he threw the car into gear.

Even Cora had no objection—there was no way for them to go but through. She and Elton tried to force their attackers away from the car and out of the way as much as possible, but the frame still lurched as one tire rolled over the legs of one of the fallen men.

"I swear," Nathan muttered through gritted teeth, punching the gas and heaving the car back up onto the road, "the moment a person decides *not* to go about causing rampant mayhem—" He paused to press his hand against the window and snapped out a curse that shoved one of the last clinging strangers loose from their grip on the driver's side door. "Just had to go and foul me up on day one, didn't you, Elton?"

"You're blaming me for this?"

Nathan didn't answer; he only tutted at the struggling engine as he forced the rental car back up the ramp onto the interstate. Cora turned to kneel in the seat and look out the back window, a deep frown on her lips as they pulled out of sight of the trail of crawling bodies still desperate to reach them.

Elton's arms were covered in raw scratches, some even bleeding through his shirt, and he knew bruises would soon form on his knees where he'd hit the ground more than once on the way to the car. His heart thudded against his ribs, and he fought to breathe. Cora dropped down facing front beside him and touched his shoulder and jaw, turning him to face her and pushing the hair out of his eyes. Sweat beaded on her forehead, and she seemed to also be short of breath, but she looked into his eyes with a scrutinizing gaze.

"Are you still you in there?"

"I'm fine, Cora."

"Just checking." She released him and settled into her seat. "Did you see it?" she asked.

"I saw something," he said with a brief nod. "It was sort of a blur. A shadow. But *something* was there. I could see it when they touched me."

She paused. "A shadow," she echoed. "You didn't see the creature we saw on the road the other day?"

"No—did you?"

"I did. It was right at the edge of the lot, just standing there, like before. I only saw it for a second—like you said, when one of them grabbed me—but everything went red, and it was like there were these...threads, or cords, or something, coming from it, connecting it to all those people, holding them by the neck like a collar or...a noose." She frowned at the floor for a moment before looking back up at him. "You had one, too. But yours was...different."

"Different how?"

"I'm not sure." Her face scrunched slightly in thought, and she shook her head. "It can't be good. What are we supposed to do about it?"

"You'll think of something," Nathan assured her.

Cora went quiet. She seemed to remember after a few seconds to buckle her seatbelt, which prompted Elton, too. He watched her prop her elbow on the door and lean her chin into her fist, scowling pensively out at the passing trees. She'd seen beyond the veil so clearly—and she'd come to Elton's rescue, without a doubt.

"Thank you," he said, hoping it was quiet enough that Nathan wouldn't hear.

She looked back at him in mild surprise, but then a faint smirk curled one corner of her lips. "Well, we can't all be this good."

Elton softened and gave a quiet snort. "I suppose not."

11

They all slept on edge that night—Elton kept his eyes on the motel door and window until he could no longer prop them open, and Nathan sat cross-legged on the bed until hours after dark, going over the notes Cora had written for him based on Thomas's advice. The string-wrapped egg had sat beside him all evening, never more than a few inches away and often gently protected by the cup of his hand and slow brushing of his fingertips.

Cora helped him mix oils and herbs, carve chunks of wax and wood, and grind insect parts to powder, but none of the methods Thomas suggested had any effect. The egg remained sealed, the twine unbroken—there wasn't even a visible line where the shell should have been able to split to release the spirit for use. Whatever Korshunov had done to shut the spirit inside, it wasn't going to be easy to undo. Nathan was convinced it really was Adelina in there—but whether it was her, or just some spirit Korshunov had caused to look like her somehow, it deserved to be set free.

"We'll figure it out," she promised Nathan in a soft voice.

"At least now I know where she is," he said as he set the egg gently on the nightstand. "The answer will come in time." He smiled at her, but she didn't quite believe it.

He left her on the bed so that he could peel off his bandages and stand under a hot shower, and she cleared their supplies off of the blanket so that he could settle in when he returned, then situated herself on the far side of the room between the bed where Elton slept and the wall.

She stayed awake well into the night, long after the two men had gone silent, staring into the black emptiness of her polished mirror. That spirit was Korshunov's—she felt it in her gut. And it was following them. Following Elton. Did that mean Korshunov himself was close behind? She didn't dare look for him directly again—not after the way he'd shown up at the lake—but whatever this spirit was, it wasn't trackable, either. She hadn't been able to feel it at all at the gas station, but once one of its...puppets? Had touched her, it had been bright as day, lurking at the edge of her vision.

Thinking about the flickering line wrapped around Elton's neck made her shoulders hunch, and she tucked her knees up closer to her on the floor and held onto her elbows. Something that took control of Elton's mind, then broke his ward, then took over thirty-something other people and convinced them it was a good idea to take leaps at a moving car—and it was tracking Elton.

With renewed determination, she stretched across the floor to reach her laptop in her bag and opened it up. The brightness of the screen almost blinded her in the dark room, but she squinted until she adjusted. Without knowing even the name of the spirit that was chasing them, information was hard to find, but she took down some notes on banishing spells she found until her head drooped so close to her laptop that her forehead hit the top of the screen. She needed to be ready the next time that thing showed up. But she needed sleep, too.

She shut her laptop, folded the soft cloth back around her mirror, and tucked it back into her bag, then stripped off her jeans, pulled her bra off through her t-shirt sleeves, and crawled under the blanket next to Elton. Maybe in the morning, things would seem a little less complicated.

They didn't.

In the morning, while the others were still waking up, Elton paced the length of the small room. He made it a few laps before Nathan bothered to question him.

"We can't just carry on," Elton said. "That creature yesterday—it's following us. And Cora thinks it belongs to Korshunov. That's what you said, isn't it?"

She nodded. "It's hard to explain, but it feels the same." She looked over at Nathan, who was now frowning at her.

"You didn't think to mention that bit."

"It's been a lot, okay?" She pushed her pillow-mussed hair out of her face. "I don't have any proof. But this spirit is…weird, and bad, and I think Korshunov summoned it like he did the other weird and bad monsters we've seen since he showed up. And I think it might be after Elton. When we saw it the first time, it controlled him, and yesterday, that…thread, or whatever, that I saw…it was like it was linking Elton to itself."

"We can't just leave this be," Elton said. "Even if Korshunov is out of commission like you say, his pet clearly isn't. We ought to stop this at the source before even more people get hurt."

Cora glanced between them with a furrowed brow. "So we're back to murder? What about all that stuff you said about trying a different way?"

"We can try a different way after the man actively hunting us is dead," Elton said flatly.

"Until the next person they send!"

Nathan stayed quiet, running his fingertips over his mouth in thought. He gave a soft hum and raised his eyes to Cora again. "I'm trying it your way. What do *you* think we should do?"

Cora hesitated with both men's eyes on her. Elton was right— Korshunov was obviously still a threat. But dealing with him the way Elton wanted meant going all the way back to Boston to find him and losing any momentum Nathan had toward being a decent person. Going on to Mexico meant risking the spirit coming after them again. No answer was good. But one was better for Nathan.

"I think…we should keep going. Put as much distance as possible between us and this thing. Marquez is waiting for us."

Elton scoffed lightly. "And just wait for the next time it finds us?"

"I found some spells last night. If it does catch up to us, I think I can send it away."

"You *think*?"

"That's enough, darling," Nathan cut in. "Let's have a little show of faith, shall we? Distance it is. Breakfast on the go, then, yes?"

Elton didn't seem happy about the decision to keep driving, but he kept his complaints to himself. Still, Cora could feel how tense he was behind the wheel.

By the middle of the day, Nathan had finished carving his pile of palm tokens and felt well enough to complain about the lack of music. When Elton finally capitulated, his reward was Nathan's drumming on the back of his seat, so when they stopped for lunch, he refused to turn the radio back on for at least the next hour.

The roads were mostly clear, only growing crowded as they passed through city after city. Cora sent Thomas a few text messages without getting a response, but that wasn't unexpected. Reception wasn't great in the cellar. She stretched her legs, curled them up under her, and ate an entire bag of cheddar popcorn by herself, and they still had only just entered Mississippi.

Nathan dozed off again, so Cora didn't object when Elton stopped replying to her attempts to chat. Nathan needed all the rest he could get—even if he said he felt better, she'd seen the damage Korshunov had done. Her poultices were good, but they still took time. After a few miles of silence, the car began to subtly drift, and the driver's side tires gave a soft series of bumps as they ran over the yellow lane markers.

"Elton," Cora said sharply as she tapped him on the elbow, and he seemed to startle for a brief second before realigning the car. "You okay? If you're tired, I can drive a while."

"I'm fine," he said without looking from the road. "Sorry."

"Don't go all tough guy on me," she teased, but her smile faded slightly when he didn't respond. She watched him from the corner of her eye as they drove, but let him be—until an oncoming car approached them, and she felt the telltale thump of the car crossing the lane markers again. "Elton!" she snapped, but this time he didn't move.

On instinct, she reached for the wheel and jerked it downward, swerving them away from the other car a moment before impact. Their rental careened into the low ditch and bounced on the grass, but Elton still didn't slow down. The engine revved hard as the tires hit the dirt, and then Cora's head hit the expanding air bag. She lost a couple of seconds to blackness, and when she stirred, she heard Nathan grunting and grumbling in the backseat. Steam rose from the crushed hood where it had met a thick tree trunk, and the windshield was thick with spiderweb cracks. Elton was slumped over the deflated bag from the steering wheel, not moving. Cora reached out to shake his shoulder.

"Elton, are you okay?" She shook him a little harder when he didn't answer and moved closer to get a look at his face. "Elton, wake up."

He gave a soft groan and shifted where he sat. Cora looked past him and out the window toward the road, and through a clear patch of cracked glass, she saw the slick, spined tail and dark mane of Korshunov's creature. Its red-wrapped face turned toward her, and even though she couldn't see its eyes, she felt the burning malice of its glare.

"Fuck, fuck, fuck," she whispered, still shaking Elton's shoulder.

Behind her, Nathan shoved the back door open. "Is that the thing you've been seeing?" he asked, but he was already too far out the door to see her nod. He took a step into the ditch on unsteady feet, bracing himself on the side of the car and scowling out toward the road as he pushed away.

"Nathan, be careful, it's—"

Elton leaned back and raised his head, but his eyes stayed on the floor. He sat still for a moment, and Cora pulled back her hand. Something wasn't right. He wasn't right. She grabbed at the backpack by her feet and tugged it with her as she forced the dented door wide and scrambled backwards out of it. Elton's gaze swept toward her, expressionless, and he pulled himself from the seat and over the center console with blood dripping down his face from his forehead.

"Fuck," Cora said one more time, arm-deep in her backpack to retrieve the packet of banishing materials she'd put together. She left the bag in the ditch and headed toward the road. Nathan was closer to the creature than she liked, and when he shouted a spell at it, nothing happened. The spirit tilted its head, curling horns seeming to absorb the light around them, and Nathan stumbled without being touched, hands gripping the sides of his head as he swayed.

"Nathan?" Cora called, but he didn't answer. Behind her, twigs in the ditch cracked, and she threw a look over her shoulder at Elton, who was now much too close and Terminator-like for comfort. When she looked back at Nathan, he too had gone still, arms at his sides, and he turned slowly to face her. *Fuck.* She clutched the satchel of herbs in her hand and set it alight with a word, then took a deep breath and hurled it over Nathan's head toward the spirit while she shouted out a likely-mangled version of the Latin Thomas had sent her. The flame burst into a broad ring around the creature and sent up thick white smoke, quickly hiding the spirit from view. Nathan and Elton both faltered for a moment, going slack as freed puppets. But then a rumbling sounded in Cora's ears, so low she almost couldn't hear it, and the sharp tips of those black horns emerged through the rising smoke, followed by jagged teeth, a long, cloth-covered face, and finally, the slow step of a slick, clawed foot. Even though its eyes were hidden, it looked straight through her, and the sunlight glinted on the near invisible red string trailing from its cloth bridle across the ditch and around Elton's throat.

It hadn't worked. The thing still stared at her, and whatever temporary effect she'd had, it was fading now—Nathan took another step toward her. She didn't dare back up into Elton, either—and she'd learned the hard way what could happen if she tried to get the help of a reg on the road. Into the woods was her only option—but then what? Go where? How far? And without Nathan and Elton?

She didn't get to make the choice. Elton reached out for her, the sleeve of her shirt tearing in his fingers as she jerked away, but before she could finish her stumble toward Nathan, something else took hold of her. Earth and leaves from the underbrush rushed to her, enclosing her in a whirlwind in seconds, and her feet were lifted from the ground. She flailed her limbs and shouted out any spell she thought might help—but then she was standing again. She held out her hands to balance herself as a wave of dizziness subsided, and when she raised her eyes from the ground, she found herself in a small clearing, so deep in the woods that the sound of the interstate had gone silent. Just a few feet from her, leaned casually against a tree, was a faun, one hoof crossed over the other at the ankle. Thick, dark fur covered his legs and up over his waist, leading into a grey human torso only slightly more sparse with hair. Lips curled into a smile beneath his broad nose, and he watched Cora through golden eyes slit sideways with black. Thick, twisting horns spiraled from his forehead, curling down around long, furry ears and back upward into small, sharp hooks. He rolled an apple between his hands and nodded toward her.

"Just in time, girlie," he said, and she furrowed her brow.

"What...uh," she began, glancing around the trees as though it would help her get her bearings, "sorry, what—"

"Such a do-gooder you can't even remember them all, huh?" The faun pushed away from the tree and clicked his tongue at her. "I'm just returning a favor you did me once."

"I...did?" She paused, then gasped out loud and pointed at him. "You were in the Magistrate jail! In Toronto!"

"Ding ding," he snorted.

"You've—you've got to take me back!"

"You're welcome for the daring rescue," the faun answered with a sneer, pausing to take a bite of his apple. "Look, kid," he went on around a juicy mouthful, "I was just trying to return a favor, not be your personal taxi. I already had to follow you around this long. We're square, now, right?"

She paused. "Wait—you've been following me?" She lifted her hands and quickly shook her head. "Never mind." She stalked the edge of the clearing, skirting the faun's imposing figure and trying to force her brain to work faster. "Fuck," she swore. "Fuck—I've fucked it up. Nathan and Elton are still back there with this thing, and it was *my* job to banish it, and it didn't work, and now it's going to follow us forever—if it hasn't already killed them—and—*fuck*," she finished one last time, coming to a halt and pressing her hands hard into her eyes. She looked up at the soft sound of hooves approaching her and tilted her head back to look the faun in the face.

He stared at her in silence for a beat, mouth drawn to one side in thought, and then he snorted. "Okay. Listen," he began with a faint air of resignation, "I'll tell you something. That thing that's got your friends is a creature of the forest, and it's not here of its own will. If you think you've got the oomph to do it, I can show you how to set it free."

Cora hesitated. "If it's set free, won't it just...rampage?"

The faun smirked and winked one strange, slitted eye at her. "Sometimes wild things are grateful to those that help them. You got the oomph?"

She frowned and stuck her chin out as she looked at him. "I've got it."

Cora's feet landed in the muddy grass of the ditch just a few feet from where Nathan and Elton lay, hands clamped to their heads as though trying in vain to block out a terrible sound and bodies twisting and thrashing. There was no trace of her prior spell now, and the spirit stood by, watching over them with an eerie stillness. She swallowed hard at the sight and fought back the frightened tears threatening to spill from her eyes. She didn't have time for them—and she needed to see clearly.

Clutching tight to the small curl of gifted horn in her palm, she walked past her suffering companions with sure steps until she stood facing the towering creature. At the first twitch of its head, she squeezed the scrap of horn painfully hard, dug her heels into the dirt, and shouted, "Ελευθερώνεοτε!"

The cord from its bridle frayed into threads and snapped, disintegrating into flecks of light that spun to the ground. The red cloth around its face came loose and drifted to the grass in heavy ribbons, falling to ash before they touched the earth. A faint shake of the creature's head tossed the last of the binding away, and the spirit focused its unveiled eyes on Cora at last—narrow black depths that made her skin prickle. She held her ground and her breath, not daring yet to be relieved at the silence that had fallen over the men behind her.

The creature flicked its spined tail once or twice, then gave a faint snort and lowered its head just slightly. The next time Cora blinked, it was gone. She whipped around and half collapsed at Nathan's side as he sat up, still rubbing at his head. Elton stirred a moment later and grunted as he pushed up onto his knees.

"Are you guys okay?" she asked, touching each of them in turn as if to make sure they were solid.

Nathan scoffed softly and looked up at her with a faint smile. "Because of you, I suspect."

Cora heaved a sob of relief and threw her arms around his shoulders, almost toppling him backwards into the mud. "I was so scared," she whispered into Nathan's shirt, and he gently shushed her and ran a hand over her back.

"You were incredible, as usual, my love."

She sat back on her heels and looked over at Elton, but he was still silent, staring at the ground with his hands on his knees. He took a deep breath, then got to his feet and moved back over to the car. He leaned inside and began to haul out their supplies, setting them carefully on a dry patch of grass. Then he moved to the trunk and added their suitcases to the pile.

"Elton?" Cora called, and he paused with his hand on the strap of Nathan's bag before letting it drop. "Are you okay?"

"We need to decide what we're doing," he answered without looking up. "This car won't move, and we're in the middle of nowhere Mississippi."

Cora softened a little and stood, helping Nathan up with her. "Well, I don't know any spells to fix a car," she offered with a shrug.

"I'm pretty sure that doesn't exist."

"Listen to you two," Nathan scolded. He winced faintly and touched his side where his stitches must have ached, but he waved away Cora's reaching hands. "Always looking to magic to solve all your problems."

"*You're* saying this?" Elton cut in, but Nathan ignored him.

"Haven't either of you ever hitchhiked before?" He was already climbing the incline back toward the road without waiting for an answer.

"Uh, no," Cora called after him, "because I don't want to get *murdered*."

"You're not going to be murdered." He stood at the side of the pavement and held out a thumb as if it was the most normal thing in the world.

"Nobody picks up hitchhikers anyway because they're afraid of being murdered. Hitchhiking is literally the only activity where both possible parties avoid it because of potential murder."

"People do pick up hitchhikers when they have a cute girl with them," he answered over his shoulder. "So get up here."

Cora groaned uncertainly but did as she was told. "That's because cute girls are easy to murder," she pointed out.

"Have a little faith, my love." Nathan turned his head to glance back down the ditch. "Come along, darling; we want them to know what they're getting into."

They waited for close to an hour, watching cars speed by without any sign of stopping. Cora tried more than once to tell Nathan it was pointless, but he insisted they give it a fair shot, since their other option was walking toward civilization carrying all of their belongings with them—"And manual labor gives me hives, you know."

Finally, a long, pale yellow tank of a car rolled to a crawl a bit ahead of them, blinking its turn signal as its brakes lurched it into a stop at the side of the road. Nathan approached it immediately and leaned against the passenger window with his best smile on. Cora edged closer to peek into the car, but after only a brief exchange, Nathan straightened and waved them both over. Cora and Elton gathered up their things and waited a few moments for the trunk to pop before they filled it with their bags. Nathan was already in the front seat by the time Elton shut the trunk, so they exchanged a quick uncertain look before climbing into the leather back seats.

The driver that turned to smile back at them was a white woman easily in her eighties, with silver hair loose around her face in wild curls and a smile creasing the deep lines in her face. "Hello!" she said brightly, plastic bracelets jingling as she offered her passengers a quick wave.

"Dolores," Nathan began with his elbow on the headrest, "this is Cora, and Elton. We really can't thank you enough for the rescue."

"Thank you so much," Cora said, choosing not to finish with "for not being a murderer."

"Not at all, not at all," Dolores went on over the top of Elton's added thanks. "I'm headed into town anyway; we'll get you all taken care of." She leaned forward in her seat to peer over the steering wheel, checked her mirrors, and pulled slowly back onto the road. She didn't turn her signal off—she didn't seem to notice the clicking sound for almost a mile, so Nathan reached over the ancient, wood-paneled dashboard and flicked it off for her.

"Dolores—beautiful name, by the way," Nathan said. "Spanish for sorrows—but that hardly seems to suit you," he added with a teasing grin. "Though you've broken your share of hearts, surely."

"Oh, I don't know," the old woman said with a laugh.

"I've an eye for these things."

"I had a few suitors, I suppose. Many years ago," she chuckled.

"With those cheekbones? Dolores, you're breaking my heart as we speak."

She swatted lightly at his arm and glanced into the rearview mirror at the others. "Where are you folks headed, anyhow?"

"Mexico," Nathan answered for them. "Just a...call it a family vacation."

Dolores paused for a moment, her pale eyes moving from Elton's face in the mirror over to Nathan. "Oh," she said a little too cheerfully. "Well, good for you two! It's so nice to see all different kinds of families these days."

"We're not a couple," Elton interjected.

"Elton is a bit traditional in his views," Nathan sighed. "In any case, I'm much more interested in you," he went on, slouching in his seat and leaning subtly closer to her.

Elton went silent and leaned back against the peeling leather cushion. He stared out the window with a thin frown on his lips while Nathan and Dolores chatted in the front seat. Cora nudged him with her elbow, then nudged him a little harder until he looked at her.

"Are you okay?" she asked in a hushed voice.

His eyes narrowed faintly, but it wasn't anger on his face. It was guilt. "You were in danger because of me," he murmured. "Both of you," he added even more softly.

"And you've been in danger because of us how many times?"

"That's different."

"Is it? Or are you just too manly to rely on other people?"

His lip curled slightly. "It's not about being *manly*—"

"Whatever," she interrupted, offering him a smile so he'd know she was teasing. "We all get each other in trouble all the time. But we're all here for each other, too, right? So who cares? It'll all come out in the wash."

He snorted and shook his head, but he'd softened, just a little. "Thank you, Cora. If it weren't for you, I—"

"Forget it," she insisted, fighting a little warmth in her cheeks. "You're stuck with us—the least I can do is save your life every now and then to make up for it. But that spell really took it out of me, if I'm honest. So could you, like, make yourself useful?"

Elton allowed a small smile of understanding to touch his face, and he shifted to stretch his arm across the back of the bench seat, allowing

Apostate

her to lean over and settle in the space under his shoulder.

12

There was only so much improvement Nikita could do in this apartment. He needed supplies. He needed to find Moore. There was no way he could ask Magister Hubbard for help again—Nikita had been warned. He was on his own. But without money, without groundings or ingredients, what hope did he have to catch up with Moore? His options to proceed were limited, but limited options were no excuse. He couldn't stay.

He still fought to swallow anything but broth and water, and his knee had mended but was still weak under the weight of his body. Collin tried to be helpful and was often frustratingly incompetent instead. Even if Nikita had had the strength to summon a potoplenyk, he wasn't confident it would be of much help to him. His injuries weren't physical—not really. They'd been caused by whatever poison Moore had forced into him.

Nikita took sleep whenever he could get it. In the middle of what he thought was his third or fourth day in the apartment, he was jolted awake by a sharp burning in his hand and wrist. It stung so deeply that he winced and clutched the wounded hand to his chest on reflex, fingers trembling when he pulled back enough to look down at it. The burn that marked the spectral leash he held the Bies by had blackened, and the skin there flaked away like charred bark. The pain lingered, but the heartbeat of magic that had pulsed under the skin since he'd summoned the creature was gone. The bond had been broken.

The Bies had finished its work.

Nikita waited until his host had left the apartment and dressed himself as well as he could. The only shoes he had were dirty sneakers with frayed laces and half a size too big. The t-shirt and jeans he took were baggy, but Nikita cinched up a worn belt and made do. His knee ached, but it was a manageable pain.

He searched the apartment for any supplies he could take. Most of the cabinets were bare of anything but sacks of rice and cans of roach spray, but, tucked at the back of the closet floor, he found a simple wooden box. Some various stones, oils, and wood for groundings, a few empty jars, zipper bags of herbs—a sparse kit, but a beginning. He ran his hands over the high shelf in the closet and touched a hidden envelope with a stack of small bills inside. He pushed them into his pocket and left the empty envelope where it fell on the floor, then picked the box up under his arm.

He had his hand on the door knob when it turned from the outside.

Collin stood just inside with a bag of groceries in one hand, confusion on his face as he eased the door shut behind him.

"You're not leaving?" he asked.

Nikita didn't answer him. He just glanced toward the door, waiting for the other man to get out of the way.

"I don't think that's a good idea." Collin frowned at him—worry? "You look dead on your feet, man. I even got some new stuff to help—if you're willing to let me try a spell I admittedly haven't practiced very much."

"No. I'm leaving," he said evenly.

"You're in no shape, man," Collin tried. "Look, I don't know who you're chasing, or what you've got going on, but you're gonna kill yourself if you go out like this. If you're worried about being a burden or whatever, don't; you can stay as long as you want. Or if you know a better spell to help, just tell me—I can get whatever from the shop if you let me know."

"No." Nikita stepped to the side and made for the door, but Collin didn't move.

"Let me at least take you to a Magistrate clinic," he went on. "You're a Chaser—they'll help you no matter what trouble you got into. If I let you walk out of here, and something happens to you—" He reached out to lay a hand on Nikita's shoulder, urging him with gentle pressure back toward the bed, and static buzzed in the Chaser's ears.

The box of groundings hit the floor, scattering stones and broken glass across the wood, and Nikita grabbed hold of the other man with both hands around his neck. Collin dropped the plastic bag of groceries to pull at Nikita's wrists, but the Chaser shoved him back against the door with the full weight of his body, and the impact jarred him enough to send them both to the floor. Nikita straddled the man beneath him, but his hands were too weak to press hard enough on Collin's throat. He leaned back to keep his face from the other man's flailing, scratching hands, and shifted to push his knee into his neck instead. He picked up a can that had rolled from the grocery bag and slammed the blunt edge into Collin's temple—again, and a third time, until blood poured from the broken skin and the frantic arms went slack.

Nikita's hands trembled as the bloody can fell from his fingers, leaving an arcing trail of red on the floor. He took shivering breaths and slowly moved back from the body, leaning against the side of the creaking sofa and resting his arms on his bent knees. He wasn't going to let him leave—he would have stopped him from going on. From moving forward. From finding Moore.

He watched the slow crawl of the blood on the floor, the rest of the apartment seeming to blur around him. He couldn't stop. He couldn't ever stop.

He had to keep moving. Moore wouldn't wait.

He needed a way to find him. A way to ensure that Moore would never get the better of him again.

Nikita crawled over Collin's legs and turned over the open box, searching through the contents and turning over jars with bloodstained fingers.

"Birch," he murmured, scanning each scrap of wood and brushing aside each incorrect piece. He repeated the word over and over again as if he could summon the grounding into his hand, and when he located it, he squeezed it so tightly it dug into his skin.

He shoved away the box and the spilled groceries, making space on the floor in front of him, and reached across to the pooling blood on hands and knees. With his good hand, he spread the blood in wide arcs, smoothing the dark stain across the wood. When he had his canvas in front of him, he took the birch in his fingertips and began to scratch lines in the thin layer of blood.

"Нечистая сила," he whispered with rasping breath as the marks began to take shape. "Найти его. Найти его."

The blood heated under his hands, thickening and darkening around the edges of the blisters forming on the surface. Clinging strings stuck to his fingers as he lifted them from the floor and sat back on his heels, and the marks he'd made burned black into the wood. Blood flowed from its source near the corpse's head into a deeper circle in front of him, each rough cyst growing and bursting with dull, damp pops. The shape of a head, then a neck, then a narrow pair of shoulders rose upward from the pool, features smoothed by the constant run of blackening fluid over the face and long, slick hair.

Nikita's weak breath caught in his chest, and he coughed, covering his mouth with the back of his burned hand. His arms quivered under his own weight, but he kept his place. "Помоги мне," he said roughly, though the spirit seemed immovable. Its low voice gurgled as if the liquid was in its throat, only a narrow slit of black showing where its mouth opened beneath the pouring blood.

"Не бесплатно."

A price. What price? Did it matter? What wouldn't he pay? Nikita curled his fingers against the floor and grit his teeth, forcing air through his dry throat.

"Name it."

13

Dolores dropped them off at a car rental in a city called Meridian, and once they'd pulled all their belongings from the trunk, she'd given Nathan a hug, patted his cheek, and then waved at them from the window on her way out of the parking lot.

"How does somebody who makes as many friends as you end up with so many people who want you dead?" Cora asked, looking up at him on the curb outside the building.

"The *Magistrate* wants me dead," he corrected. "Government bureaucracies don't take charming personalities into account, I'm afraid." He smiled at her. "Now let's get something spacious, hm?"

While Nathan went inside to glamour them a new ride, Elton stood on the sidewalk with his arms folded, frowning down at their suitcases like he was trying to intimidate them into keeping still.

"You okay?" Cora asked, but he didn't look up right away. When he did, his frown didn't soften.

"I can't go on to Mexico with you."

"What? Why?"

"That spirit took control of me. More than once. It put bystanders in danger. It put you and Nathan in danger. It...caused *me* to put you in danger. And Korshunov set it on me. I can't just carry on with this humanitarian field trip knowing he's still out there."

Nathan emerged from behind the glass door with an employee who directed him to a car parked nearby, passed him a key, and thanked him for his business. Nathan turned to his waiting companions but paused as he glanced between them.

"Are we having an argument?"

"Elton says he's not coming to Mexico."

Nathan's eyebrows lifted as he turned on the blond. "What? No; you must."

"I can't leave with Korshunov still out there. It's just delaying the inevitable. He's going to get more people killed coming after us, and we're going to have to deal with him eventually. It should be sooner rather than later."

Cora lifted her hands and let them slap back against her thighs. "We're moving backwards. Now you're both team murder?"

Elton shook his head. "I never said we shouldn't kill him. I just didn't want Nathan killing himself and a dozen other people in the process."

Nathan put a hand to his chest. "Darling."

"Shut up."

Cora took a step closer to Elton and frowned up at him. "How has all this death worked out for *you*, huh? All this serial killer bullshit has really put a dent in the world's problems, hasn't it? Oh yeah," she cut him off when he had the audacity to look offended, "I heard all kinds of gory details about the things you did from Thomas's people. That's really how you want to keep going?"

"Korshunov is trying to kill *us*, Cora."

"And he's the bad guy!" she said much more loudly than she meant to, hands flailing in frustration. "At least, he's supposed to be! I want us to be the *good guys*. You both act like that's what you want, too, but then everything is just dead."

Nathan put a light hand on her shoulder. "What do you suggest, my love?"

She scowled at the ground, keeping her mouth shut for a few moments to keep her anger and guilt from bubbling out. She'd made the wrong call before. She knew it. Just running away, hoping things would turn out—Elton said he'd been the one to put them all in danger, but she was just as responsible. If they just kept going again, Korshunov was sure to catch up to them eventually. And every time he'd gotten the drop on them, something terrible had happened.

"We have to turn him in," she finally said.

"Turn him in?" Nathan echoed. "To whom, exactly? He's a Chaser."

"Yeah, but Chasers still have rules, right? Elton went to *jail* for doing way less than this guy has! He has to be responsible to someone."

Nathan tapped his lips with the metal end of the car key and exchanged a long glance with Elton, who exhaled quietly as though agreeing to something Nathan hadn't even said.

"What's happening?" Cora said. "I don't like this telepathy. Include me."

Nathan hummed in amusement. "I did join up with this comedy of errors because I liked the sound of the word *vigilante*," he chuckled. "Perhaps turning over a corrupt Chaser to a slightly-less-corrupt Magister, if we can find them, would be satisfying. And less bloody," he added with a smile.

Cora perked up. "You really think we can?"

"We can surprise him for once," Elton said. "He's sure to be after Nathan again before long; we can be waiting for him. And maybe Marquez knows someone trustworthy we can hand him off to."

"We're gonna, like, lay a trap for him?" she asked, unable to keep from bouncing on the balls of her feet. "Man, he deserves a good trap."

"He certainly does," Nathan agreed. "But we'll need somewhere to be still a while until he catches up, won't we?" He turned to make for the car, apparently trusting that Cora and Elton would carry all of their bags to the trunk. "And as I can hardly be expected to withstand an extended stay in *Mississippi*, I humbly request that we get a move on so that we might be somewhere more inhabitable before midnight."

Elton loaded the trunk of the car while Cora passed him suitcases and grounding kits, calling through the car while Nathan settled himself in the driver's seat. "I hope you don't mean New—"

"New Orleans!" Nathan cut him off with a cheerful laugh.

Elton sighed as he shut the trunk. "Great."

Nathan's glamour paid for a much more luxurious rental than Thomas's credit card had. Elton didn't complain about this, at least; they were all tired, and the soft seats were a blessing. Cora stretched out in the back and used one of Elton's suit jackets as a blanket while she read a cheap romance novel on her phone.

Even Elton dozed off for a while, head lolling against the passenger side window. It was a boring ride, but peaceful—and Cora thought boring was a price she'd pay if it meant going a single evening without being attacked, chased, or beaten up. It was nice to listen to Nathan's soft humming with the radio after being away from him for so long. She hadn't realized just how much she'd missed him over the summer—even if sharing motel rooms with him again meant waking up and seeing his dick first thing in the morning.

Nathan brought them to a stop on a narrow street lined on both sides by two-story brick buildings with wrought-iron balconies, and he got out of the car at a pair of broad green double-doors. Elton was jerked awake by the sound of the car door slamming shut, and Cora sat up to get a better look out the window. Nathan already had the trunk open by the time she and Elton stepped out.

Cora rubbed at one eye and peered up at the swinging wooden sign above the door. This place didn't look up to Nathan's usual standards— but at this point, she'd take anywhere with a bed.

She was proven wrong as soon as they went inside. Everything was old-world chic, polished floors and thick rugs, and antique furniture lined the entry hall. It was more like visiting a wealthy Victorian person's house than a hotel. The suite they were led to was crowded with furniture Cora felt too poor to touch, let alone sit on—each of the three bedrooms they were shown had its own small sitting room, each separate accommodation linked by a narrow, wooden hallway. The space Cora chose contained a massive four-poster painted teal, a high-backed bright red sofa, and a jungle painting hung above the fireplace. Nathan carefully placed the egg trinket in a small sweater nest on the nightstand, then settled himself on a bed surrounded by a canopy of delicate, green patterned roses on a cream background in a bedroom that was a short stairway up from the leafy-green sitting room. Elton was left with an ochre floral four-poster and garden-bloom furniture, but he didn't seem to pay much attention to the decor anyway.

"This place is nuts," Cora laughed as she fell down on Nathan's blanket beside him. "How much does it cost to stay here honestly? Wait—don't tell me. I'll just get mad."

Nathan chuckled softly with his hands laced over his stomach. "Back some hundred and fifty-odd years ago, this used to be a house belonging to a friend of mine," he said. "The decor has improved since then."

"What? Get out," Cora laughed. "Really?"

"Of course. He was an older gentleman by then, and after he died, he left his weeping, lonely widow all alone in such a sprawling house as this. The poor dear was positively forlorn. I couldn't bear to see it."

"And let me guess," Cora snorted as she rolled over onto her stomach to look at him, "you comforted her in her time of need, right?"

"Naturally."

"You're so full of shit," Elton spoke up from beyond the wall.

"I am not!" Nathan called back defensively.

Elton appeared in the doorway and leaned against it with his arms crossed. "You did not fuck some 19th century plantation owner's wealthy widow."

Nathan leaned up on his elbow to grin at him. "Well not just the one."

Elton scoffed and went away again, shutting the door to his bedroom with a definitive clack. Cora smiled as she heard the familiar sound of shuffling paper even through the wall, and a moment later, Elton was down the hall and setting his wards all over the antique windows.

"So," Nathan began, tipping his chin at Cora as she looked back at him, "tomorrow, I'll call Señora Marquez and see if she has any input on Magisters who might be trustworthy."

"And we're not worried about Korshunov, like...getting the drop on us again?"

He shook his head. "I have his personal concerns now. I'll smell him coming."

"Even if he's a bear?"

Nathan huffed. "Can you believe?"

"I *know*, right? Why can't you turn into anything?"

"Trust that I'll be looking into it," he answered with a smile, then sat up and glanced toward the nightstand and the waiting egg. "You ought to get some rest. I'm going to try a few more things."

"As if. Let's get that thing open."

Nathan's smile softened slightly, and he nodded at her.

Cora stayed up helping Nathan test spell after spell on the egg trap until she fell asleep next to him. He wasn't there when she woke up, but the egg was nestled safely in his sweater on the bedside table. She glared at it as she rolled out of bed. There must be something they could do—there was no way Korshunov had made an actually impenetrable spell. There was probably no such thing at all. And if Cora was this frustrated, she could only imagine how Nathan was feeling.

He passed by the bedroom door in his underwear and carrying a steaming mug, and he paused when he spotted her awake. "Ah, there you are. Ready to go shopping?"

"Witch shopping?"

Nathan chuckled and gestured toward the window. "We're in New Orleans. Laissez les bon temps rouler."

"Fuck. Yes."

After a quick shower, a change of clothes, and a weakly-argued protest from Elton that they ought not draw attention to themselves, the three of them left the hotel and made their way through the French Quarter. Nathan walked as if he could have shown them the way with his eyes closed, smoking a cigarette and exhaling it above him in a plume as he went.

Cora got Thomas on the phone once they'd found a shop that Nathan approved of, and she wandered the shelves, describing them to him and scooping anything he said might be useful into her basket. Nathan seemed to know precisely what he wanted, and he chatted with the clerk while Elton picked through a few baskets of stones near the back wall. Cora was even able to find some of the rarer ingredients Thomas suggested, once Nathan smiled at the woman behind the counter and gained them access to the back room. Cora paid for the groundings and ingredients with a good chunk of her online earnings—even Nathan rarely tried to glamour a fellow witch.

They ate beignets while they walked back with their new supplies, which was nice and quiet until Nathan put a powdered sugar handprint on the back of Elton's pants and earned himself a scolding.

Once they made it back to the hotel, Nathan was eager to shut himself up in his bedroom, and Cora went with him. Elton even joined them, though his face made it clear he thought the effort was a waste of time. Cora couldn't be sure whether Adelina's real, actual soul was trapped inside the egg or not, but Nathan clearly thought it was.. It being important to Nathan was enough for her—and Elton, too, it seemed.

Cora made an infusion of burning bush bark and passed it on to Nathan to cool, then boiled another of pokeweed and shook it up with angelica and rue. She took the egg from Nathan's soft nest and carefully lowered it into the murky jar, sealing it up tight and setting it aside while they made the rest of their preparations. Elton made a circle of herbs on the floor—dried avens flowers, white clover, and horehound. Nathan was on incense duty—he mixed vetiver, frankincense, myrrh, fumitories, and furula gum into a sticky mass that smelled bad to begin with and turned to awful once he lit it.

Cora had read the instructions Thomas sent more than once, and everyone seemed to know their part, so they worked in silence. Nathan had a constant soft frown on his face as he placed the burning incense at the center of the circle Elton had made. He really needed this to work. Cora steeled herself with a light huff of determination, then carried the floating egg in its jar and kneeled beside him before twisting open the lid. Nathan scooped the twine-wrapped egg out and held it over the burning incense, turning it slowly in his dripping fingers to coat the shell with the smoke.

Elton and Cora sat by, watching Nathan as he focused on the small, precious token in his hands. Cora thought she saw his eyes narrow faintly, and when he was satisfied that the smoke had done its job, he laid aside the lid of the jar of burning bush infusion next to him. He wiped his hand on his jeans and dipped his fingers into the warm liquid, cupping the egg in his palm as he traced a slow, careful cross-shape over the shell. Cora handed him the wispy tamarisk twig she'd set nearby when he reached back for it and held her breath.

Nathan gave the center of the drawn cross a single light tap with the wood and paused. A tiny, barely audible crack sounded in the quiet room, and Nathan dropped the twig to cradle the egg in both hands. The air in the room dropped a few degrees, and something like living smoke rose from the now broken shell in Nathan's palms. It never quite took form, but a deep smell like spices filled Cora's nostrils. A moment later, the room was clear and warm again.

All three of them sat very still, until Cora dared to whisper, "Did it work?"

Nathan let out a slow exhale and crushed the eggshell in his fingers. Already his body seemed more relaxed, and when he turned back to them, he had a calm, genuine smile. "I believe it did."

Elton seemed skeptical, but he kept any nay-saying to himself. He just snuffed the incense and began to gather up the scattered herbs. Cora scooted forward to squeeze Nathan in excitement, and he shifted to put an arm around her, then pressed a firm, swift kiss to her temple.

"Let's call Señora Marquez."

14

Nikita forced himself to sit up in the stranger's bed. His head swam, and he flinched when he caught himself on his blackened hand. He looked slowly around the room, craning his head to get a full view and frowning as he pushed the balls of his hands against his sockets. The ache behind his left eye hadn't subsided even after sleep.

Though the thought turned his stomach, he needed food. He rose from the bed slowly, stepped over the unmoving ankles on the floor nearby, and leaned against the kitchen counter to steady himself. He pulled open the bag of bread and tore away the spots growing mold before pushing the rest of the slice into his mouth. It dried in his mouth like ash and chewed like sand, but he swallowed it down.

On his way back to the sofa, he stumbled, and his shoulder hit the wall. Warm, humid air hit his face, and a smoky smell filled his nostrils—Moore was standing in a doorway in what looked like an ostentatiously-decorated home, mostly nude, sipping from a heavy mug then saying something Nikita couldn't hear.

He stayed against the wall, taking shallow breaths until the apartment came back into focus around him. Had that been a house, or one of Moore's usual hotel suites?

Nikita rubbed his knuckles into his eye as if it would ease the throbbing there, and he blinked it open to blackness—all that remained on his left side after the spirit had taken its payment. He'd seen the haze that had overtaken his vision as he'd washed the blood from his hands the night before, the sickly grey soaked through the blue of his iris. This vision must have been his reward, but it told him nothing. How was he supposed to find Moore with only the knowledge that he was in a room—somewhere? More would come. The spirit had assured him his request would be granted. He only had to be patient.

He sank down onto the sofa and leaned his head back against the cushions. Impossible to relax his body. He was hungry, but his stomach revolted at the thought of anything more substantial than bread. But he'd lived on bread before. Sour, grey bread softened by thin cabbage soup that would have to last until the end of the week. Complaining of hunger meant being beaten, so he didn't complain.

Nikita flattened his hands against the thighs of his borrowed jeans and tried to focus his flattened vision on a single spot on the ceiling. Collin's clothes didn't fit him, and the worn jeans and pocket t-shirt felt slovenly. He'd scrubbed himself in the shower, though standing upright for so long had made him vomit into the drain, but he still felt intolerably dirty.

Her voice was in his ear, jerking his small body as she tugged up the collar of his secondhand shirt and fastened the highest button tight at his neck. *Look at yourself. A disgrace. You look like a serf.*

He grit his teeth and winced faintly at a throb behind his eye. His clothes didn't matter. Patience mattered. Just wait. Moore had no way of escaping him now. All he had to do was wait.

Every time Nikita's vision shifted, it made him tense. He saw Moore walking down a city street, laughing and smoking a cigarette. Hours passed; Nikita didn't move. He stayed on the sofa, watching the ceiling, waiting for each flash of sight to give him some clue. He fell asleep at some point, slid sideways on the sofa with his legs tucked up. Late in the morning, he woke with a jolt—he saw small hands holding a paper basket of sugary pastry, and Moore, face marked with white powder, leaning toward a larger man who recoiled from him.

Nikita's black-burned hand stung as he gripped the cushion near his face. Willis. Willis was alive. But the Bies—Nikita's breath caught in his throat, the rage in his gut rising up to choke him. The Bies had failed. They'd destroyed it somehow. And now they were on a fucking vacation. Moore had been satisfied to get away with the rusalka and leave Nikita behind. He wasn't chasing him—after everything Nikita had done, Moore wasn't chasing him. He didn't matter. He wasn't a threat.

His jaw hurt from holding it so tight, and his ragged breaths came even faster. Without thinking, he slid from the couch, his fingers seeking some of the shards of glass still littering the floor around the spilled groceries, and he sat with his back to the sofa, pulling the sharp edges across the skin of his stomach. With each breath and each droplet of blood seeping into his t-shirt, his heartbeat slowed, until he finally let the glass slip from his hand and took a long, slow exhale.

The city looked familiar.

Nikita spent time through the afternoon sorting through the groundings and supplies still scattered across the floor. He piled them more neatly and took note of what he had. He sometimes had to stop, his surroundings overtaken by the smell of chemicals and wine and the sight of Moore lounging in a soft chair while a woman filed his fingernails. Every time, Nikita exhaled through gritted teeth, stopped himself from scratching at his blinded eye, and forced his attention back to his task.

The body smelled.

He ate some of the canned soup Collin had brought and the last of the bread, but most of it ended up in the toilet when his stomach rejected it. He was growing weaker—he couldn't carry on like this. He took some incense from the kit he'd put together, lit the cone in a clean space on the floor, and laid down. He let the smoke fill his lungs and settle over his body, thickening the blood in his veins while he whispered his incantation. Sweat beaded on his forehead and fell in winding rivers into his hair, but he did his best to slow his breathing.

The tiny, airy spirit jolted his body as it slipped into his lungs, seeping into his skin from the inside. If the curse Moore had laid on him could be lifted, this was the only thing Nikita had left to try. His body had healed its wounds, but he would need to be clear-headed when he saw Moore again. He wouldn't be put down by a stomachache—and he wouldn't let this spell kill him before he finished his job.

The spirit had no say—this was its duty. To come when Nikita called, and to do as he asked. They weren't living creatures; not really. They were just energy, drawn together by his will and dispersed just as easily. His grandmother had told him so. She used to hide small objects around the house so that he could practice calling spirits to find them, and, once their duty was done, she would snatch them in her long, thin fingers and grip them tight until he banished them. The first time, he had cried at the thought of destroying the little sprite he had summoned. So she'd done it herself, and she'd hit him. When she'd caught him in his room late the following night, whispering to a watery spirit no larger than his own small hand, she'd crushed it immediately. She'd made him kneel with his nose against the wall and whipped him until he bled.

That was the last time he'd cried.

He laid still for well over two hours, fingertips occasionally twitching against the wood floor, until cold air filled his chest where thick incense had been before. He turned on his side to cough and choked out the last wisp of smoke, watching it pool briefly on the floor before sinking beneath the wood. The spirit was dead—but he would finally be able to recover some of his strength.

Nikita breathed easy as he sat up, his lungs clear for the first time in days. He still felt queasy, but he was able to stand, even if it was slowly. It was enough. He ate two granola bars one after the other and kept them down. He slept.

A jerk woke him up after a few hours, and he gripped the pillow in his arms tighter to his chest as his vision lurched him from sleep and onto a narrow city street, lit with iron streetlamps and bustling with people who passed underneath iron balconies. Moore had a drink in his hand and a smile on his face, but above him, a sign hung between dark metal columns caught Nikita's eye—*Maison Bourbon.*

Of course. That's why the city looked familiar.

He was on fucking Bourbon Street.

Nikita lurched out of bed so quickly that his head swam for a moment, and he gathered up the groundings he'd left around the apartment, piling them all back into their box and stuffing it into the backpack. His hands trembled faintly as he worked, but he paid it no mind. He knew where Moore was.

He knelt on the floor and patted the corpse's pants pockets, then reached in and retrieved the cell phone from the one nearest him. Its battery was dead, but when he found the charger, the screen lit up right away. He dismissed the few missed call and text notifications and began to scroll through the contacts. One entry was listed only as "Station." Promising. Nikita tried it, waiting through a few rings before a curt voice answered.

"Yes?"

"Is this Boston?" he asked, aware suddenly of how rough his voice sounded.

"Please state your name and registry number, sir."

He swallowed before answering. "Nikita Korshunov, out of Ottawa, Ontario. Registration number 8957624."

A pause. "Thank you, sir. How can I help?"

"I need to book a flight to New Orleans."

Once he'd been given the details, he hung up the call, then left the phone behind on the floor and crossed the room to wash cold water over his face. It was finally time to go—he would have to be well enough.

He found his way back to the station, where he was able to request a replacement ring and identification, and then paid for a taxi to the airport with money from Collin's hidden envelope. He made it through the gate with the help of a Magistrate clerk, since he was also lacking his mundane ID, so he made his way to the proper gate as briskly as his still-aching lungs would allow. He was glad to be able to sit.

Everyone who passed watched him from the corner of their eye, scanning his ill-fitting clothes, his scarred hands and forearms. The ones who noticed his blinded eye gave a start or stared with curiosity or pity. Nikita wasn't interested in either. He was only interested in the brief glimpses that made him shudder and clench his hands around the backpack in his lap—Moore and his companions sitting together in a smoky bar, surrounded by people. They looked relaxed—unconcerned. Chatting. That was fine.

They could underestimate him one last time.

15

Marquez and Nathan had talked on the phone for some time; Elton wasn't thrilled that the entire conversation happened in Spanish, but he supposed Nathan had very little to hide from him at this point. He seemed cheerier, lighter on his feet, and unconcerned with what injuries he had that remained to be healed. He honestly did believe that he'd freed his daughter's soul from that eggshell this morning. If it made him more focused, Elton wasn't going to argue, no matter how skeptical he was.

He was focused enough, at least, to remember to ask Marquez for advice about a Magister willing to arrest an off-the-rails Chaser—at least, Elton was fairly sure he heard the word "Chaser" more than once during the call. He watched Nathan with his brows lifted in expectation as he hung up and tossed the phone onto the nearby sitting room sofa.

"Fate is occasionally kind," he said, and Cora finally looked up from her laptop. She'd given up trying to pay attention to the conversation fairly early on. "Señora Marquez says that the Magister right here in New Orleans should be open to hearing us out. She hasn't met him, but he apparently has a reputation for using his position to stick it to the higher-ups when he can, which means he may be just our sort of person."

"That's great news," Cora said with a smile, but it faded when

Nathan kept his eyes on her.

"I did ask after your Magister friend from Miami," he went on. "And it seems he was one of the unfortunate resistors. He was hanged two months ago."

Her whole body slumped a little, and she chewed her lips and huffed through her nose as she shook her head. "They just...crush anyone trying to do good, don't they?"

"They seem to do their level best," Nathan answered gently. "I'm sorry, Cora."

A few beats of silence passed before she answered. "Well. I've got high expectations for this new guy."

"As do I. Shall we go pay him a visit?"

"Now?" Elton asked, and Nathan shrugged at him.

"Why not?"

"It's the middle of the day. Shouldn't we wait until this evening, try to catch him at home?"

"Nonsense." Nathan picked up his phone again and slid it into his jeans pocket. "What's the point of making good with a Councilor if you've still got to skulk about? We're *expected*."

Elton stared at him. "*We're* expected, or he's been told to expect *someone*?"

"Does it make a difference?"

"Yes. It does. If this Magister thinks Nathaniel Moore is going to show up at his office, don't you think it might be a trap?"

"All right, I'll rephrase—does it make a *practical* difference? We go and he helps, or we go and we kill him."

"Nathan!" Cora piped up, and Nathan groaned loudly as he swung his head back in frustration, arms dangling as if they were too heavy.

"Fine," he sighed. "We go and he helps, or we go, he tries to arrest us, and we firmly but kindly request that he reconsider."

"I'll take it," Cora laughed.

Elton considered a moment, then shook his head, resigned. "I'll find out where the office is."

The building that housed the Magister's office was beige and nondescript, a stark contrast to the historic look of the surrounding streets. A single glass entrance door sat beneath a stretching second-story window, and the only signage on the outside wall was an iron-wrought silhouette of a stag.

"Do we all go in?" Cora asked, glancing between the two men as they all stood by the corner of the building. "I *think* I'm still slightly less wanted than you guys."

"No half-measures," Nathan answered with a smile as he flicked the butt of his cigarette away. Without waiting for agreement, he swung the front door open and stepped inside, forcing Cora to hurry after him.

Elton allowed himself a soft sigh before following them in. The building was surprisingly empty—the offices they passed held only desks and chairs, the conference room was abandoned, and even the kitchen seemed to be percolating coffee for no one at all. When they reached the end of the hall and went upstairs, they found a desk with another empty chair just outside a closed door. The computer's screen was still on; this place hadn't been empty for long.

"This looks appropriately official," Nathan chuckled, already reaching for the shut door's metal handle.

"Hold on," Elton said in a low voice. "Don't you think it's strange that there's no one here?"

"It is," Cora agreed quietly. "Seems kind of...trap-y."

Nathan hummed briefly, then nodded and tilted his head toward the door. "Then Cora can go in first. She's the least wanted."

She huffed but didn't argue as Nathan held the door for her. Elton followed right behind her, and at the far end of the room, they found a desk that wasn't empty. A balding Black man who must have been at least seventy sat in a high-backed chair with his hands folded on his considerable belly.

"I hope you're the ones I've been asked to listen to," he said evenly, watching them file into the room, "or else I've sent the whole office to lunch for nothing. It's not every day I get a call from a member of the Council—" He stopped, and he stared a moment in stunned silence before standing and leaning his hands on the desk. "I'll be damned. Nathan, is that really you?"

Elton glanced sidelong at the man beside him. Nathan? Not "Nathaniel Moore," or maybe just "You?"

Nathan's eyes narrowed faintly as he stepped past Cora to inspect the old man, but he didn't answer right away.

"You don't recognize me, do you? You've put a few years on, too—

though not as many as you're owed, I see."

Nathan hesitated with a hand on his hip, but then his eyebrows lifted, and he gave a sharp laugh. "Ray?"

The man let out a whistling laugh and nodded, happily accepting the hug Nathan skirted the desk to give him. Elton and Cora exchanged a confused look, but neither of them spoke.

"Look at you," Nathan said, leaning back with his hands on the other man's shoulders. "You're old as hell."

Ray cackled in return. "You're one to talk."

"How on Earth are you a Magister?"

"Same way anyone else is. I busted my butt."

"Exceptional," Nathan laughed. He finally turned back to his companions. "This is Cora, and that's Elton. This is Ray Morris—who was, what, perhaps seventeen when I saw you last?"

"That's about right." He gestured to the pair of chairs in front of his desk. "Come on and sit down now." He settled back into his desk chair, not seeming to mind that Nathan took a seat with one leg folded under him at the edge of the desk.

Cora smiled as she sat, but Elton couldn't uncrease his brow.

"All right, darling? You look as if you've swallowed a bug."

"This is just the first time we've come across someone who's *happy* to see you."

"Ray and I used to knock around and get into a bit of young man trouble," Nathan explained. "I wouldn't have expected you to go into politics," he added, leaning his weight on one hand on the desk.

"Well, I heard you talking up such a storm all the time about the Magistrate this, Magistrate that, all the things wrong with it. I thought it could do with a few more good folks."

Nathan paused a moment, his smile faltering just slightly as though this wasn't the answer he expected. "Well. I suppose it got one," he said. "At any rate," he carried on, "did Señora Marquez fill you in on our predicament?"

"She said you've got a Chaser after you who's putting civilians at risk? Regs?"

"Not just regs," Nathan said quietly. "And my new boss," he went on with a brief gesture toward Cora, "has forbidden me from committing unnecessary murders. We were hoping that said Chaser might be brought to justice some other way, but officers of the Magistrate willing to accept our offering are likely to be few and far between."

The Magister watched them from underneath bristling white eyebrows and rocked back a little in his chair. "Well I've got cell space, if that's all you're asking for. Drop him off. I can make sure he's put in the system."

"That's it?" Elton said. "Just on our word?"

"Nathan's a lot of things," Ray said with a light chuckle, "but he's no liar. If he says this Chaser is a danger, I believe it." He looked up at Nathan, and a warm smile wrinkled his cheeks. "Besides, I've heard a lot of good things about you lately. They all true?"

"Mm," Nathan hummed, "sixty-forty."

A small laugh shook the Magister's shoulders. "I'll take that, I guess. Anyway, what's a political office for if you can't protect your friends? If you catch this Chaser, bring him in, and I'll show him the way we do things in the Big Easy." He wrote a phone number down on the back of a business card and held it out to him. "Just give me some warning."

Nathan slid from the desk and offered Ray his hand, which the Magister took and squeezed with both of his own. "Thank you, Ray. Sincerely. I'll do my best to keep any trouble to a minimum."

Ray wheezed out another brief laugh. "Minimum for a normal person, or minimum for you?"

He grinned. "I said I'd do my best, not work a miracle."

"Just be careful. We haven't had much in the way of protests here, but there's not a witch around who's not on edge. We had a number of people taken from the city—there wasn't much I could do to stop it. All this terrible camp business. But from what I hear, you know all about those, don't you?"

"We've all got to do our part, Ray." Nathan gave the man a wink and held up the business card. "I'll be in touch."

Once they were all safely outside again, Nathan briefly inspected the card before putting it into his jeans pocket. "Well," he said brightly, "now that business is sorted—shall we enjoy the city?"

"We're not on vacation, Nathan," Elton reminded him. "We have to keep our guard up if we want to have the upper hand when Korshunov shows up."

"Darling, before lunchtime today, I've freed my murdered

daughter's soul from its cage and reunited with an old friend in an unexpectedly high place. Now I have nothing to do until a Chaser shows up ready to be brought to book. *I'm* on vacation."

"Me too," Cora added. "I know there's a lot to do, but if we have to wait anyway...when's the last time we had a couple of days off?"

"It's a free afternoon, at the very least. Just enjoy yourself, darling," Nathan pressed, touching a hand to his chest that Elton peered down at with blatant distrust. "I understand that, as guests of our hotel, we have access to the local athletic club, which includes a salon—and I'm in desperate need." He smiled back at Cora. "What do you say, my love? A bit of pampering?"

"Uh, yeah," she answered with a scoffing laugh.

"You really think that's—"

"Abup bup bup," Nathan interrupted with a quieting finger on the blond's lips. "I've had quite enough of this now, thank you. You'll spoil my good mood." He offered his arm to Cora, who took it with a teasing curtsy, and led her down the sidewalk without looking back.

"God damn it," Elton sighed.

The athletic club *was* nice—though Elton had no interest in joining Nathan and Cora in their foot baths and cucumber masks. He had no packed clothes fit for exercising in, and he wouldn't have wanted to agitate his shoulder just in time for dealing with Korshunov even if he had. So he took a walk on his own, confident that his companions would be contained for at least as long as a massage and a manicure took.

A couple of blocks away, he found a pair of wooden doors with worn white paint at the top of a short set of steps. A pair of plastic crates sat on the top step, filled with books and marked with a cardboard sign that read, "$1 each—pay inside." He took both steps in one stride and opened the door.

The inside of the shop was all narrow aisles made tighter by the haphazard piles of books stacked up against the shelves, so tightly packed in places that Elton had to pick his way over the top of the gap between two towers. The whole interior smelled like musk and vanilla, the warm and pleasant scent of slowly decomposing paper. He took his time through the aisles, scanning the crowded and mismatched spines and occasionally reaching out to brush his fingers over leather-bound copies.

He'd had nothing to read for months but whatever mysteries or detective thrillers were available at airports they'd passed through. Not that he had much time for reading these days. Or that he ever had.

Maybe taking an afternoon off wasn't so bad.

By the time Elton realized it was getting dark out, he'd been slouched on a back bench in a bar-slash-coffee shop next to a long-ago-emptied cup of Irish coffee and was halfway through *The Red Garden*. He snapped the book shut, picked up the copy of *Ficciones* he'd laid aside, and started back toward the hotel, cursing himself. He had no questioning messages from Nathan or Cora—which definitely meant they were making trouble.

When he got back to their suite, however, he found the pair of them lounging on Nathan's sitting room sofa in fluffy bathrobes, eating from a tray of fruit and sipping champagne.

"Darling, you made it back," Nathan called when he spotted him. "Just in time. Cora and I were about to go drinking."

"You're already drinking," Elton pointed out, passing them by to tuck his books into his suitcase.

"Well, yes," Nathan went on, a little louder so as to be heard beyond the door. "But we're going to get sexy first and then go and drink with strangers."

"For the record," Cora spoke up with a mouthful of strawberry, "I'm getting sexy for my own enjoyment only, as I now have a very nice boyfriend."

Nathan grunted in distaste. "Must you?"

"Shut up. Or I'll refer to him as my lover instead."

"That is worse, yes. Carry on."

"Thank you," she ended with a nod as she sipped from her tall glass.

"I don't think anybody should be out drinking," Elton said, taking a seat in a chair nearby them. "We don't know when Korshunov is going to catch up with us—or send some other creature."

"I'll know when he gets here," Nathan assured him, and Elton snorted.

"Even drunk off your ass?"

"Absolutely." Nathan rose from the couch and set his glass on the tray. "Now doll yourself up for me, darling, while I do the same." He shut the bedroom door, and Cora brushed by Elton a moment later with a smile and a shrug.

Elton didn't change, since anything he might put on would just be a different variation of the slacks and button-down he already wore, but he did roll up his sleeves in the humid night air, and Nathan undid his second collar button for him on the way out the door, which wasn't worth arguing about.

He didn't look particularly dressed up himself—he had his usual dark jeans and V-neck shirt on—and Cora had chosen a pair of high-waisted denim shorts with ragged edges and a shirt that Elton was fairly sure was Nathan's. She'd applied perfectly winged eyeliner and berry-pink matte lipstick and left her hair a stylish mess around her shoulders, and she leaned a hand against Nathan to balance herself while she zipped up her black ankle boots. A far cry from the hunching, timid girl in the moth-eaten sweater.

Nathan led the way out of the hotel and onto the street, and Elton held the door once he'd gone to let Cora out ahead of him.

"Hey," he said quietly as she passed him, and she paused. "You look really nice tonight."

Cora stared at him for a moment with slightly wide eyes, and then she smiled, put a hand on his chest, and tilted her head back to look up at him more dramatically. "You had your chance, sucker." Then she breezed past him onto the street and linked arms with Nathan.

Elton smiled faintly as he followed them.

Nathan had a drink in everyone's hand before ten minutes had passed. Apparently it was legal in New Orleans to just have a plastic cup full of alcohol in your hand as you walked the streets—which seemed to Elton like a monumentally bad idea, but Nathan and Cora were enjoying themselves. Elton could have done without quite such a tight crowd, but once they found themselves a table in one of the dimly-lit bars along the loud street, it was actually enjoyable.

Nathan told very animated stories about their time in the RV, Cora shared how much she'd learned about herbs—and blood eating—from Thomas, and Elton laughed when Nathan tried to argue about how abysmal he was at pool. Cora demanded they find somewhere to play, so they gave up their spot in search of a pool hall, and Nathan brought another round of drinks while Elton racked the balls.

Cora was pretty bad at it, too. Elton could have made a fortune off of them—if they'd had $10 between them.

By the time Cora started to get sleepy, Elton was happy to help her back to the suite. Nathan briefly complained that it was *only* two in the morning, but he relented, taking slow drags from one last cigarette as Cora walked between the two men, holding onto their hands and humming lazily to herself.

Elton helped her through the door of her bedroom and watched to make sure she actually made it onto the bed when she dropped, then retreated to his own room, where he had to physically peel Nathan's hands from him before shoving him out. He locked the door, then undressed, drank some water from the bathroom sink in his cupped hand, and laid down.

Not a bad night, overall.

16

Nathan didn't go to the club to swim the next morning. He stayed in his room, pillow held loosely at his stomach, staring up at the canopy of his bed. Adelina was free—he should have been pleased. Satisfied. But he'd expected to see her in his dreams. Be given some sign that she was unbound. None had come. She was loose from her confinement, that much was clear; but if she still wasn't free to visit him from the waters, what still held her?

He didn't like it. But there was nothing to do at the moment but wait for Korshunov—perhaps he would have an answer that could be pried out of his mouth.

Cora and Elton were already up by the time Nathan left his room, and neither of them looked the worse for wear from their late night. That was good. He had more of the city to show them, yet.

Even Elton had no protests when Nathan suggested they take a cruise on one of the riverboats and have a leisurely lunch—he finally seemed resigned to the prospect of having a good time where they could get it.

Cora rushed ahead of them as they drew close to the dock, and she pushed her way through a handful of people in her eagerness to get to the railing above the muddy river.

"It's really one of those old-timey things!" she called back to them, pointing out over the water. "With the big wheel on it and everything!"

"Did you think they were fairy tales?" Nathan chuckled.

"Listen, I'm from the desert," she answered with a laugh. "Come on, let's get on!"

Nathan glanced over at the blond beside him as they approached the line of people waiting to board. "Do you like jazz, darling?"

"Not particularly."

"Of course not. Well, you like drinking, and you like my company, so you'll just have to make do with that."

"Do I like your company?" Elton asked with a slight frown, but Nathan paid him no mind. He got them on board with a simple glamour, and the two men spent some time following Cora around the steamboat while she explored the decks.

It was a pleasant morning—not too sunny, with a warm breeze off the water. The blithe music and wandering tourists were a very different atmosphere from the time Nathan had spent on a trade ship up and down this same river, but he liked it better, he thought.

The three of them had a drink, ate some lunch, and sat near one of the open windows, watching the riverbank go by. Nathan could probably have stayed here happily for some time, with the pair of them to keep him company—but there was more to do. Cora wouldn't be satisfied to leave the world the way it was. Nathan couldn't be sure he would be anymore, either.

Elton sat up straighter in his chair as the riverboat rounded a broad turn in the water, and he locked eyes with Nathan. The same prickling feeling must have been creeping up the back of his neck, too. Nathan couldn't help the smile that crept across his lips.

He was here.

Before either of them had time to warn Cora, a heavy crack sounded below them. The whole boat rocked and shuddered so harshly that they had to catch themselves on the table to keep from toppling over in their chairs. It tipped sharply sideways, and Elton snatched Cora by the arm to stop her hitting the window, bracing himself against the now almost horizontal wall. Tourists and employees shrieked around them, grasping at each other and sliding across the rising floor until a number of them fell from the deck into the dark water below.

Nathan planted his feet on the window frame, but the wood split almost immediately. A jagged line shot up the floor, and the hull snapped apart, exposing the lower deck to the air and rushing water as the two halves were pulled down toward the sinking mud.

There in the gap, a creature rose from the muck—four massive, clawed hands pried at the boat as if opening it in search of food, and it stood hip-deep in the water on a third pair of limbs, all six of its extremities covered in thick, jutting scales. It wore a cloak of moss and algae over the breadth of its back that dripped mud and river water from its edges, clumps of the foul-smelling peat lodged in its scales and joints. A mass of gnarled horns twisted like driftwood from its flattened face, and when it opened its broad mouth full of slick fishlike teeth, a deep, deafening sound like a foghorn filled the air, forcing Nathan to slap his hands over his ears.

"—fuck is that?" he heard Cora shouting as the cry dulled. She struggled to keep her footing on the sinking wood even with Elton's arm around her, her attention on the former passengers flailing in the water below them. "We have to get these people out of here!"

The creature stilled ahead of them, its deep-set black eyes locked on Nathan. From in front of it, the wood where the boat had split gave a creak, and a much smaller figure stepped calmly up into view, balancing himself on the broken wood and looking down at the three of them with quiet fury hidden behind cold eyes—one of which had faded from clear blue to milky white.

Korshunov. Finally.

Voices screamed in terror and pain all around them as the buckling wood of the riverboat gave under the creature's weight. Electricity crackled from a dangling wire that swung down where it had snapped loose from the ceiling, but Koshunov didn't flinch. Behind him, the creature leaned deeper into the watery gap and reached one of its four massive arms across the broken decks, reaching for the trembling body of a woman who had managed to secure herself against the corner.

Elton snapped out a hand from his breast pocket, and the paper talisman flew from his fingers, lengthening and tightening around the monster's scaly fingers. It howled in a deep, booming cry that rattled the bones in Nathan's chest and tore back from the damaged boat, bringing a section of the deck with it as it curled its injured limb to itself.

Korshunov had raised his hand toward Nathan, and whatever spell he spoke was drowned out by the creature's roar, but the force of it still hit Nathan square in the torso and knocked him backward into what used to be the ceiling of the upper deck. His wrists hit the wood and stayed there, and he had to try more than one of the spells on his bracelet to wrench them free and drop back down to the window frame.

"Elton, the people!" Cora shouted next to him. The blond hesitated to release her waist, as she was already unsteady, but she shoved him until he turned his attention to the passengers frantically treading water below.

The monster's lower limbs had torn the cutting spell paper free from where it dug into its thick skin, and now it pulled purposefully at the few parts of the boat that remained above the surface of the river. The water flooded over Nathan's feet, and he swayed as the bowels of the deck buckled somewhere underneath him. With his eyes on Korshunov, he crouched down to dip his fingers into the swirling water, the carved chunks of wood hanging around his neck warming with intent.

"Leve kanpe," he growled, and as he rose, the water swelled with him, rising into a dripping wall that crashed itself forward into the Chaser and his creature. Korshunov was slammed from his place on the edge of the deck, but he snatched hold of one of the broken planks before he could be thrown completely from the boat and planted his foot on one of the monster's arms to push himself back up. His ragged voice shouted out a word that knocked Nathan from his feet, and the muddy water washed over his face, spilling into his nose and mouth. He coughed out a burst of bubbles as his body was pressed under the water, his limbs held fast to the crumbling deck. It only took a moment for him to tear free and breathe air, but it wasn't by his doing—Cora was hauling him up by the arm. She helped shove him to his feet and then turned her eyes on the dripping teeth of the monster still tearing at the boat. It had a man in one set of claws now, but Elton was distracted by the barrier he'd built around the largest group of swimmers, the shimmer of green forcing bits of falling wood and metal to be knocked harmlessly aside.

Cora clambered up onto one of the disrupted tables nearby and shouted to get the creature's attention, drawing one of its black eyes over to her. She tugged the cord around her neck, freeing the shaved curl of horn from underneath her shirt, and laced both hands around it. She took a deep breath and seemed to steel herself, then she shouted, "Ελευθερώνεστε!"

The creature jolted as if startled, and then it went briefly still with its victim still struggling and screaming in its grip. With a final quick glance of empty eyes surveying the destruction it had caused, the monster gave one more chest-vibrating foghorn cry and sank underneath the water. Cora cried out and tried to leap forward as the man it held disappeared beneath the surface with it, but Nathan grabbed her by the elbow to keep her from tumbling in after them.

Korshunov turned his head to watch the swirling water the creature left behind, and then, with a deadly fury in his eyes, fixed his gaze on Cora. She flew backward and crashed into the former ceiling, shattering a stained glass lamp underneath her. Nathan tried to catch her before she hit the water, but his own feet were knocked out from under him, his arms twisted behind his back so that he hit the foot of the upended table face first. The wood beneath him groaned, and the water rushed higher, flowing over the top of both of them. Nathan jerked upward enough to uncover his head and caught sight of Elton hip-deep in the water nearby, arms pushing forward as the entire barrier below them shifted and dragged through the river. The passengers below were being forced toward the shore and away from the wreckage, but moving the barrier was slow work.

Cora gasped for breath beside him but took in water instead, and Nathan could barely find the air to speak a spell. Korshunov splashed into the water beside him and fell on him, hands on Nathan's shoulder and head to force him back into the rising mud. He had little recourse—the Chaser's spell kept his body pinned, and if Nathan dared open his mouth, all he would do is swallow river water. If his connection hadn't been severed—if Kalfu would still answer him—

Nathan was jerked backward as the weight on his back was thrown away, and the pull on his arms faded, allowing him to push himself up and take a breath. Korshunov was on his ass in the water with blood pouring from his cheek and mouth, and Elton stood over Nathan with a dripping plank of wood in both hands. Korshunov spat blood as he snarled out another spell that threatened to crush Nathan's ribs, but the sudden pressure was cut short as a tendril of pale blue shot from beneath the water and snared Korshunov's head. It wrapped translucent threads over the Chaser's mouth and dragged him backward, his arms splashing up brown water as he flailed. In a flicker of light, Nathan could make out the skinless back of the woman he'd seen that day in the woods—Adelina's curls falling over her shoulders and exposed bone. Korshunov fought, but slips of incandescent blue had wrapped themselves around his limbs and forced him down.

The water was up to Nathan's chest now as he found his footing, and Cora seemed to be already treading water. In another few seconds, they would all be swimming. Nathan pushed through the water toward Korshunov but reached instead toward the barely opaque figure of the woman.

"Kè mwen," he called with anguish in his voice. She turned her head to him and extended slender fingers, but before he could touch them, her hand drifted back toward the Chaser as though guiding him forward.

Elton waded past him and snatched Korshunov around his middle, paying no mind to the spectral wisps binding him, then climbed over the top of what sinking wreckage still remained above the surface and hauled the struggling young man with him through the water. Nathan lingered despite Cora's urging pull at his arm, but the flickering woman in the water ahead of him faded and seemed to slip back beneath the swell of the river.

"Nathan, we've got to go," Cora begged, so he went, helping her away from the swirling pull of the deck and toward the shore while she clung to him.

The people in the thick reeds along the river were coughing, crying, checking on each other and speaking in frightened, confused voices. They were outside of the city now, but the crew must have gotten some message out—distant sirens were already beginning to echo over the flat swamp.

Elton dropped Korshunov face down in the mud and bound him with a word. They had nothing to tie him with, so Cora approached as soon as she was able to find her footing in the dirt and reached out a hand as Elton turned him over, her touch to his forehead and the wearily-murmured word "Enkonsyan" dropping the Chaser into a heavy sleep. Elton began to check his pockets for groundings and paused. Nathan pushed through the grass to stand beside him in time to see the blond pull the boy's t-shirt up to his chest. In a jagged pattern from the Chaser's stomach up to his shoulder, swollen red welts seeped watery blood from where scraps of stone had been pushed halfway into the skin and shoddily stitched over with black thread.

What rage had built in Nathan's chest as he drew near to the boy seemed to cool inside of him as he took in the weeping infection spreading spiderwebs of red across his torso.

"Are those his groundings?" Cora whispered.

Elton frowned and looked up at Nathan. "What do you want to do with him?" he asked, and Nathan felt the weight in the words.

He should kill him. He should step on his neck and push until the bones broke. Maybe hold him under the water and pin down his thrashing body. Snap every one of his limbs and leave him to bleed out into the river. Adelina had pointed him toward this Chaser—toward her murderer. Vengeance was what she wanted, wasn't it? Only that would truly set her free—for her spirit to see her death avenged. That was why she hadn't yet finished her journey. Why she still lingered here. That was why she'd helped restrain the boy, allowed Elton to take him. Vengeance.

Cora's hand touched Nathan's bicep and squeezed. She watched his eyes with an uncertain frown on her face, and she didn't have to speak for Nathan to understand her. Vengeance wasn't what they were after—and it wasn't what Adelina would want. This boy had been trained up and broken down by the Magistrate, and now he lay in mud littered with crushed soda bottles and decaying potato chip bags, having become so desperate to catch his target that he'd disfigured his body and thrown himself against what he must have known were slim odds. For what?

Vengeance wasn't what Nathan wanted now. What he was looking for—what Adelina needed—would be much harder to come by. Justice.

"Ray is waiting for us," he said. "Let's make our delivery."

It wasn't difficult to slip away from the scene in the chaos of ambulances, fire trucks, and police cars, but it was trickier to find a ride back into the city. Nathan eventually made an executive decision and borrowed one of the police cruisers parked nearby despite Cora's protests that it wasn't exactly a low-key option. Elton didn't object— he just tossed Korshunov into the back seat and climbed in with him so that Cora could sit up front beyond the dividing barrier. Nathan got them back into the city without incident, though he felt his weariness in his bones by the time they pulled up close to the Magistrate office. Ray could handle the inconvenience of a stolen police car, he was sure.

Since all three of them had lost their cell phones—again—Cora went inside the building alone, as she was the least immediately-recognizable of the three of them. Soon, a pair of Chasers emerged from the building and collected Korshunov from the back seat, carrying his unconscious body between them across the sidewalk and into the glass doors of the station. Nathan leaned his arms on the steering wheel and watched them until the boy disappeared into the hallway, then turned to rest his forehead on his folded arms.

"You think this is the right call?" Elton asked from the back seat.

Nathan shook his head. "We'll see, I suppose."

Cora came back onto the street and opened the passenger door to lean inside. "You smart guys want to maybe get out of the cop car now? We should get out of here."

Nathan forced himself out of the car, though he wasn't sure any of them were less conspicuous for walking—they were all still soaked and muddy and exhausted. At least the hotel wasn't too far, and New Orleans wasn't a city that asked a lot of questions.

Once they made it back, Nathan was ready for a long, hot bath—but Cora lurked in his bedroom doorway, so he sat down on the bed instead and waved her inside.

"Are you okay?" she asked softly as she settled beside him.

"I'm all right, my love. We did what we set out to do."

"That...spirit that helped us," she began, peeking up at him as though afraid her words might sting, "it...looked like—"

"Yes," he agreed. "I believe it was. Perhaps now that Korshunov has been given to the authorities, she'll be able to rest easier." He leaned back on his hands and gently nudged her. "Are *you* okay?"

"Yeah, I...that was so crazy. All those people, and the thing just— that poor man, he was...and who knows how many more when the boat was destroyed—" She stopped, and she inhaled slowly, then let it out in a shaking huff as she turned to hide her face in Nathan's shoulder. "I'm so tired of all this *death*," she said, punctuating it with a soft hiccup.

Nathan wrapped an arm around her and shushed her with his chin resting on her head. He spotted Elton paused by the door and exchanged a silent look with him before the blond walked on with a faint shake of his head.

The telephone in the room rang loudly, startling both of them, and Nathan tilted his head to look Cora in the face as she pulled back from him. She nodded and offered him a faint smile as she wiped at her wet cheeks with the ball of her hand, so he rose from the bed to answer.

"Hello?"

"Nathan—it's Ray."

"Hello, Ray; how are you? Did I give you this number?"

"No—but I'm supposed to be surprised you're staying at the oldest place in town?"

"Fair enough," he chuckled. "Everything all right?"

"This Chaser you dropped off is a god damned mess, Nathan. What the hell did you do to him?"

"Would you believe very little?"

"Not really."

"I think he's done more damage to himself than can be blamed on me," Nathan said quietly. He glanced over at Cora, who gave him a brief wave to excuse herself from the room. "He's dangerous, Ray. Don't give him any room to breathe, or you'll lose people."

"I hear you," the Magister assured him. "He'll need a hospital bed before a jail cell. But we'll make sure he's tried—especially after what happened today. A riverboat full of mundanes getting torn in half by some giant creature is way too big to cover up."

"That one can't be put on me. That boy you're holding summoned that thing."

"I thought as much," Ray said with resignation in his voice. "But it doesn't change anything."

Nathan paused. "You're going to tell me to leave town, aren't you?"

"I'm sorry, Nathan," he sighed. "It's not because of me. After something like that, anyone who's looking for you is going to guess where you are. It won't be safe for you here."

"It's fine." Nathan put a hand on his hip and glanced toward the bedroom door. "We have places to be, in any case."

17

Cora was too tired to ask questions when Nathan woke her in the middle of the night to tell her it was time to leave. She'd only just gotten to sleep—she couldn't stop seeing the Frankenstein work that had been Korshunov's chest in her mind's eye. She called Thomas to tell him what had happened, but he had no answers to any of her questions. Why had Korshunov done that to himself? And his eye—she was sure one of them was blind. How had it happened? And now that he'd been taken to the Magistrate, was he going to be tried and hanged? Killed anyway, only the blood wasn't on Nathan's hands directly? What difference did that make?

She wasn't sure any of this was doing any good. But it was nice to hear Thomas's voice, anyway.

Elton had their rental car pulled around by the time she got her things downstairs, so she threw her suitcase in and crawled into the back seat to lie down, tucking her hoodie under her head as a makeshift pillow and doing her best to get some more sleep.

It didn't work. She jolted awake almost instantly, it felt like. The car was stopped—and she was the only one in it. She sat up so quickly that her vision blurred for a moment, but when she focused, she spotted Nathan and Elton standing outside the car in a scene she'd had to bear witness to more times than she could count—Elton was scowling, gesturing around him in exasperation, and Nathan had his elbows in his hands, his head tilted back, eyes shut and mouth open as if the scolding had put him to sleep.

Cora opened the car door and leaned on it once she put a foot on the ground. The car was parked in a lot at the end of a long pair of docks lit by yellow lampposts. The air smelled, and she scrunched her nose as she spoke up to interrupt Elton's next words. "What's happening now?"

Nathan huffed as he lifted his head to look at her. "I simply proposed a very sensible, time-saving alternative to driving through the entirety of Mexico to get to Yucatán, and Elton is objecting for completely irrational reasons."

"He wants to steal a boat," Elton pointed out, as if his argument required no further explanation.

"It makes sense," Nathan pressed. "We'll cut straight down instead of going all the way 'round. I got us some new phones and even picked up a few nonperishables before I woke you; we'll be fine."

Cora was already fully out of the car, hooking her fingers under the handle of the trunk to pop it open. Elton stared at her with disapproval on his face as she let the wheels of her little suitcase hit the asphalt.

"What?" She shrugged. "I've never been on a boat. Anyway, didn't you spend all summer in a stolen RV murdering your way across the country? Get a grip."

"You see?" Nathan moved by her to take his own bag from the trunk. "Out of the mouths of babes. Let's get a move on, darling."

"That had better mean 'babe' as in, 'wow, Cora, you're such a babe,' and not as in 'baby,'" Cora grumbled as she pushed the car door shut.

"Naturally," Nathan said with a smile. He hauled a few plastic bags and packs of bottled water from the trunk and passed some off to Cora before urging her down the dock.

"That looks like more than a few nonperishables," Elton noted, but Nathan shrugged and carried on without looking at him.

"Sailing is hard work, darling, and I do get peckish."

Elton stared after him for a moment or two, but he made no further argument. He took his suitcase in hand, glanced through the inside of the car to make sure they hadn't left anything behind, and then followed them down one of the docks.

Nathan strolled down the wooden deck, pausing in front of each docked boat and leaning over the edge of the pier to inspect it. Elton kept quiet for the first three, but when Nathan simply passed by the next without even pausing, he had apparently had enough.

"What the hell's wrong with that one?"

Nathan paused and looked back over his shoulder at the blond with an incredulous curl of his lip. "I'm not sailing a *catamaran*, Elton. This isn't a bachelorette party."

"For fuck's sake. Just pick a boat."

Nathan wasn't listening. He continued down the row, carefully considering each moored vessel before moving on. He got all the way to the end of the long dock and then finally stopped in front of a long, white boat with gleaming silver rails and two wide steering wheels at the rear. The name "The Codfather" had been painted in block script along the side of the hull.

"Aha," Nathan said as he reached out to touch the silver rail ebbing near the pier. "This one is lovely. All aboard," he called, already putting a foot on the slick surface to haul himself over the rail. Cora passed him her suitcase when he reached back for it, but Elton stayed back with an uncertain frown on his lips.

"Are you sure you can even drive this thing?"

"Elton," Nathan scoffed, perhaps more honestly offended than Cora had ever heard him, "do *I* know how to sail a boat? Honestly."

"I mean one with a motor."

He laughed. "Don't be ridiculous. It doesn't have a motor."

"You want to take a *sailboat* across the Gulf of Mexico."

Nathan stood with his hands on his hips and glowered down at the other man. "Darling, I once made a living helming a sixty-meter brig through the Atlantic; I rather think I can manage a day-cruise with a ten-meter single mast. Now are you coming, or not?"

Elton stared for a beat or two, but then took Nathan's offered hand and accepted his help up onto the boat beside him. He set his suitcase on one of the seats at the rear, muttering, "Two hundred fucking years ago."

"Look at this thing!" Cora shouted from inside the low door to the cabin. Two long, sleek couches ran along either wall beyond the small kitchen at the base of the stairs, flanking a folding wooden table and ending at a set of double doors open to reveal a large bed. Cora checked the door beside her and found another small bedroom, as well as a bathroom. "There's a whole apartment down here!" She leaned against the stairs to stick her head back out the door. "I didn't know boats had insides!"

Nathan chuckled. "What did you think was in there?" He moved by them and began to check what seemed to Cora an infinite number of different ropes, unfastening this and unzipping that with an air of practiced routine.

"I don't know—engines, or something. Or just air so they float better. I don't know anything about boats."

"We'll make a sailor of you yet," he promised. He climbed back up and over the thin rail to the dock now that Elton was out of the way, safely positioned by one of the rear seats. "Everybody ready?"

"Ready!" Cora called, kneeling on the bench with a tight hold on the top cord of the railing.

Nathan bent down to untie the ropes from their moorings, tossed them onto the deck, then leaned the balls of his hands against the side of the boat, pressing it away from the dock with a steady heave. Cora thought he might fall into the water, he leaned so far out from the pier, but then he hopped up onto the side and swung his legs over the cord as they began to drift. He started back to the rear of the boat and nodded to Cora on his way.

"Pull the bumpers up, will you?"

Cora started to move, then paused. "The what?"

"The fenders," he tried again, scanning the inner sides of the seats and bending down to a small built-in holster.

"The...what?"

"Oh, for—the big rubber things bobbing on the side, there. Just pull them up."

"Oh!" She slid from her seat to do as she was told, hauling up the miniature punching bags along the hull of the boat and leaning each one along the inside of the railing.

"Don't know what sort of life you've been leading," he sighed as he rose with a handle in his hand, and she snorted at him.

"A landlocked one."

Cora did her best to stay out of the way, holding onto the handle Nathan passed her and tucking her feet up onto the bench seats next to

Elton to watch him work. He seemed exceptionally at home here—he turned the wheel with sure hands, positioning the nose of the ship until he was satisfied. He reached out to guide Cora's hand onto the wheel and smiled at her.

"Just there, if you please," he said, then moved up to pull on one of the ropes looped around one of the pinball bumpers dotted around the upper deck. It gave a whirr with each tug, and the sail leapt upwards, easily at first, and then more slowly, until Nathan leaned his weight against it and finally wrapped the long end of the rope a few times more around the bumper. When he reached out his hand to her, Cora offered him the handle on a guess and watched as he slid it smoothly into the center of the spool and pulled it round to tighten the rope further. He leaned out to check the sail, one hand on the long beam swinging out over the seats, and adjusted the rope there to his unknown specifications.

Cora and Elton watched curiously—one less obvious about it than the other—as Nathan stepped back to the wheel, dropping the detached handle back into its holster on his way. There wasn't much of a breeze, even now that they'd drifted a fair bit from the dock, but Nathan checked the ropes again and turned the wheel, and the boat picked up speed as wind filled the tall, white sail. Cora was happy to let go of the wheel so that he could take over, and she smiled at the calm way he stood, his hands relaxed on the wheel as he guided the boat easily away from the small marina and deeper into Lake Pontchartrain.

"I assume it's pointless to ask if you have any idea how to *get* to Cancún in a boat?" Elton asked, glancing over his shoulder as though he didn't trust the railing to keep him aboard.

"I'm sure there's a map in the cabin somewhere, and these modern boats all have navigation built in; I'll manage. It's a trip I've made once or twice," he added with a faint smile. "We'll have to dock at Port Eads for the night, regardless. I'm going to need some sleep, and I'm not keen to leave the sailing to either of you."

"Good choice," Cora agreed. She wrapped her arms around her knees and leaned her cheek on them to smile up at him. "Know any shanties?"

"I do, as a matter of fact," Nathan said with a chuckle. "But I'll spare you. It's not as impressive without two dozen of you, at any rate."

"Maybe I can find you a captain's hat."

"I would far rather be on this little daysailer with the two of you than back steering that brig full of unwashed mercenaries," he answered with his attention steadily on the water ahead of them. Elton glanced past her to look up at Nathan with a faint knit in his brow, but he didn't speak.

Nathan maneuvered the boat across the lake, underneath a few interstate overpasses, and into the narrow strip of water leading into the broader sound, as easily as if he were driving a car. He warned them that he was "about to tack, so mind the boom," which neither Cora nor Elton comprehended until the long metal pole holding the sail swung dangerously close to their heads.

The water was smooth, and so was Nathan's steering, so they made quick time around the southern bend of Louisiana's uneven coast. Sailing in the darkness, putting steady distance between themselves and the lights of civilization along the shore, felt secret and special. Even Elton's shoulders had relaxed, his face turned into the breeze and his elbow resting on the top cord of the rail. Cora wished they could keep going, but when a lighthouse came into view near the mouth of the river, Nathan swung the boat around and into a narrow channel beside a thin strip of beach. He put Cora's hand on the wheel again to keep them steady while he lowered the sail and slowed the ship into a drift. He worked the thick canvas with ease, folding it back and forth over itself until the entire thing lay flat along the pole—the boom, Cora corrected herself. He unhooked one of the ropes and latched it to a metal hook near the cabin door, then hopped back down and pulled the rope on the boom tight. She didn't think she would ever be able to work so smoothly, even with two centuries of practice.

Once he was satisfied, he took over the wheel, then bent down close to the console near his feet. Both passengers gave a small start as a low rumble churned the water at their rear, the scent of diesel fuel drifting up from the surface.

Elton stared at him. "So it *does* have a motor. Why weren't we using it the whole time?"

"Don't steal things, Nathan," he grumbled as he straightened to steer, "don't make a scene, Nathan, but of course, use the engine and glamor some poor portworker out of enough fuel to take us across the

Gulf of Mexico, Nathan—"

"I get it," the blond cut him off.

As they drew close to the inlet opening into the docks, Nathan called to Cora to drop the bumpers again, and she gave him a brief salute before clambering up onto the deck to obey. He turned the engine off and let the hull ease against the dock, then stepped onto the wood with the tie-off ropes in his hand and swiftly lashed them to the waiting metal moorings.

"What now?" Cora asked, and Nathan gave a small shrug and let his hands drop to his sides.

"Now sleep. We'll head out first thing in the morning."

"Sleep on the boat?"

"Or the dock, I suppose, but the cabin is likely to be more comfortable."

"This is the *coolest*." She laughed and dropped down the stairs into the small floating apartment, scooting suitcases out of the way to make for the bed at the other end of the room. She spread out on the mattress and tested the bounce while the men filed in after her, then turned to lay on her stomach and peer out at them.

"You're welcome for choosing one with actual beds," Nathan said. He picked up his bag and hefted it up onto the bed almost hidden by the tiny kitchen.

"Tomorrow will you teach me how to drive?"

"If you like."

Elton glanced briefly between the two opposing bedrooms before settling on the bench sofa. "How long is this trip supposed to take?"

"With good wind and weather, we'll be there tomorrow evening."

"And without good wind and weather?"

Nathan paused to look back over his shoulder at him. "We die? I'm not sure what you want to hear, darling. We'll get there when we can, and it will still likely be faster than driving. Relax," he went on as he crawled up onto the bed. "People pay good money for vacations like this. Enjoy it."

Elton gave a soft sigh as Nathan shut the narrow door behind him, enclosing himself in the bunk. "Enjoy it," he muttered. He slid a finger under the knot of his tie and pulled it undone, dropping it onto his suitcase on the floor.

Cora leaned her chin in her hand and frowned. "You're not going to try to sleep on that thing, are you?"

"It's fine," he answered without looking at her.

"Don't be stupid. Come sleep up here if you don't want to risk Nathan. This bed is huge. I mean, for being on a boat, it's huge."

"Cora, it's...not really—"

She let out a groan before he could finish. "Elton, are you serious? We've shared a hotel bed, like, a hundred times. I'm pretty sure I trust you not to molest me by now. And I think, if I try, I can withstand your raw animal magnetism."

He looked down at the floor with a touch of a reluctant smile on his lips. "And what if I'm just worried about being drooled on?"

She flung a pillow at him that he didn't even try to dodge, and she moved over closer to the wall to make room for him as he approached.

18

Nathan was up before his companions in the morning. He pulled on his pair of dark blue swim trunks in what little room the cabin bed left him, then slipped from the bed and up the cabin stairs with light steps, careful not to let in too much morning light. He freed the boat from the cleats on the dock, heaved it outward, and hopped back aboard to pull up the bumpers and lay them aside. He returned to the cockpit and took the wheel, shutting his eyes and taking a long, deep breath of the saltwater air flowing up from the Gulf. He turned the bow to face the wind, then refastened the halyard, hauled up the mainsail and winched it flat, and left just enough slack in the mainsheet to give the boom some freedom.

The sun hadn't been up long, but its light already warmed his bare shoulders as he guided the boat out of the port, down the broad mouth of the Mississippi, and out into the warm waters of the gulf. The built-in navigation made it simple to chart their course. A modern marvel. He was grateful for more time sailing and less time doing arithmetic.

If he'd been on his own, he would have stopped to have a swim—but if Elton caught him in the water when he woke up, it would mean a scolding Nathan didn't want to listen to. Somehow, he needed to teach the broody former Chaser to ease up. On himself, if no one else. Nathan thought he'd seen a touch of it back in California—an Elton who could have a beer and shoot pool and forget the world for an evening. An Elton who could even laugh. He was glad for the blond's surly nature when it came to fighting off Chasers, but on a day trip to Cancún on a sailer crewed by what seemed like the only two people left in the world who cared about him, Elton ought to try to slow down some. Perhaps Nathan would tell him so.

He passed a few other boats out early—mostly charter fishing, he guessed—but the company thinned as he followed the heading South. This was what he'd wanted. Just the sea, and the wind, and the sun on his skin. He'd been out sailing countless times even once it stopped being his mode of employment, but rarely had occasion to make such a long trip.

He should have taken Adelina.

With a frown and a shake of his head, he glanced up to the mainsail and adjusted the wheel slightly to port. He'd done nothing but sit with his rage and guilt ever since Korshunov had slipped away from him in the Massachusetts woods, and what had it helped? Not himself, and not Adelina. It had never helped anyone he'd lost.

The answer was plain. It was Elton and Cora who would be in harm's way. And they weren't something Nathan was willing to risk. He'd caused enough loss.

The breeze was hot on his face, and the boat had begun to heel hard, so he settled against the cockpit seat with one hand steadying the wheel and the other between the bars of the railing to skim the surface of the water with his fingers. She'd tried, back then, to touch the water.

María had leaned half her body over the edge of the sloop as it heeled, so far that he'd been afraid she would fall in and be dragged to the bottom by her voluminous skirt. But when he'd warned her, she'd lifted her head, holding her broad straw hat in place with one hand, and she'd laughed. Her dark green dress brushed her ankles in the wind, and she clutched at the cream-colored lace shawl around her shoulders. It was how he always remembered her—smiling, with her dark hair set free in loose curls around her neck, the sun warming her porcelain skin and brightening her honey-colored eyes.

She was always smiling. Laughing. Even when she tore her dress, or when the salt water soaked her skirt as it washed up over the rocks in the little cove where they escaped to be alone. She just looked up at him, hair stuck to her forehead by sweat and ocean air, and wrapped her arms around his neck when he kissed her.

He'd snuck into her room more than once and had to hide from the servants, and she'd smiled as she shut the door behind them and turned back to him. She'd smiled when she'd seen him beneath her window, cupping a folded paper bird in his palm and blowing it to flap gently upwards into her waiting hands. And she'd laughed when he promised that her sapphire engagement ring wasn't stolen, when they both knew it was a lie.

He remembered her this way so that he didn't have to remember the way he saw her last—frightened and confused and calling for him, dragged away by the arms by Magistrate Chasers while he was pressed helpless to the floor. He'd let his pain and guilt overwhelm him then, too. And he'd died for it. Pointlessly, in a rage, shot down in the street. Ever since, he'd been keeping that bitterness in his gut.

Cora had asked him to think about the man he wanted to be. That answer was plain, too. He wanted to be one who deserved the care of the people he'd lost—and the ones who remained.

He turned toward the sound of the cabin door opening and smiled as Cora emerged, squinting in the morning sun. "Good morning, my love."

"Nice shorty-shorts," she answered with a grin as she straightened and shielded her eyes with one hand. "Did you pack a pair for Elton?"

"If only he would," Nathan sighed dreamily.

She came slowly up the steps, steadying herself on the doorway and leaning a little to peer toward the water. "Is it meant to be so...sideways?"

"It's called heeling. It's just what happens when you have wind like this. It's a good thing."

"Well it made me wake up crushed against Elton in the corner of the bed, so maybe good but not great."

"We should all be so lucky." He tilted his head to the wheel. "Want to have a go?" When she nodded, he pushed out of his slouch and moved aside for her, only helping to balance her with a hand on her back. He showed her how to read the display on the small screen nearby and instructed her to hold their heading, then left her to it and stretched out on the bench dipped closest to the water.

Elton appeared looking preemptively miserable; he'd only buttoned about half of his shirt and he'd already rolled up his sleeves, but he still had on slacks.

"You look dressed for the occasion as always, Elton," Nathan said, earning himself a quick scowl.

"I wasn't given much warning we'd be sailing."

"If you had, would it have changed anything? Would you lounge barefoot in your little khaki shorts, linen shirt open and fluttering in the sea wind?" When Elton began to bite back, Nathan held up a hand and shut his eyes. "Hush, darling; I'm imagining it now."

Cora spoke up before Elton could begin his berating, her voice sounding unsure. "This is really sideways," she pointed out. "And the land sure is...gone, isn't it?" She was almost leaned perpendicular to the side of the boat, and she glanced anxiously at the water. "You guys know I don't actually know how to swim, right?"

Nathan gave a long sigh and nudged Elton gently backward as he stood, then tugged up on the bench seat to reveal the cargo underneath. He found the fluorescent orange vest right where he expected it and stepped back to the wheel with it in hand. "That's another thing I'll have to teach you," he said with a smile as he took the wheel from Cora's tight hands.

"This is cute," she sighed, but she pulled the vest over her head and buckled it in front anyway.

"You're a tangerine vision, my love."

"Where are we?" Elton asked, glancing around as though the open ocean would give him some indication.

"South of where we were," Nathan answered with a teasing smile. "Didn't I tell you to relax?"

"There isn't anything you need me to do?"

"Well, we are luffing a bit; tighten that mainsail if you insist on being a first mate."

Elton's frown suddenly dropped, replaced by confusion as he turned to look over his shoulder at the multitude of cables latched onto the deck. "Which one is that?" he asked after a moment's pause.

"Never mind; Cora, hold this a moment, will you? Elton, you just use the winch handle and pull the jib while I take the main halyard." He edged by Cora on the bench and dropped the handle heavily into the blond's hand. "Don't worry—it's a rolling jib, easy to open. It'll come right around off the forestay."

He waited with his hands on his hips, but Elton hesitated, glancing at the handle in his hand and back across the deck as if trying to guess where it might be of use.

"...Which—"

Nathan took the handle from him and shooed him away to the bench by Cora. "Softened city folk, the both of you," he scolded lightly, already setting to work fulfilling the commands he'd given the other man. Once he'd finished tending the sails, he returned to his place at the wheel and double checked their heading. "Now if you're quite convinced that precisely one of us knows what he's doing out here—relax. It's a boat ride, darling."

Elton frowned at him, but didn't argue. Cora leaned against him for stability, and, after a time, she seemed to regain her confidence and her smile. Elton was slower to relax, but eventually he slouched just slightly against the cord.

Around the middle of the day, Cora cobbled together a lunch from the food Nathan had brought—which wasn't impressive, he had to admit, but it did the job. Nathan spent some time in the afternoon teaching her some of the proper names for various parts of the boat and sails, and by the time Elton retreated into the cabin because he realized his skin was burning, she had grown comfortable enough to climb up onto the coachroof when he asked her to adjust the jib.

Once they were all relaxed on the deck to eat a simple dinner of chips and convenience store sandwiches, Elton interrupted the quiet.

"How much longer? Are we spending the night out here?"

"I'm afraid so," Nathan answered. "It's over seven hundred nautical miles, after all."

"And that translates into how long?"

He gave a small shrug with one shoulder and leaned back against the railing cord. "With good wind and weather, you know—"

"Nathan—how long?"

"Another three days, most likely," he said easily.

Cora choked on her bite of sandwich. "Three days?"

Nathan didn't have to look to feel the weight of Elton's glare.

"You *said* this would be faster," the blond ground out.

"I *said* it made sense to cut straight down. And it does."

"God damn it," Elton spat, and he ran a hand over his eyes in frustration. "I knew it. I fucking knew you just wanted an excuse to get out here, and I didn't say anything, and now—"

"Elton," Nathan interrupted, leaning over on the bench to catch the other man's eyes. "Are we on a timeline?"

He paused, as though the concept of *not* being on a timeline was one completely foreign to him.

"The camps have been liberated. The Magistrate's wrongdoing exposed. There are protests. There is movement—for once. Even Korshunov has been removed from the board. We have no deadline to meet. We can, for the first time, afford to *take* our time. The world and all its flaws will still be waiting when we land." He paused to light a cigarette in his cupped hand and breathed out his first lungful of smoke. "You'll give yourself an ulcer with all this worrying, darling."

Cora smiled and nudged Elton with her shoulder. "Don't you think we deserve a little break where we can get it?"

He sighed, shaking his head and watching the floor between his feet for a moment before giving a small snort. "Cancún isn't going anywhere, I guess."

"That's the spirit!" Nathan said with a laugh. "We'll relax you yet, darling. Do you want to try the wheel?"

"I'll pass. I need to replace the talismans I've used." He rose without waiting and stepped down into the cabin, clicking the door shut behind him.

Nathan chuckled and flicked the ash from his cigarette into the soda can he'd emptied. "Baby steps, I suppose."

Cora moved to sit beside him, taking a moment to tug off her bulky life jacket before nestling herself under the arm he'd laid across the railing's top cord. They stayed there in silence for a while, Nathan breathing his smoke over her head so it didn't blow into her face and Cora watching the purpling sky at the horizon.

"I know why you did this, you know," she said, just loud enough to be heard over the wind.

"You do?"

"You needed a break, too. It can't have been easy—the decision you made. To leave with us. To...spare him. But I think it was the right one.

It's good for you to be out here; I can tell. I hope it helps you."

Nathan looked down at her profile in the fading sunlight—the gentle touch of a smile at the corner of her mouth and the faint crinkle in her nose as her fingers pushed a flyaway lock of hair back behind her ear. He moved his arm to tug her head more tightly against him by the crook of his elbow and leaned over to press a long, firm kiss to her dark hair. When he released her, she stayed against his shoulder, and they sat that way until long after the setting sun had given way to night.

Elton wasn't pleased the following morning when he found that Nathan had cut a pair of his slacks off just above the knee, but he did accept the other man's apology in the form of a bottle of sunscreen found in the cockpit's dry box—and he was undoubtedly more comfortable in short pants and bare feet. He still didn't want to take the wheel, but Nathan caught him with a faint smile on his face more than once over the course of the day. He and Cora played cards and shared a bag of trail mix, and he even sat with Nathan in companionable quiet for a time while the girl had a nap below deck.

By the third day, Cora had been able to help tighten or loose the mainsheet at Nathan's request and seemed secure enough on her feet to forego the life jacket. They passed through a brief storm in the afternoon, but Nathan ordered them both into the cabin and got the vessel safely out the other side with only minor concern for his well-being.

As they finally drew near enough for the Northern shore of Yucatán to come into view on the horizon, Elton and Cora both leaned over the railing to get a better look. Once they came into usable cell phone range, Nathan gave Cora the wheel and called Señora Marquez for advice on where to land. After assuring her that yes, he did indeed mean to say that they'd come by boat, she directed him toward Playa Blanca with a description of a dock where he could moor, then said she would call him in a few hours.

Nathan wasn't keen to put on real clothes for the first time in four days, but the darkening scruff on his jaw had grown itchy, and a long shower and a good meal would be welcome. Cora and Elton both swayed uneasily on the solid ground of the dock for a few steps before settling on the pair of beach chairs at the end of the long deck, leaving Nathan to secure the boat.

Apostate

After a while, a call from the beach drew their attention, and they turned to see Señora Marquez waving her arm at them from the edge of the water. She gave each of them a long look up at down with a thin frown on her lips as they approached, but she took Nathan's hand when he offered it.

"We have a lot to talk about, Mr. Moore."

19

Councilor Marquez's house was one of the fanciest places Cora had ever been—and that was after weeks traveling around with Nathan. It had an infinity pool you could step out of straight onto the beach, a built-in bar beside a wall of windows, and marble floors so shiny they might have been cleaner than the plates Cora usually ate off of. Marquez led them upstairs to settle their things—in separate bedrooms, thank god—and then they regrouped in the massive living room.

Cora liked the look of Marquez herself—she was small, and a little hunched, but the wrinkles on her face seemed more like laugh lines than scowling ones. Cora got the distinct feeling that the cane she carried was mostly for show.

"Well, Señora," Nathan began, already moving behind the bar with his fingertips skimming the marble counter, "we've come willing and able to help. When we spoke previously, you mentioned damage to the city?"

"This city has many problems," Marquez admitted. She sat down on one of the soft chairs, but stayed to the edge of the cushion without seeming to relax. "The damage to the homes along the coast is extensive. People are homeless or living in shanty houses. But, as I told you on the phone—as upsetting as it is, it isn't an issue for the Magistrate."

Nathan had found a short glass and poured an inch of rum over a cube of ice, and he ducked down below the bar to the sound of the soft suctioning of a mini fridge door. "Why shouldn't it be?" he asked as he twisted the cap off the bottle of Coke. "Don't witches generally live in homes?"

"Of course, but *housing* isn't generally considered something under our jurisdiction."

He filled the glass to the top and set the half-empty bottle aside, then paused, turning back to scan the bar shelf behind him. "Limas?" he asked, holding up his thumb and forefinger as though framing a small object.

Marquez gave a light sigh. "I'm afraid not."

Nathan sucked his teeth in disappointment but picked up his glass to return to the sofa regardless. "How many witches live in Cancún, Señora?"

"I don't know the precise number offhand," the Councilor admitted, "but close to five thousand."

"And how many of them live in the damaged areas?"

"Many. What are you getting at, Mr. Moore?"

He swallowed a mouthful of rum and soda and leaned his elbows on his knees. "Why hasn't it been repaired?"

"I told you it isn't something I control. The city itself, the state— they handle these things. There has to be money, supplies, labor. It's complicated."

"Must it be?" Nathan watched the Councilor with a furrow in his brow. "What if it could be done? Homes repaired or rebuilt. By us."

Marquez gave a small, uncertain snort. "You want to go down there with a hammer and a box of nails?"

"All of us," he clarified in a soft voice, his dark gaze steady on her face. "How many witches live in Cancún, Señora?"

She watched him for a moment or two in silence, the wrinkles at the edges of her mouth deepening with her frown. "You don't mean by magic?"

"And why not?"

"That kind of magic would require—" She lifted her hands from her lap as if the answer was too large to express and shook her head. "Not to mention the impossibility of explaining in mundane terms how a house was suddenly rebuilt."

"We don't owe them any explanation at all," Nathan insisted.

"You're proposing an exceptionally severe breach of the Concordat, Mr. Moore."

Cora shifted from her seat to the floor, laying her arms on the cool surface of the glass coffee table. "Could that be done?" she asked, drawing Nathan's attention. "Really? Could we fix a whole house with magic?"

"With enough palm tokens," he answered with a faint smirk on his lips, and her eyebrows lifted in understanding.

"For real?"

"For real."

"That many local witches willing to cast a spell like that is a big ask," Elton pointed out. "Not everyone is so eager to commit crimes."

"They're eager to stop living under tarps, though, aren't they?" Nathan cut back.

"The Magistrate is not in a position to sponsor or condone such exposure," Marquez said with a sigh. "I'm grateful that you want to be of help, Mr. Moore, but this..."

"The Magistrate *exists* to govern witches," Cora said. "Governing doesn't just mean they tell us what to do and what not to do. It doesn't mean they punish us for breaking laws and leave us in the wind when we need help. At least, that isn't how it should be. If the Magistrate can't even help keep its people housed and fed, what good is it? Then the people have to take care of themselves."

Nathan gestured appreciatively toward her and looked back to Marquez. "Your people are capable of taking care of themselves, Señora, but it would be easier with help. Today, we aren't asking you to sponsor or condone. Only to blink, and it will be done." He tilted his head at her with a smile so charming Cora wondered how often he practiced it in the mirror. "And perhaps to continue offering your kind hospitality."

Marquez pursed her lips in thought, folded her arms on her crossed knees, and bounced her foot lightly in the air with her eyes on the braided rug below. After a pause, she went still, and then she raised her gaze to look into Nathan's eyes. "Tell me where you plan to be, and I will make sure there are no Chasers to interrupt you. That is all I can offer—for now."

"I'll take it," Nathan said with a chuckle as he sipped from his glass.

"Thank you, Señora. I will try not to get you into any trouble directly."

"That is unlikely," she answered dryly. "But...your friend is right," she added with a nod toward Cora. "Perhaps the Magistrate can be better."

Cora's face grew a little hot, but she smiled as she looked up at Nathan. "So let's get started."

Marquez took the guests into her office and showed them photos, maps, and damage reports from the worst-hit areas of the city. It was bad—there were an awful lot of tarps, and a number of houses were little more than soaked wreckage. Shelters had been set up, some temporary homes provided, but there wasn't much in the way of actual aid. It didn't look good.

Nathan chose a neighborhood at Marquez's suggestion, and Cora helped him word a simple flyer asking for any witches willing to help their neighbors to be present the following morning. Marquez agreed to send it out through the Magistrate's system of threatening white envelopes, which Cora didn't think was ideal for actually getting people to show, but it was the only option they had for getting the message out quickly, so it would have to do. Maybe word would spread once they showed what they were really trying to do.

The night spent in the Councilor's soft guest bed was the best sleep Cora had gotten since she'd left Thomas's house. It hadn't been as bad as she'd expected on the boat despite Elton's furnace body in the bed next to her, but being able to spread out and use as much of the blanket as she wanted was infinitely better.

She stayed under the downy comforter and held her phone above her face to send Thomas a brief update and a good morning, and she smiled when the phone vibrated almost immediately in response. It was still early—she pictured him at the kitchen table with his usual cup of coffee and slice of toast and wished it could have been bread she made for him. It must have all been gone by now.

Cora smiled faintly and curled up on her side, hunching under the hem of the blanket with her phone like a kid afraid of being in trouble for staying up too late.

Are you fasting right now?

With the bottom of her grin caught in her teeth, Cora held the phone in one hand and lifted it to tent the blanket upward, then pulled up her shirt and flashed a photo of her bare chest. She sent it along with the message, *Miss you.*

She couldn't be *positive* that he spit out his coffee in time with the read receipt, but she chose to believe it was true. She got out of bed and stretched, and she hid her laugh in her knuckles on the way down the stairs as she read his reply.

Thank you. I miss you too.

She smiled down at the screen before turning it off to focus on her footsteps. What a dork.

Nathan was nowhere to be seen, but when Cora found Elton in the kitchen, he pointed with his mug toward the tall windows making up the back of the house. Cora squinted into the distance, but it took Nathan walking out of the gulf and up onto the sand for her to spot him. He came back into the house still dripping and laid his wet head on Elton's shoulder as he passed, earning an elbow to the ribs from the blond. He didn't seem bothered.

"Have a good swim?" Cora asked as Nathan poured himself a cup from the coffee pot. By the time he turned to her to answer, Elton had already returned with a towel and was now scooting it across the floor with his foot to mop up Nathan's puddles.

"Usually," Nathan said over his steaming cup. "Ready to make a nuisance of ourselves?"

"So ready."

The damaged neighborhood they'd chosen was a fair distance from the stretch of fancy beach houses, but once they were in the city itself, Nathan stopped their taxi and urged them out. He double-checked that they were headed in the right direction, then thanked the driver and gave the top of the car a pat to send it on its way. He actually felt slightly guilty paying the man with a glamour—there wasn't much wealth to be had in this town to start with, and Nathan was depriving him of more. But, in his defense, Nathan didn't have any of his own to share, either.

Cora seemed mildly uncomfortable as they walked along the side of the road, but she kept her thoughts to herself. Perhaps she was imagining herself as one of the kidnapped tourists on the news, or was looking out for violent, roving gangs. He didn't blame her—Mexico, especially the vacation cities, certainly had a reputation. But a poverty-stricken neighborhood didn't necessarily mean a dangerous one. She would understand.

Elton guided them with the map on his phone, but it was easy to see when they reached the right area. The streets weren't paved here—stone walls with metal gates made up the buildings opening directly onto the roads, roof tiles had been torn away from their now bare rafters, and piles of debris filled empty yards and overgrown gaps between houses. Spraypaint marked the walls around the doors of open-air shops with Coca-Cola signs hung over the door. Some homes had nothing more than a pinned-up blanket for an entrance, and many had filthy, tattered tarps attempting to cover the holes in the roofs. Most walls had high-water lines on them and broken or missing window shutters. A handful of people walked the dirt street in bare feet or flip-flops, a few gathered around a small wooden fruit stand—one man passed them cradling a rooster in his arms. There was a lot to be done here.

Nathan almost drifted off course as they walked through the warm smell pouring out the open door of a shop labeled PANADERIA, but Elton kept him on the sidewalk with a tug on his sleeve. When they turned the corner into a small, bare lot, Nathan stopped near the open fence gate. A dozen people stood along one of the surrounding stone walls, anxiously chatting with each other. Nathan gave a small hum.

"Well, it isn't as many as I was hoping for," he murmured, "but it will do."

Their arrival drew the attention of the pair of women standing nearest the gate. They exchanged a quick glance, then scanned the foreigners with uncertain frowns. Nathan greeted them brightly, and a few shoulders in the group relaxed at the spoken Spanish, but the tension in the lot was thick. The soft buzz of a barrier passed over them as Elton hid their voices from the surrounding streets.

One of the men at the back called out, cutting Nathan off before he could continue. "I know you," he said in a tight voice. "You're

Nathaniel Moore."

The recognition felt nice, but it sent a ripple of suspicion through the gathering. Someone else shouted at him, "What are you doing here? We didn't come to make trouble!"

Nathan glanced briefly back at his companions, who both watched him with frowns of concern.

"Famous everywhere you go, huh?" Cora muttered softly, and Nathan shrugged and offered her a helpless smile.

"I didn't come to make trouble either," he promised as he turned back to the small crowd. "You all want to fix the neighborhood, right? To help the people living here that the government and the Magistrate won't. So did I."

"We don't want your kind of help," one of the women close to him spat. "This place is destroyed enough without you making things worse!"

"So you know what I'm capable of," Nathan answered evenly, and the woman took a half step back. "There is help I can give. I came to give it. Will you listen?"

"He helped my friend's cousin in California," a man said, drawing the eyes of the others around him. "Helped him get away from the Chasers with his mundane wife."

"I heard it was him who stopped the factory in Miami where all those people were being taken," someone else spoke up.

A few murmurs of cautious agreement made their way through the gathering, and Nathan didn't bother arguing with any misinformation—if word was getting around that it was him who'd freed the prisoners from the Magistrate camps, who was he to correct it?

A woman raised her voice above the whispers. "What is it you want to do?"

Nathan held his hand out to Cora, who passed him the cloth bag full of palm tokens from her purse. "I want to repair these houses," he said. He shook the bag lightly to jostle the bits of wood inside. "But I can't do it alone. This magic will take all of us."

"And nobody is going to notice that the buildings fixed themselves?" another voice asked. "The Magistrate isn't going to notice?"

"So what if they do?"

"We all get arrested!" a man shouted. He pushed by the people standing between him and the gate, and a few others moved with him.

"Wait," Cora said, "are they leaving? What happened?"

Nathan let out a small sigh and looked between her and Elton. "They're afraid."

"But—wait," Cora said again. She stepped in front of the fleeing group and held out her hands. "Wait! You can't just leave!" When they stopped, she stood up a little straighter. "The Magistrate isn't going to help you have homes again." The gathering glanced around at each other in mild confusion, and Cora shoved Nathan's arm and gestured outward as if what she wanted should have been obvious.

"Oh." Nathan touched the girl's shoulder and nodded toward her, then began to translate out loud as she continued.

"How does the Magistrate help you?" she asked, raising her voice to be heard at the back of the small lot. "What do they do except tell you how *not* to use your magic? What's the point of this gift if we can't use it to help ourselves? To help each other? What good is it if all we let it do is keep us tied down?" She looked up at Nathan, a tender crease in her brow. "Without magic, I wouldn't be...anybody. I wouldn't have anybody." With a quick, deep breath, she subtly squared her shoulders and looked out at the listening crowd. "My magic gave me a home, and it set me free. I've seen witches—*this* witch," she added with a hand on Nathan's arm, "do incredible, impossible things. *I've* done things I wouldn't have believed if you'd told me about them five years ago. The Magistrate tells us what's allowed because *they're* the ones who are afraid. They're the ones who want to hide, and cower, and pretend we're the same as everyone else! But if we work together, we can do more than they want to let us do. We can be more than they want to let us be. We can change things—for everyone. I want to fix the damage here. With your help. We can do it, but we have to stand up. We have to fight that fear they've worked so hard to put inside us. And we have to prove to them that they can't stop us from doing the right thing. From making our own lives *better.*"

Nathan kept up with her words, but he couldn't hope to match her verve. By the end of her address, even his translation had slowed down—his attention was on the faces of the gathered witches, moment by moment losing their uncertainty and steadily gaining set jaws and frowns of determination. Cora took the bag of groundings from Nathan and opened it, drawing out a handful of wooden tokens to extend to the others.

"Let's show them," she said, Nathan echoing her in a quiet voice. "Let's show them they're wrong about what we can accomplish."

After a heavy pause, one of the women stepped forward first, reaching out to take one of the groundings from Cora's offered hand. Two or three in the crowd still shook their heads and brushed by Elton to escape into the street, but as the rest approached to take their token from Cora, and the smile on her face beamed, Nathan took a step back with a pleasant heaviness in his chest that he couldn't quite name.

She was incredible. Centuries ago, he'd convinced Kalfu that with a little help, with a second chance, he could change the Magistrate. Change the continent. And in the years between that moment and this, he'd done very little to make anything better for anyone but himself. He'd accomplished nothing. He'd been selfish and indifferent.

When he was lying on the parking lot pavement in Yuma with a Chaser's bullet in his skull, the moment before he recovered had passed like minutes—Kalfu had wanted to take him then, and in the black nothing between this life and the next, he'd pleaded for one more chance. Elton was the one. He'd been sure of it. The one who would become the force Nathan never had and turn the Magistrate upside down. But he'd been wrong about that, too. Elton had become as bitter and violent as Nathan himself. Even Adelina might have gone on to be great help to the people of Haiti, but she had no interest in large-scale change.

It was Cora.

Nathan's expression softened as the girl turned to him. He'd been blind. Cora could change things. In the end, it wasn't his role to lead anyone to any kind of glorious coup. He should have realized it when his first attempt earned him nothing but a musket ball to the gut. Better late than never.

"Can you split them up?" Cora asked. "We'll need some people on barrier duty."

He nodded with a smile. He was, for once, precisely where he was meant to be—following Cora's lead. "At your service, my love."

On the advice of the locals, they selected a house to test the spell on first—a run-down two-story with water damage on the bottom floor and only half a roof. Currently home to an extended family of seven. Elton arranged the two other witches who would help maintain a barrier surrounding the house, at least attempting to shield their work from mundane eyes and ears, and Nathan helped organize the rest into a staggered circle around the home, each with a carved palm token held tightly in their hands.

"I can carry the bulk of the spell," he said loud enough to carry across the circle, "but I'm going to need to borrow some strength from each of you." He took his place at arm's length from Cora and rolled his own grounding between his palms as he looked over at her. "Are you ready?"

She turned back to call to Elton, and once the shimmering barrier washed over them and closed off the crumbling house from the outside world, Cora looked back to Nathan and nodded with a fierceness in her eyes that made him smile.

"I'm ready."

He took a quick breath, pressed the token between his hands at his chest, and raised his eyes. This wasn't really wise. It may not even work. But it was worth a try—even if he ended up being carried home.

"Retounen sa ou te pran. Remèt sa ki pèdi a."

The wood burned the skin of his palms, but he held tight, and he heard the soft hisses and grunts of surprise as the heat spread around the circle to either side of him. The air within the barrier thickened and grew warm and damp, and the dirt at Nathan's feet began to darken. The moisture sank his shoes an inch into the ground as it spread, spattering dark droplets across the earth inside the circle. Water began to gurgle up from the edges of the walls, drawing itself upward into thick vines swirling with mud. It swelled and rolled until it reached the bare rafters, then stretched like reaching fingers, lashing around the beams and hauling the rest of the water up with it.

Nathan's hair was already stuck to his face with sweat, and blisters were doubtless forming on his hands—the others must have felt the pressure too, but he didn't dare take his eyes from the house to check. The entire structure was now encased in a gently swaying bubble, roiled by sediment where it met the ground. The mud thickened along the lower wall and crept higher, filling the water with dark sand and grit. As it reached the apex of the orb, the whole house was lost to view, hidden by rolling chunks of mud and stone. Nathan held it there, the muscles in his arms beginning to quiver from holding the grounding so tight between his hands.

"Remèt sa ki pèdi a."

The earth at the base began to harden and crack, slowly spreading narrow fissures up the sides of the walls toward the roof. The house gave a grinding, groaning sound, and bits of the drying mud flaked away—but something was wrong. Nathan grit his teeth, settled his heels into the damp earth, and sent a flare of burning heat into the token in his palms—but the caked mud remained. This needed to work. Cora needed it to work. If Nathan failed here, these people wouldn't believe either of them again. They'd lose heart. They'd lose what spark had begun to form in them. And Nathan needed them not to.

Cora needed them not to.

A moment before his knees gave under the weight of the spell, a searing pain burned at the back of his neck, and his vision blurred. He flinched, and when he regained his focus on the house, it was as if the air was tinged red. The dried earth around the house grew damp again, and the water cleared, and Nathan straightened his shoulders under a diminished burden. The risen water broke away, rushing back to the ground to wash over Nathan's ankles and sink back into the dust. He let his hands drop, his carved wood falling to the dirt.

The walls of the house were solid, smooth white stone, and the green paint on the wooden door shone fresh and bright. Terracotta tiles lay in neat rows over the roof, providing shade to the small balcony garden. Even the front step had been repaired and washed clean.

Nathan dropped back into a seat on the ground and let his arms rest heavily on his bent knees. He scrunched his face and shook his head, then blinked his eyes open to clearer sight. Cora was kneeling at his side with a hand on his back, sweat covering her flushed face and breath heaving.

"Are you okay?" she asked. "Your face—"

He reached up to touch his cheek and drew back fingertips coated in black, slick tar. A laugh fell out of him, and he nodded, drawing her close with an arm around her neck to touch her forehead to his.

"Perfect," he murmured. He released her and gently urged her away, a smile on his lips as she laughed and touched the hands of the other witches. They didn't need to speak the same language to understand the tears in the eyes of the family whose home now stood sturdy as the day it had been built.

Elton approached him from behind and offered a hand to help him to his feet, so he took it. He lifted the hem of his shirt to his face to wipe away the black stains and leaned his shoulder against the blond's.

"This should have been impossible, you know," Elton said quietly, not commenting on his use as a support as he crossed his arms.

"I do," Nathan laughed. "And yet." He gestured toward the house as if no further explanation was needed.

"What's this about?" Elton tapped his own cheekbone with one finger to indicate Nathan's. "Were you possessed?"

"Perhaps," he mused.

"I thought you weren't connected anymore."

"Hm." Nathan eased away from the other man and brushed some of the dust from the back of his jeans. "I suppose even a wastrel such as myself can be vindicated under the right conditions. Now come along. More work to be done." He left Elton behind, knowing without looking that the blond was frowning after him. It didn't matter. Cora was laughing, and when Nathan approached, she latched her arms around his waist and hid her face in his shirt. He touched her hair, and he smiled.

20

The whole neighborhood had come alive by the time the sun was high overhead. More witches had gathered, as well as curious mundanes—but they had more joy on their faces than questions on their lips when they saw the state of the repaired home. An entire party seemed to spring up all around them. By the time Elton had realized what was happening, someone had set up a small grill, others had arrived with coolers in hand, and now there were even a handful of people playing music at the side of the street. Someone had pushed a bottle of beer into Elton's hand and clapped him on the shoulder.

Nathan had swallowed down half his beer already, and Cora was sipping at hers, though she made a face after each mouthful. Nathan chatted with people in Spanish and helped translate for Cora, and once one couple started dancing together on the dusty street, the dam seemed to have been broken—Elton had never seen such a sudden eruption of good spirits in all his life. It was strange to be around. It felt separate from himself. Nathan and Cora had made this happen, without a doubt. All Elton had contributed for months was complaints, protests, and bloodshed. He'd shared the weight of the violence with Nathan, too, of course—but maybe he was onto something when it came to choosing another way.

Across the street from him, Nathan took Cora's bottle from her, set it down beside his on the ground out of the way, then offered her his hand. She laughed and accepted it, allowing herself to be led into the street. Both of them were smiling as they danced, Cora's hair making a dramatic swirl as Nathan spun her out and back into him. He held her hand and waist lightly, and she gave a small shriek that dissolved into laughter when he turned her suddenly and dipped her low to the ground. When the musicians finished their song and paused to accept the grateful clapping from the gathering, Nathan lifted Cora's knuckles to his lips for a brief kiss and said something that made her smile.

She released him and came trotting over toward Elton, which immediately cast a pall of dread over him.

"Your turn," she said brightly, and he shook his head.

"I'm good."

"I didn't ask," Cora shot back. She took his beer from him and handed it off to Nathan as she dragged the blond forward just in time for the music to start up again.

Elton was not a dancer—which shouldn't have surprised anyone who'd met him. He had no sense for it and knew it. Cora didn't seem to mind; she held him by the hands and moved them for him, swinging them in exaggerated motions back and forth until he finally snorted and smiled. He gave in and put a hand on her back when she moved in and touched his shoulder, but he still didn't have much in him but a simple sway.

"Nathan did good this time, huh?" she asked.

"You both did," Elton agreed. "You inspired these people to take action. They'll be better off moving forward because of what happened here today."

"I hope so. It still feels like there are infinity things to do."

"There always are. But I'm proud of you."

Cora smiled up at him. "I'm just glad we did *something* that didn't involve hurting anybody. Let's keep doing that, okay?"

"You mean instead of my serial killer bullshit?"

"Exactly. Skip it. Wasn't going well."

"I think I can do that."

She gave his shoulder a pat and stepped back from him. "You're free to go. Thanks for the awkward prom dance."

"Glad I could be of service," Elton answered dryly, but he took the out and moved out of the street, accepting his returned beer when Nathan held it out to him.

"That was distressing to watch. Want me to teach you?"

"Pass."

"Promise I'll keep my hands above the waist," Nathan pressed with a smirk on his face, but Elton ignored him in favor of taking a drink from his bottle. "Your loss."

Elton glanced sidelong at him. "So what's next? The house next door? The one next to that?"

"No," Nathan said, shaking his head. "I think there will be enough of them now that they won't need me to carry on. Juan Carlos over there," he said with a brief point of his bottle in the direction of a young man across the street, "I believe, will be able to bear the brunt of it. He's got talent."

"How do you know?"

Nathan tapped the side of his nose with one finger. "You get a sense for these things. And besides—he offered. Willingness counts for a lot."

"I guess. Seems like a heavy spell to pass off to someone that isn't you."

Nathan leaned his head against the blond's shoulder and smiled up at him. "Darling, are you trying to say you want to retire to our beachside home already?"

Elton shrugged his shoulder sharply to bump the other man's head off of him, but Nathan only laughed. "So you don't know what's next."

"It isn't up to me." Nathan emptied his beer and nodded toward Cora, who was smiling and talking with a couple of women trying to feed her. "I'll do whatever Cora decides."

Elton watched the young woman laugh across the street and softened slightly. That sounded fine by him.

When the three of them returned to Councilor Marquez's home late in the day, she was waiting for them. She brought them into the dining room, where she had laid out a couple of open file folders, and she took her seat at the head of the table with Nathan at her left.

"I have something I would like to ask you to do," she began.

Nathan was already peering down at the file, so she turned it toward him. From across the table, Elton could see the paperclipped photo on top of the stack of papers—it looked like a standard registry photo of a dark-skinned black man in his twenties, thin dreadlocks pulled back from his face.

"This is Eli Brooks," Marquez continued. "He's the face of a group called Freedom to Be. They're based in Philadelphia, but they've organized protests all over the Northeastern United States. The Council—or some of us—have dubbed him and his movement 'Anti-Magistrate.' But they have done good work. They go through the right channels. They forward petitions, file lawsuits—and they've caused some minor reform to be pushed through over the last couple of years. Mandatory sentences for possession of certain controlled substances have been reduced, and restrictions on certain poisonous herbs have been lifted—such as ones that can also be used for medicine. A lot of those improvements went out the window with the Order of Repression, of course, which is why we're seeing such an increase in demonstrations these last weeks."

"So what is it you'd like from me, Señora?" Nathan asked, not taking his eyes from the young man's photo.

"What you did today will change lives. Word will spread, and it will change the way people view what is possible with magic."

He looked up at her with a small snort. "Are you trying to flatter me before you ask?"

"You told me once, Mr. Moore, that you were a weapon." The old woman leaned forward in her chair, making certain she had Nathan's full attention. "Have you considered being a shield, instead?"

"How do you mean?"

She tapped the file in front of him. "Eli Brooks is an important young man. His movement can and will improve our system, if he's given the chance. But right now, protestors are gathering in Philadelphia from all over North America as a show of solidarity in their unrest. The Magister there has let it go on for now, but more people are arriving every day, and none are leaving. She's called in Chasers from neighboring areas to try to disperse them, and now there are arrests being made. Things are starting to get violent, and it's impossible to keep hidden from the mundanes. The Council is gathering to meet with the regional Magisters and come up with something that can be done to placate them."

"Forgive me, Señora—I'm still not understanding my place in this."

"Come with me," the Councilor pressed.

"To a *Council meeting?*" Elton cut in, but Marquez shook her head.

"To the protest. Brooks is surely there—and he has a reputation for becoming...heated. He may get himself arrested, or worse. I don't want that to happen. I would like you to come to Philadelphia and collect him for me—so that Councilor Anderson and I may speak with him, even if the others won't. I want you to keep him out of the Chasers' hands."

Nathan seemed to hesitate, lowering his gaze to the photo again. Elton could guess what was on his mind—the last time Nathan had attended a Magistrate protest in Philadelphia, it hadn't turned out well for him. But things were different now. He had the blessing of some strange, powerful spirit, for one thing—and he had Cora and Elton, for another.

"Of course," Nathan said after a moment. He shifted the file toward Cora. "If it's all right with the boss, that is."

"Anybody we can keep from being arrested for protesting is a win to me," she answered with a nod.

Marquez looked pleased. "I would bring you with me personally, but I'm sure you understand the potential consequences of arriving at the airport with Nathaniel Moore."

"We've been avoiding flying entirely," Elton added. "Too many Chasers around."

The Councilor frowned and glanced between the two men. "This is urgent; it would take days for you to go back by boat *or* car."

"We have another way," Cora spoke up. "Thomas is close to Philadelphia. He can bring us. We could be there tonight."

"Who is Thomas?" Marquez asked.

"Another lawbreaker we know," Elton answered.

"He can be trusted," Nathan said when Marquez seemed skeptical.

"I won't tell him you said so," Cora teased, and Nathan cast a quick sidelong smirk at her.

"The less I know about it, the better," Marquez said. "I'll be leaving shortly; you're welcome to stay until your arrangements are made. Contact me as soon as you arrive in Philadelphia, and I'll give you the latest information I have."

When the three of them stood to leave, the Councilor lifted a hand toward Cora.

"Actually," she began, "Ms. Daniels. One more thing."

"Ma'am?"

"I also heard about what you did today. You stirred those people—made them feel strong enough to stand. That is, in many ways, an even more important skill than raw magical talent."

Cora smiled at the floor and pushed her hair behind her ear. "Thank you, ma'am."

"I've also heard about your actions in Miami a few months ago. Have you ever considered a career with the Magistrate?"

No one in the room moved for a beat or two.

"...Pardon?" Cora finally said.

"We can always use young, idealistic people with drive like yours. God knows we have enough old, traditionalist ones. Have you thought about it?"

"I'm...pretty sure they don't want me," Cora said with a shrug. "I'm a known accomplice of dangerous witches, right? And anyway, I skipped out on my scholarship back in Vancouver. I don't think I qualify for any positions with the government, even if it was something I wanted."

"Anyone can have a clean start if they want one," Marquez said gently. Her eyes flicked between the two men. "Almost anyone," she clarified, then returned her gaze to Cora. "I believe you could have a meaningful future. If you want one."

Cora hesitated to speak, so Marquez went on.

"Think about it. I'll be leaving for the airport soon. If you would like to see what a difference you could make...consider joining me."

Marquez rose from the table and excused herself, cane tapping on the tile floor in a diminishing echo down the hallway.

"Well," Nathan chuckled, "that's a job opportunity that doesn't present itself every day." He tilted his head at Cora. "You ought to go."

"You're joking, right? Work for the *Magistrate*? Doing what?"

"Whatever Marquez asks, to begin with. From there, who knows?"

Cora frowned at him. "I thought the whole point of everything we're doing was that the Magistrate sucks."

"The Magistrate does suck," Nathan agreed. He glanced over her at

Elton, who gave a small shrug.

"But it doesn't have to forever, right?"

Cora frowned back and forth between them. "If you guys are actually agreeing on something, does that make it...a good idea, or a bad one?"

Nathan scoffed. "As if I've ever had a bad idea in my life." He laid a hand on her hair so she'd look at him. "You can't just follow me around forever, my love. If you want to, you should see what Marquez can offer you."

Her eyes narrowed. "You're just trying to get me away from this protest."

"I can't say that keeping you out of harm's way is the *furthest* thing from my mind, exactly," Nathan admitted. "But if you'll recall, I once told you that there was nothing wrong with giving normal a try."

"I tried normal at school. I'd rather be with you."

"Of course it's your choice, my love." He smiled at her. "Just don't overlook a possibility for a better future for my sake."

Cora nodded. "I'll...ask Thomas if he can summon us." She left them behind and trotted upstairs.

Elton watched her until she disappeared around the corner, then looked back to Nathan. "You think she'll go?"

Nathan snorted softly with his eyes on the floor. "She'll go."

Once Thomas had confirmed that he would be able to bring them to the house, Nathan and Elton set about drawing the circle they'd practiced many times over the summer in charcoal on the Councilor's back patio. Cora set out the incense they needed, and soon they all stood with their bags at the edge of the circle, waiting for the go ahead from their friend.

Cora looked down at her phone as it vibrated in her hand. "He says he's ready." But when Nathan and Elton stepped into the drawn circle, she hesitated. She looked up at the two of them as if she needed to ask their permission for what she was going to say next. "I'm...I think I'm going to go with Ms. Marquez."

"Good," Nathan said with a smile. "We'll need someone on the inside when Elton inevitably gets us arrested again."

"When I what now?"

Cora chuckled. "I just...if she thinks I could really do something, I think I should try, you know? At least for this big...meeting, or whatever. Maybe I can help." She pointed an accusatory finger at Nathan's chest. "But that doesn't mean you go back to killing people!"

He placed a hand over his heart. "You have my word, my love. I will do my very best not to kill anyone unless they really, truly deserve it."

She sighed and shook her head. "I guess that's the best I can hope for. Be nice to Thomas. I'll see you again once we're all in Philly, okay?"

"Of course. Take care, Cora."

"*You* take care. Both of you," she said with a glance toward Elton, and he nodded.

"I'll try to keep him honest," Elton promised, and Cora snorted at him.

"Yeah, like I can count on *you* to not kill anybody either. Shit," she huffed. "Maybe I shouldn't leave you two alone."

"Go on," Nathan shooed her.

She smiled at them, picked up her suitcase, and hurried back into the house just as the edges of the charcoal circle began to smoke.

21

The transportation spell wasn't unpleasant, exactly—but Elton wouldn't want to do it again. He felt as if he'd blinked and then been standing in Thomas's cellar instead of Marquez's patio, but his organs took a few seconds to catch up with the rest of him. Nathan swayed next to him, and Elton didn't even fight when the other man reached over to snatch at his forearm for support. Elton used him to keep on his feet, too. It passed quickly, at least. By the time Thomas had slipped his black veil from his eyes and laid it aside, Elton had shaken Nathan off and taken a couple of puffing breaths to settle his insides.

"I've got a car," Thomas said as a greeting. "It's five or six hours to Philadelphia—we can be there by morning."

"You're coming?" Elton asked. "I thought you said you didn't do 'field work.'"

"If everything Cora told me about the situation is true, then I think I can be of more use in person. I have a friend who will let us stay with him—he's already involved in the protests, and he was keen to help when I told him I'd be bringing Nathaniel Moore."

"You see, darling?" Nathan cut in with a chuckle. "Brand recognition."

"I'll take it," the blond agreed. "And I'll drive."

Thomas didn't complain about Nathan calling shotgun—he was probably just as happy not to sit next to Elton for five hours. He did

162

take over driving after the halfway mark, though, since Nathan and Elton were more than a little drained from their work that afternoon. Nathan especially; he passed out against the window almost as soon as the car started moving, like a sleepy toddler. Elton took the back seat when they stopped for gas, and Nathan didn't stir at any point during the process. Elton couldn't imagine the stress the spell must have put on his body—even if Kalfu was helping him again. Would the locals in Cancún be able to replicate it without Nathan there to anchor them? Elton's gut said no—but he couldn't be sure. A day ago, he would have said the spell was completely impossible to begin with. So who knew?

Thomas parked the car outside a tall building, its bottom floor made of marble lined with Ionic columns. He nodded toward the arched glass doors. "This is Oliver's place," he said. "I trust him."

Nathan finally pushed away from the car door and peered out the window, rubbing at one of his eyes with the ball of his hand. "The *Public Ledger,*" he chuckled. "This is a residence now? It's fared well since being burned down."

"Burned down?" Elton echoed as the three of them climbed out of the car to gather their bags from the trunk.

"By pro-slavery rioters," Nathan answered dryly. "So, an apropos place for a Magistrate protestor to be, I think. Let's meet your friend, Mr. Proctor."

The apartment they were let into was all mottled wood floors and polished white and silver surfaces, but the man who greeted them was untidily dressed and had a days-old beard. He beamed a bright smile at all of them as he guided them past the kitchen to the living room, which was littered with paints and white poster boards both pre-sloganed and not.

"I can't believe Nathaniel Moore is in my apartment," Oliver said, gesturing broadly for them to make space for themselves on the leather sofa. "I've heard—well, I'm sure you know how much I've heard about you." He stood in front of the couch and looked down at his guests as they settled.

"What's the situation in town?" Nathan asked before Oliver could start to chat. "Has there been any violence?"

"Not really. Some scuffles. But it's been...tense. There have been Chasers out there every day, all over the place. So far they haven't started anything too bad, and neither has anybody else, but everybody's on edge."

"And this is in the courtyard area in front of the Magistrate Hall mostly, yes?"

"Right. You know it?"

"I know it," Nathan agreed, sounding slightly subdued, but he perked up immediately. "Is there anything to eat here, perhaps, Oliver?"

"Oh—for sure. You guys make yourselves at home."

Their host rushed off into the kitchen, and Nathan relaxed against the back couch cushions with his head lolling over onto Elton's shoulder. The blond frowned down at him but didn't move.

"Are you good?"

"Just still tired, darling," Nathan murmured, eyes already closing. "Don't fuss. Right as rain tomorrow."

"I mean are you good going to a protest outside the Magistrate Hall in Philadelphia?"

Nathan peeked one eye open at him, and a smirk pulled at the corner of his lips. "I'm touched by your concern, Elton, but there's nothing to worry about. They wouldn't dare kill me twice."

"So they *did* kill you," Thomas cut in, but Nathan put a shushing finger to his lips as he let his eye shut again.

By the time Oliver came back with food, Nathan was dead asleep. Elton didn't move him.

The streets approaching the courtyard outside the Magistrate Hall were full of people, and the crowd only got thicker the closer they got to the building. Painted signs blocked the view around them—dozens of hands held up a variety of slogans to support the shouting. *CAMPS ARE CRIMES. SILENCE IS COMPLICITY, NOT FREEDOM. GET IN LOSER WE'RE PROTESTING SYSTEMATIC OPPRESSION.* They'd seen the photo of Brooks, but Oliver had assured them he wouldn't be hard to find regardless—he was the type to stand on an empty crate with a megaphone.

At the far end of the courtyard, the Magistrate Hall stood large and imposing as ever; the marble almost gleamed in the morning light, columns and tall windows at increments across its broad face. Nathan paused as the building came fully into sight over the crowd, but he didn't give Elton time to question him before pushing forward.

The courtyard itself was surrounded by a wide ring of Chasers, some standing guard and others focused on maintaining the barrier that hid the protest from the regs—but all of them marked by dark blue armbands with gold edging bearing the profiled stag of the Magistrate. They were struggling. This was a massive barrier to keep up, and they must have been at it for days. It was too large an area, and too many people passed in and out. They would drop it at the first real interruption.

Elton didn't like the armbands at all. Chasers had never been so clearly separated from the people they were meant to protect before, and the Magistrate's choice of identification was foreboding.

"Do you see what you missed, darling?" Nathan said, leaning his head closer to Elton to be heard over the noise of the crowd. "This could have been you."

"I am way too blond to ever wear any kind of armband," he answered, and Nathan chuckled and tapped Elton's bicep with his knuckles.

"Come on. Let's go find our lucky winner."

The crowd was dense, so their progress through the courtyard was slow, but occasionally someone would turn and look Nathan in the face—and then there was space to move as they backed out of his way, pulling companions with them to make a path. It wasn't fear Elton saw on them. Admiration, maybe. That had to be a new one for Nathan.

Brooks was, as expected, easy to spot. He was young, handsome, and energetically shouting into his megaphone. Nathan had to gently brush aside a small cluster of people who had gathered around him, but when Brooks laid eyes on him, his calls for chanting stopped. He dropped down from his upturned box and smiled as he let the megaphone hang from its strap around his shoulder, reaching for Nathan's hand before he'd even offered it.

"I knew you'd be here," Brooks said as he gave Nathan's hand an energetic shake. "I'm glad. Seeing you will really give people a boost."

"Will it?"

"Are you kidding? After everything you've done? You're practically the poster child for the abolition movement."

Nathan paused. "Pardon? The what?"

"We're demanding the abolition of the Magistrate prisons and for the Chaser agencies to be defunded."

Elton spoke up over the jostling people around them, skepticism in his voice. "No more Chasers?"

Brooks shrugged one shoulder. "Not as they exist now, anyway. We want them to have more training, more accountability—and for there to be other alternatives for people to call when they need help. The regs are talking about it too. People don't need to call a cop when they have problems related to poverty, mental health, addiction—what is a Chaser going to do? The Magistrate should be the organizing force that allows the people to support each other, not the hammer that comes down on us when we get out of line. And the prisons?" He scoffed. "Let's not pretend the Magistrate does any better with racism than the regs do."

Nathan glanced over at Elton with a smile. "I can see why Marquez wants to talk to him."

The boy leaned in a little closer as though he hadn't heard. "Marquez? Councilor Marquez?"

"I've been asked to come and fetch you," Nathan explained. "Señora Marquez wants a meeting with you—you've caught her attention, and she thinks you can help her."

A broad smile flashed across Brooks' face. "Well that's a hell of a good sign. Didn't know one of the Councilors would work with someone like you. No offense." He hesitated a moment, then shook his head. "But I can't go now—not when we're right in the middle of things. I can go meet her when stuff slows down, or maybe tonight, if they break us up—but I won't leave my people."

"You don't want to be in the thick of this if things go poorly," Nathan said. "Marquez wanted me to get you out of here before things went bad."

"No way. I can't leave now."

"If you're not careful, you might leave your people in handcuffs or a body bag. If you make a target of yourself, these Chasers won't hesitate to haul you in."

Brooks' lip curled slightly. "And why should I get special treatment?" He gestured around at the crowd. "Nobody here deserves to get arrested or killed, so why am I the one who gets an escort?"

"Because Marquez asked for *you*," Nathan answered plainly.

"Oh, and when some Magistrate higher-up says jump, you say how high? Man, come on," the boy scoffed. "That's not who I thought you were."

Nathan watched him with faintly narrowed eyes, considering. "You're right," he said after a pause. "They don't deserve to be arrested or killed." He tilted his head toward the blond at his side. "So let Elton take you to see Marquez—and both of you put a stop to the whole thing. I'll stay," he cut Brooks off when he started to object again. "The Chasers won't take anyone. Not while I'm here."

Brooks glanced between Nathan and Elton, clearly wary. He licked his lips in thought. "If anybody else said that to me..." He shook his head again, then locked eyes with Nathan. "But I've heard the stories. So okay. I'll go—temporarily. I want to hear what Marquez has to say."

"Good lad."

"But one thing," Brooks added. "I've heard *all* kinds of stories. This isn't a violent protest, and I don't want it turning into one. If anybody out here starts killing Chasers, it's going to hurt our cause, not help it."

"Don't worry. I've been rehabilitated. I'll take care of your flock, Eli. You go meet the politician." Nathan clapped him on the shoulder to urge him toward Elton and found the blond frowning at him.

"I don't like this."

"You don't like anything, darling. This isn't news. Go on."

"I don't want to leave you alone here." The words were out before Elton realized he was about to say them—and the slow, gleaming smile that spread across Nathan's lips immediately washed regret all over him.

"Elton, can it be that you're—*worried* about me? Little old me?"

"Forget I said anything," Elton grumbled, already tapping Brooks' elbow to lead him away. Before he could fully turn, Nathan's hand reached out and gripped Elton's arm, so the blond looked back at him.

"I'm fine," he said, uncommonly sincere. "This time will be different." Nathan gave his arm a light pat to send him on his way, so Elton and Brooks began to weave their way through the packed crowd.

They didn't get far before something crashed halfway across the courtyard. It sounded like a bottle breaking, or something else glass—

but either way, the sound rippled like a shockwave across the protestors. The closest Chasers started to shout at people to back up, and some did—which only served to press them back against the ones who wouldn't. People on both sides began to shout at each other, pushing and jostling in the crowd either to get away into the streets or up tighter against the threatening Chasers. Brooks was tense, standing on tiptoe and craning his neck to scan the protestors like a sheepdog looking for signs of danger.

"Let's get moving," Elton said, but he was looking for someone, too.

Nathan was at the center of a cluster of shouting people, now exposed to three Chasers who had forced themselves into the space. One of them gave a last warning, and when the protestors didn't move, the Chaser threw a bottle from his belt, smashing it on the ground and spilling a sickly smell into the air. It burned Elton's eyes the moment it reached him, and he hid his nose and mouth in his elbow just like the others around him. This was *loiscnech*—a fast-spreading gas that seeped into the lungs and made a person weak. Elton had never seen it used before, but he'd seen the rows of yellow bottles in the storeroom at his station in Vancouver. He knew the spell to protect against it, since it wouldn't be much good to a Chaser who also felt its effects, but he didn't even get a chance to use it—back at the closest source of tension, Nathan had pushed his way to the Chasers.

It only took a gesture from him to create a gale that knocked the Chasers back and, even at this distance, swayed Elton on his feet. It cleared the air, but one of the protestors hit the ground as a Chaser snapped at him, knees against the concrete and arms behind his back. Once one had been bound, others tried to push forward in protest and found themselves pulled down as well. As more Chasers rushed in, doubtless as word spread that Nathan had appeared, the protestors fell like dominos. A dozen were bound against the cement in an instant, and Brooks moved to go to them, but Elton held him back with a firm grip on his arm.

"They're fine," he said.

Even as Brooks looked back at him in anger and confusion, Nathan was moving. Without a word, the cracking sound of broken bindings echoed across the courtyard, and people began to pull to their feet, hauled up by their companions. A hush came over the area as Nathan stepped past them, even the Chasers going still and wary across the small clearing.

"That's Nathaniel Moore," someone whispered nearby, causing a ripple of soft murmurs to spread through the crowd.

"If you lot can't behave yourselves," Nathan said, "you're going to ruin everyone's day." He gestured back toward the people now inching away and getting themselves fully off the ground. "If you ruin these people's day, you're going to ruin *my* day, and then I'll have to ruin *your* day," he finished with a sigh. "You don't really want me to ruin your day, do you?"

Before any of the Chasers could speak, one of them raised a hand and called out a binding spell. Nathan didn't even flinch. He just paused, then lifted his shoulders and dropped them again in one last dramatic sigh. In the next moment, the offending Chaser was off the ground, flung backward into a pair of his compatriots, and all of them hit the concrete.

"Nathan," Elton groaned under his breath. He should have known better than to think Nathan was capable of de-escalating literally any situation.

The other Chasers didn't hesitate to press again, and the surrounding protestors didn't back down. In seconds, people were being bound, bottles of loiscnech were being broken, and more Chasers began to appear from the steps of the Magistrate Hall. Protestors shoved, some eager to get in the way of the Chasers and some simply trying to flee the courtyard unscathed. These people weren't fighters. Even the ones itching to *start* a fight weren't fighters. Elton kept his grip on Brooks' arm to stop him from taking off into the chaos that spread through the courtyard, pulling him back from the center and toward the street.

Nathan's presence definitely emboldened people—but even in the quick glances Elton took over his shoulder as they weaved through the growing tension, he could tell the other man was at least trying to behave himself. Chasers were being knocked around, occasionally singed and scratched by the spells of protestors protecting themselves, but nobody was bleeding. The people who dropped into bindings nearby were freed almost before they could touch the ground—Nathan was keeping his promise, but Elton suspected the courtyard was too large for him to protect everyone.

Almost as soon as he thought it, a woman gave a shriek from the arms of the Chaser physically heaving her off the ground. Her legs kicked against the hold, but a moment later, the Chaser was knocked to the ground, and the woman lurched forward like she was on strings. Suddenly Nathan was between Elton and the flung body, and she hit him so hard that he fell and skidded on the concrete himself. He let her up once they came to a stop and pushed to his feet, urging her along with a light hand on her shoulder and not a care for her breathless thanks. The back of his shirt was striped with a few small tears, but he didn't seem to notice them, either. He spotted Elton and waved him away with both arms.

"Why are you still here? Go on!"

Elton hesitated, frowning, but then he pulled Brooks with him and shouldered his way through to the edge of the courtyard, stopping only once or twice to help up someone who had fallen in their rush. They passed through the barrier and onto the streets of mundane Philadelphia—the pedestrians oblivious to the brewing riot only a block away. The Magistrate was good at keeping itself secret, at least.

Once Brooks was safely back at Oliver's apartment, all it took was a phone call to Cora, and a black car arrived at the building within minutes. Elton shut the back door once Brooks was inside, waited until the car had turned the corner down the block, then gave a small snort and started back toward the courtyard. Nathan wasn't going to do this alone.

22

There was no way for Cora to keep her cool once she stepped foot on Marquez's private jet the next morning—Magistrate Councilor present or not. She touched every cushioned, swiveling chair before choosing one, and she gave it a few test turns back and forth as she leaned toward the window. There were even real tables in between the chairs. This was more like a flying conference room than a plane.

The pilot seemed friendly with Marquez, but Cora couldn't understand their Spanish. When the Councilor gestured toward her, the pilot smiled at Cora and made sure to point out the minifridge toward the back of the plane, then disappeared into the cockpit.

Marquez settled into the seat across from Cora with a small, tired sigh, her walking stick leaned against the arm of her chair. She didn't speak until the plane had circled the runway and taken off, so Cora kept quiet too, despite her excitement. She needed to let Marquez set the tone. And if she was honest, there were nerves mixed in with that excitement. This *was* a Magistrate Councilor. She'd seemed helpful and trustworthy so far, but she was still definitely the most powerful person Cora had ever been around. Politically, anyway. But something about the worn, gnarled walking stick propped against the seat told Cora the old woman could still hold her own on other fronts, too. Nathan liked her—that had to count for something.

"I don't imagine you've ever been to any kind of Magistrate sitting before, Ms. Daniels?" Marquez asked, snapping Cora's gaze back to her face.

"Uh, no," she answered with a small laugh. "Even when I got approved for my scholarship, I just got a letter. And I ducked out before I could do my required service."

Marquez watched her with focused eyes for a beat or two. "Yes, you mentioned a scholarship. Required service, hm?"

"Yeah. I was adopted by mundanes in the US, and then Nathan found me and taught me some stuff, and Elton helped me get enrolled in school in Vancouver. But then I got involved in all this other stuff with Nathan, and...never actually graduated."

"Well. I'm sure that's something we can fix."

Cora frowned. "Fix?"

"Never mind for now." Marquez shifted in her seat and leaned one elbow on the armrest. "What you can expect when we get to Philadelphia is a whole lot of nonsense, mostly. When it's only the Council, we can—sometimes—have civil conversations. But when you try to get every Magister in a room together, it's just a lot of old people trying to talk over each other and convince everyone else that they're the most important one in the room."

Cora snorted. "That sounds about like how I expect politics to be, actually."

"The situation is that we're still outvoted. As far as pushing the sorts of changes I believe are necessary, I can only really count on myself and Henry Martin—he's the newest addition to the Council, thanks in part to our mutual friends. We'll need at least two more on our side if we hope to sway Morris—that's Morris Gagnon, the current Council Chair. He will approve what the majority presents. No opinions of his own. Lucky in this instance," she added with mild disdain. "As for the others—Eliseo Araya is a lost cause. He's an anti-mundane fascist, and he isn't shy. He's been profiting personally from the Order of Repression and the camps." The Councilor frowned out the window, a faint sneer on her lips. "I don't condone killing, but if a Councilor had to be murdered, it is truly a shame it wasn't Araya. But we don't need him," she went on, waving her hand as if to dispel any thoughts of the man. "We only need to drown him out."

"I'm hoping this is leading into you telling me the others are more reasonable?"

"Of the others, I believe the most likely to listen to reason are Sylvia Young and Paul Humbridge. Sylvia is the oldest of us, and she can be set in her ways, but she isn't *un*reasonable. If we can give her numbers and facts to support our position, she'll come around. And Humbridge is an ass, but I believe he's simply latched himself onto all of this repression nonsense because of people like Araya bullying him. Very concerned with his image. We can use that."

Cora nodded along as Marquez explained, but she was being thrown a lot of names and information very quickly. Maybe she should have brought a notepad. "Councilor, I'm sorry, but...what is it you think I can do to help with all this? Why am I here?"

Marquez paused a moment, then rose from her seat and moved over to the minifridge. "You have a powerful voice, Cora," she said as she bent down. "If our friends can get you and Eli Brooks into the same room, I believe you can provide the passion needed to get our point across to the other members of the Council."

"That's it?" Cora stared at the older woman as she returned, taking the offered soda automatically. "You want me to come and...give a speech? In front of the Council?"

"Not a speech," Marquez clarified, "so much as...a viewpoint." She sat back down and opened her own bottle of soda. "I've seen you inspire people to action. Sometimes that's enough. As for the other aspects of working for the Magistrate...I suppose we'll see if you have a head for it or not."

"What does that mean?"

"Let's get you through your first sitting, and we'll talk more. For now, just try to relax. There will be plenty to do before you know it." With that, she took a paperback book from her purse and opened it on her knee, ending the conversation.

Cora waited for a minute or two, in case Marquez had anything else to say, then resigned herself to a quiet flight on a luxurious private jet stocked with snacks.

When they landed in Philadelphia, a car was waiting for them right on the tarmac. A young woman in a navy blue dress suit and holding a tablet to her chest stood by the open back door, watching them approach. She smiled, subdued but gentle, her dark hair pulled into a neat, low bun away from her round face.

"This is Ana, my aide," Marquez said, and the woman gave Cora a brief nod.

"Pleasure to meet you, Ms. Daniels."

"Uh. Cora, please."

Ana only smiled and gestured toward the car door, urging them both inside. She took her place on the rear-facing seat across from them and clicked on her tablet as soon as the car was in motion. She seemed to have a hundred updates for Marquez—which Magisters had arrived when, her meeting schedule for the afternoon following the sitting, reminders of paperwork that needed her attention. It was professional, rapid-fire assistant-ing that left Cora feeling a little lost. At least she was polite enough to do it in English, so Cora had a chance of keeping up. After the quick debriefing, Ana glanced over to Cora and seemed to notice how out of her element she was. Her expression softened.

"During the sitting, you'll be with me, Cora. I'll take care of the official note-taking; I understand Señora Marquez wants you to observe today."

"Okay," Cora answered, relief lifting a little weight from her shoulders. "I can observe."

The Magistrate Hall wasn't quite what Cora expected. It was big, and imposing, but it kind of looked just like the rest of Philadelphia and the other cities in the Northeast—columns and wide walls done in Founding Fathers white. She'd expected it to be different, somehow. But it was just another building where politicians yelled at each other.

A mass of people filled the courtyard beyond the building, holding signs, chanting, but generally being peaceful. The sight made Cora happy. People really were speaking up. They were demanding to be treated better. The horrors of the camps had shocked people into action—finally. Cora smiled to herself. Nathan was getting a lot of the credit for all this, but, even if he never bothered correcting a single person, Cora knew the truth. This was because of Thomas.

The driver let them out at the front steps of the Magistrate Hall, beyond the row of Chasers at the foot of them. Were those armbands? Yikes. Who made that decision? Cora could see the faint shimmer of the barrier they held, but it would only keep mundanes from seeing and hearing the protest within. Nathan might already be down there. No—it still looked peaceful.

Cora trotted to catch up as Ana and Marquez reached the top of the stairs. All three of them were let into the building without question by the Chasers standing guard, and Cora dutifully followed the two women ahead of her who clearly knew where they were going. They passed through the formality of security and into the tall, wide corridors beyond. The floors were all dark and polished, illuminated by the stately windows along one side, and the hallway bustled with people—Chasers in their new armbands, men and women in suits. Everyone looked busy and important. Cora pulled up the sagging shoulder of her baggy shirt, feeling underdressed.

They went straight to the meeting room—which was more like an auditorium. It was round, with stadium-style seating all around the room. It looked like the kind of United Nations room you might see in a movie. People were already settling into their seats behind their desks and little standing microphones. A separate, more spacious area stood out at the top of the ring, and that was where Marquez led them, taking her seat among the other Councilors. Ana graciously named them all for Cora as they turned to greet the last arrival. Cora hung back with Ana and a few other professional-looking young people, suddenly feeling like too many eyes were on her. Magisters passed them on their way to their places, and many gave her the quick up-down Cora had long ago identified as "you don't belong here." Some even whispered as they went by.

"Um," Cora began, leaning closer to Ana so she could speak softly, "isn't it likely that people here are going to...recognize me? They mentioned me on Nathan's wanted poster; I saw it. Won't Ms. Marquez get in trouble?"

Ana shook her head. "Señora Marquez had me notify security that you'd be with her, and I've released a memo stating that your time with Mr. Moore was in the capacity of a confidential informant. Pending charges against you have been cleared, and though I admit there was some pushback from some of the Magisters, Señora Marquez told me to tell them...well, a basic translation would be, 'a Council pardon is a Council pardon, so shut up.'"

Cora covered her mouth to muffle her quick laugh. Marquez was her kind of lady.

Once the meeting started, it went exactly like Marquez said it would—a lot of people argued over each other and tried to make their own voice the most important. Marquez formally proposed repealing the Order of Repression. That apparently would require a separate hearing, but it didn't stop the Magisters from arguing about it now anyway. No wonder everything stayed the same shitty way it had always been.

A surprising number of the Magisters seemed to be in favor of repealing the Order already, but the loudest voices were the ones claiming that "backing down on this issue" would be giving in to the demands of rioters and inviting "further chaos." What a crock.

Every Magister who spoke up made Cora angrier. *We need more Chaser supervision, not less. Crime is out of control as it is.* But what really made her want to go over the desk was the Magister who said, far too calmly, "We might do *something* to placate the protestors and get all this to die down again. People have a short memory. If we throw them a bone, they'll gnaw at it until they forget."

If Cora had known where the hell she was, she would have left. This was disgusting. She'd always known, on a surface level, that anyone in politics was likely in it for the power or the money or both, but to see it laid out so blatantly churned her stomach. She hadn't anticipated this level of disregard for the people they were supposed to be representing and helping. At least—at the very least—there were some who were speaking up for progress. That was fucking something, she guessed.

She began to tune them out for the sake of her own mental health, but after a while, a Chaser came through the back stairs to the Council's pulpit and whispered in the ear of Morris Gagnon, the Council Chair Ana had pointed out to Cora on their way in. He spoke quietly to the other Councilors, his hand over his microphone, and then abruptly announced the end of the session, to reconvene tomorrow morning.

Cora looked up at Ana, who had a similarly questioning expression on her face. As the Councilors and Magisters began to shuffle out of their seats, a grumbling of confusion sounding through the hall, Marquez approached them with a tight frown on her lips.

"It seems there has been some violence outside."

Cora didn't get the feeling it was the time for asking questions, so she just followed as Ana and the Councilor filed out of the room along with the others. They weren't allowed to leave the offices for some time, since security didn't want to risk the Councilors' safety, so they waited in tense silence in the Council chambers while a pair of Chasers guarded the door. Did they expect the protestors to raid the building? They'd seemed peaceful enough earlier.

Cora's phone vibrated in her purse, startling her, and she sighed with relief as she saw Elton's name on the screen.

"Hey," she said, "are you guys outside the Hall?"

"Nathan's behaving, mostly," Elton answered. "I have Brooks. Where does Marquez want him?"

"Oh. Hang on."

After a quick exchange, Marquez arranged to send a car to pick up their new friend. Cora made Elton promise to keep himself and Nathan as safe as was reasonable, then left the Magistrate Hall with the Councilor and her aide—Marquez wasn't prepared to listen to safety protocols anymore.

They went out the rear exit of the building to avoid the protest, which made Cora nervous—how bad were things on the other side of the Hall?

By the time they made it to the hotel and up to Marquez's suite, Ana had verified for them that while there had been some injuries at the protest, there had been zero arrests—despite the Chasers' best efforts.

"It seems," Ana said, glancing back down at her phone screen with a faint smile curling one corner of her lips, "that Nathaniel Moore was present and assisting the protestors. The Chasers don't seem to have been prepared for that."

Cora smiled, but Ana put a finger to her lips to quiet her as a knock sounded on the suite door.

The boy who was ushered in looked about Cora's age—younger than he'd seemed in his stern-faced photo. He was cute. He had short dreads pulled up into a knot and a sweet smile. But when it was time to talk to Marquez, he was all business. He had a lot to say about what the Magistrate had been up to these last few months, and he didn't seem shy about saying it to a Councilor's face—but he settled down once he realized she was agreeing with him.

She let Cora tell him about what Nathan had done in Mexico, and how it was only the beginning of what they hoped people could accomplish. Eli talked about harm reduction and community action and prison abolition—concepts Cora had never heard verbalized before. She liked him a lot. He was idealistic and uncompromising as he laid out his plans and expectations to Councilor Marquez, but very clear in that he was unwilling to be dirty to accomplish his goals.

"We have to be better than the people we're trying to replace," he said, looking at Cora with a frown on his lips and fire in his dark eyes.

When they all shook hands late into the evening, Cora was given the key to her own room down the hall from Marquez, and she dropped down onto the bed with her arms splayed wide. Today had been a roller coaster—but she had a smile on her face as she turned over onto her stomach and reached for her phone. She wanted to tell Nathan and the others everything.

23

Cora was up early the next morning—and she was still the last one to arrive at Marquez's suite. Eli and the Councilor had already settled themselves at the long dining table and were poring over some files when Ana led her in. Eli had his laptop open and was typing away furiously, but he did pause to look up as Cora sat down across from him.

"Morning," he offered. "We're working on a proposal demanding the repeal of the Order of Repression."

"Just some light work over breakfast," Cora said with a chuckle, and Eli flashed a brief smile at her.

"This is only the first step. But without this, nothing else we try to do is going to matter."

"But how do we convince the Magisters? The rest of the Council? These are all the same people who passed it in the first place, right?"

Ana lightly cleared her throat from the end of the table. "Last night's poll of the attending Magisters indicates that about 42% of them would support repealing the order—but that isn't enough for a majority, of course. And a repeal would require the Council's approval as well."

"I have a few favors and liens I can use with some of the Magisters," Marquez said. "I intend to press them."

"Some of the Magisters who initially supported the Order *have* changed their minds," Ana went on. "It seems many were not expecting it to be executed quite as harshly as it was. A few commented on the camps, calling them excessive cruelty. They would be in favor of repealing the Order, if it were replaced by something with clearer guidelines." She glanced down at the tablet in her hand and shook her head. "Some only care about the bad PR the camps caused. This information wasn't polled, obviously, but it's common knowledge that some Magisters had money invested in the companies that were charged with managing the camps. Or in those supplied by the materials produced by the prisoners. These companies will certainly pressure them to maintain the new status quo."

"*Companies* managing the camps?" Cora interjected, turning her incredulous attention on Councilor Marquez.

"It's become a more standard way of doing things, I'm afraid," Marquez said.

"Private-run prisons have been the norm in the States for decades," Eli spat. "Why should concentration camps be any different?"

Cora's brow furrowed. "I didn't know there were private-run prisons, either."

"Why do you think so many people do time for things like driving without a license? Violate your probation by getting pulled over, and bam—prison. Why do you think states have started legalizing pot, but none of the people in prison for possession have been released? The Magistrate isn't any different. They oversee the prisons on paper, but the companies running them cut corners wherever they can, and the suits get richer with every inmate."

"It's always about money, isn't it?" Cora said. Eli saw all the flaws and corruption in the system as if they were highlighted in yellow—things Cora had never even thought about. She'd been fighting against something she didn't even understand. Not really. She only saw the individual injustices. But the scope of the problem was much larger than she'd imagined. It wasn't just that Chasers were jerks. This was Magistrate-wide. Systemic. From the top to the bottom.

Eli softened as he took in the look on her face. "Not to everyone," he said.

Marquez pointed one finger across the table at Cora. "For today, I want you to try to work on Humbridge. Find out what you can about him. His reasons for supporting the Order. See if you can make any progress. Ana can point you in the first direction. And I want you to work with Brooks to put together some reports to show Young."

"Okay." Cora nodded and hoped she sounded more confident than she felt. She didn't have much to contribute while Eli finished the proposal Marquez half dictated to him, and she was left even more out of her depth when the Councilor started to talk to Ana in the same kind of rapid exchange of information the aide had given the day before. The Councilor had planned out a dozen back room exchanges and deals in the time it took Cora to pour herself a cup of coffee.

What was she doing here?

When they were finished, Marquez left the hotel to attend the morning's Magistrate sitting, Eli left to meet Nathan at the day's protest, and Cora sat at the table with her half-drunk, room temperature coffee.

Ana slid back the chair beside her and sat down. "Shall we begin?"

"I don't even know *where* to begin," Cora admitted.

"It must seem overwhelming," Ana said gently. "But one thing at a time." She leaned in a little closer, a catlike smile on her lips. "Would you like to know how many Magisters are secretly gay?"

Cora snorted out a laugh, some of the weight lifting from her shoulders. "That's a good start. Is Councilor Humbridge one of them?"

"Not that I know of." She laid her tablet down on the table between them so that Cora could see the file she had pulled up. "Paul Humbridge—sixty-five, white, from Surrey, British Columbia, Canada. I'm sure he's not far off what you're expecting. In the summer, he golfs; in the winter, he skis. He and his wife have two adult children together. Their son is in finance, and their daughter has her own boutique clothing store in Vancouver. Humbridge himself has always been seen as something of a centrist, but he's also always taken a hard line against fraternization. I wouldn't say he's as bad as Araya—Humbridge has never said out loud that the mundanes are inferior, at least—but he's definitely been an advocate for as much separation from them as possible. He's made jokes before about private islands with nothing but witches on them, that sort of thing."

"Separate but equal, huh?"

"If that."

"Great. Good start." Cora frowned at his photo staring up at her from the tablet. He looked like every other old white politician she'd ever seen. And Marquez expected her to be able to do something about the way he'd been doing his Councilor-ing for the past how many years? She looked back up at Ana. "Can you tell me where he's staying? He doesn't live here, right?"

"Correct. He's staying at the Ritz-Carlton."

"Of course he is," Cora sighed as she scooted back her chair, and Ana smiled. "Thanks. I'm going to see what I can find out."

"I'll be at the Magistrate Hall for the remainder of the day, but do feel free to text me if there's anything you think I can help with."

"You got it. Thanks, Ana."

Cora shut herself back in her own hotel room down the hall and hauled her bag up onto the bed, pulling out the cloth-wrapped obsidian mirror Thomas had bought for her—it seemed like forever ago now.

She shut off the lights, lit her candle, and settled herself comfortably on the floor by the bed. She'd gotten so used to doing this in the warm, quiet creaking of Thomas's house that the sterile hotel room seemed unwelcoming. But she had a job to do.

Cora let her eyes fall half-shut as she stared into the soft candlelight, allowing herself to drift the way she'd done so many times before. Philadelphia was an unfamiliar city, and she'd only seen Humbridge a couple of times, so it took her some time to sink into the shoulder-slumping, soft-edged vision.

The suite at the Ritz was nicer than Marquez's—modern and sleek and boring. It made Cora long for the leopard-print pillows and bright teal rugs in the hotels Nathan normally chose. She wished she could be back with him and Elton and Thomas, instead of in her own bland, monochrome hotel room. On the other hand, she got to wake up this morning without seeing Nathan's bare ass before coffee, so there were pros and cons.

She let out a long exhale. Focus.

She scanned the suite's rooms, looking for anything out of place, or at least that would give her some information she could use. There was a closed laptop on the coffee table in the living room. Some papers here and there. The dining room still had last night's leftovers on it, it looked like. Two plates, two wine glasses. One with a lipstick stain. Cora was surprised the Councilor had brought his wife to something like this—the only perk of being married to a politician must be how often they're away, right? Maybe the wife was also a jerk, she guessed.

In the bedroom, one suitcase lay open on the folding stand at the foot of the rumpled bed. Just one? Something was making noise—the shower. Cora didn't particularly *want* to check on this old man while he was having his shower, but another sound caught her attention. The glass shower door was fogged, but smearing handprints cleared it in swipes, and the noises coming from inside were...identifiable. Good for Humbridge and his wife still having an active relationship, but—she paused. Cora distantly felt her fingertips curling against her knees as she tried to focus more closely.

The woman in the shower couldn't be Humbridge's wife. No way. This woman looked like she was in her twenties. If Humbridge had been the sort of skeez to have a young trophy wife, Ana definitely would have mentioned it—and she said they had adult children together.

Could Cora be so lucky? Was it possible that the old, white, right-leaning politician had...a *mistress?* Or at the very least, he was seeing a sex worker while he was away on business. How unexpected for someone like him.

But this wasn't something they could use. Well—maybe it was—but it wasn't proof. Marquez might have believed Cora personally just from a report from a scrying vision, but the rest of the Magistrate wouldn't. She needed to find out who this woman was. Maybe Cora would get extra lucky, and this woman *was* a sex worker, and there would be some kind of payment paper trail. But no matter what, Cora needed to get into that hotel room in person.

After a long post-scrying nap, Cora met up with Eli and Ana to put together some reports for Councilor Young. Neither of them were any more surprised than Cora had been that Humbridge was sleeping around. Eli already had most of the statistics they'd need for the report, so it was mostly a matter of laying everything out in a way that would convince a member of the Magistrate—frame things as cost-benefit, show where resources might be better allocated, prove the Magistrate had the funding to begin with, and show how similar programs had worked elsewhere.

When they'd taken a break for some coffee, Cora leaned her elbows on the conference table with her cup between her hands.

"How are things outside?" she asked, and Eli looked up at her while he stirred the creamer into his own mug.

"You're asking about Nathaniel Moore?"

"He really likes to be called just Nathan."

"Well he was fine when I left him. Things were calm this morning, but I think everyone's still on edge from what happened yesterday. We'll see how it goes. I'm going to head back out tonight."

"Can I go with you? I feel like I'm being benched, staying in the hotel all day."

"You said you got a lead on Humbridge, right? And now you're here putting together this report with me. Everybody's part looks different, Cora."

"I know," she admitted in a begrudging mumble, turning her cup with her fingertips. "But my part feels a lot less cool than yours and Nathan's."

Eli chuckled and opened his laptop again as Ana returned from the small kitchen with her own cup of coffee. "If I could make this happen without the help of somebody with his set of skills, I would. This kind of work is more important. It's longer-lasting. Protests might show up on the news for a while and draw attention, but it's all for nothing if things don't actually change. Like naming a holiday after Dr. King and still perpetuating a system that maintains a prison population that's five times more black than it is white. Pointless." He shook his head with a dry smile and a sidelong glance at Cora. "Us witches are just lucky, having to deal with *two* governments."

"Hooray," Cora said blandly, but she smiled. He was right. This was what she'd been telling Nathan, wasn't it? They can kill as many people as they want, but that won't change the laws. This was the work that really needed to be done. Cora could leave the flashy stuff to Nathan— that suited him better, anyway.

In the morning, Cora let Marquez know that she was hunting down some info, and would hopefully have something real to tell that afternoon. Ana promised to look into things on her end, and also to be Cora's lookout—she would need to let Cora know right away if Humbridge left the Magistrate Hall for any reason.

Cora was already standing on the street outside the hotel by the time Humbridge got into the back of his black car to be driven to the day's meeting. He was alone, of course. The woman might still be upstairs in the room—but that was a risk Cora was going to have to take. She'd talked her way out of worse situations.

She walked through the marble-columned lobby and found the elevators, trying not to look too out of place. She was sure she did anyway in her lace-up boots and slouchy t-shirt, but walking with purpose could take you far. The elevator needed a key to get to the room floors, so she put her hand over the scanner and pressed her palm tight against the plastic, muttering the word that heated the leopard jasper on her bracelet. She wasn't sure the spell would work on digital locks like this—she'd only used it on things like deadbolts before. The red light beside the scanner didn't change, so, with a frown, she took a step closer to the panel and cupped her hand with her mouth against the open space she made, then tried the word again, forcing that tight feeling in her chest that Nathan called will out through her lips. The scanner gave a small ding, and the elevator shifted as it started moving upwards.

Good enough.

She walked down the corridor like she belonged there—no doubt there were cameras in the halls, and the last thing she needed was some reg security guard thinking she looked suspicious. When she reached the room, she paused at the door and laid her fingers on the handle. It was warded, of course—but they were Magistrate standard. They were easy enough to dispel, and they would be easy enough to replace when she was done. They were probably more of a deterrent, anyway. Most people weren't likely to risk breaking into a Magistrate Councilor's hotel room in the first place, she guessed.

The door lock chimed itself open easily now, so she let herself in and shut it quietly behind her. She waited just inside, listening for any sound of occupants, but there was nothing. Cora made her way through the suite room by room, searching any papers and files left behind but finding nothing except the same generic reports she was sure Marquez was also getting. She pawed through Humbridge's suitcase as carefully as she could and tried to put the contents back the way she'd found them when she was done. Nothing there either. The laptop was missing from the coffee table—he must have taken it with him.

There were signs someone else had been there—another wine glass, and too many wet towels. A woman's lip gloss sat on the bathroom vanity. Cora could have taken pictures, but what would they prove? Only that someone wearing lipstick had once been in this room.

"Fuck," she said out loud, breaking the stillness of the room.

She couldn't linger. Humbridge might not come back, but any of his security or aides might, and Cora didn't want to still be in the room when housekeeping came around. So she left the suite, replaced the wards on the door with a few hasty words, and took the elevator back down to the lobby.

What the hell was she supposed to do now? Maybe she wasn't really cut out for espionage.

As she trudged back through the lobby, she glanced into the restaurant to one side of the lobby, separated only by yet another set of Greek-looking columns, and stopped short. Right there, sitting alone at one of the tables, was the woman Cora had seen in Humbridge's room. She looked different dressed and with her mouth closed, but it was definitely her. She had her phone in one hand, looking down at whatever she was scrolling through while her other hand reached for the mimosa flute beside her plate.

Cora moved to press against one of the columns as nonchalantly as someone can creep, and she chewed her lip. What could she do? This woman wasn't likely to talk to her. If she was still here, had been in Humbridge's room again the night before, then that tipped the scales toward mistress, not sex worker, right? But even if Cora could put the pieces together, that didn't mean—

She paused, gripping the strap of her purse at her chest. The woman was on her phone. A phone had information. A phone might have texts, emails, pictures...proof. If this woman could be distracted, maybe, Cora could take the phone no problem. She could give it to Ana. Find every scrap of evidence, every bit of dirt this guy had tried to hide.

Blackmail wasn't exactly playing fair—Eli probably wouldn't approve. But maybe it didn't even have to be blackmail. They could just tell everyone what he's done and let his public image take the hit for it. That wasn't playing dirty. That was just making someone face consequences.

The petty theft was worth it.

Cora waited by the entrance of the restaurant, smiling at the hostess and telling her she was waiting for the other members of her party before she wanted to be seated. She looked down at her phone, tried to play it casual, but she kept one eye on the woman finishing her breakfast of fancy toast and champagne. When she finally finished her meal, and the server came to take her plate away, Cora slipped by the absent hostess's podium and rushed through the restaurant. She waved as if trying to greet someone across the seating area, and she forced herself to slam full-speed into the server and his tray. The leftover food scraps and mimosa drippings went all over the table and the sitting woman, and Cora and the server hit the ground.

She started apologizing immediately, and the poor server did as well, visibly bracing himself for the shouting he must have known was coming. But the woman at the table waved him away, clearly startled but not seeming angry. She smiled at the server's apologies, assured him it was fine, and started helping him scoop up bits of toast and tomatoes with her napkin. Cora bent down to help pick up the fallen silverware, and on her way back up, slid the woman's phone from where she'd laid it aside on the table. She pushed it into her back pocket in a quick motion and began to move away, still apologizing. Before the server could finish clearing up the mess, Cora left. She strode out of the restaurant, then out of the lobby, and she didn't stop until she was two blocks away from the hotel entrance.

She stuffed the phone into her purse and zipped it shut. There had better be some useful information on this thing.

She waited until she was back in her own room with the door locked to look through the phone. The passcode had been 1-2-3-4. The phone itself must have warned her about the security of that choice when she'd entered it, right? But Cora wasn't going to complain. There were definitely photos of the two of them together—even a few pictures of the Councilor naked that he'd sent to her. Could have done without seeing that. But it was good news for them, if not for Cora's eyeballs.

Everyone's part was different, she reminded herself. Cora's part was breaking and entering and theft—then more paperwork later, probably. Working for the Magistrate was turning out to be just about as up and up as she'd expected.

Back in Marquez's suite that afternoon, Cora passed the phone to

Ana and let her work her information magic on it. She was delighted—this woman lived on drama. Cora liked her more all the time.

It was easy to get the woman's name from her phone, and from there, Ana was able to track down the rest of her life within half an hour. Lindsey Baker was twenty-three, lived in Vancouver, and seemed to have no job. She had a fairly successful social media presence, though—a decent number of followers apparently wanted to see her in her puffy jacket at Whistler, or at the beach, or eating a salad in her nice apartment.

"Humbridge must be taking care of her," Ana said. "That can't be cheap. And that means paper trails. I'll find them."

"This all sounds like good news," Cora said, looking across the table at Marquez's pensive face. "We can use this, right?"

"We can," the Councilor agreed. "The best case scenario would be getting him to resign, but...unfortunately, a Magistrate official having a mistress isn't exactly a surprising secret."

"There is one more thing," Ana cut in. She let her tablet rest on her knees and held it at the top with both hands. "This woman is mundane."

Cora scoffed. "Is that supposed to be a surprise either? Some witch separatist not following his own rhetoric? That's no different from the anti-gay Congressman being caught with their boyfriend." She snorted and tucked her feet up under her in her seat. Witches all over sure did like to act like they were better than the regs, but really, they got into all the same kind of stupid, self-serving, harmful bullshit as everybody else.

She paused when she saw the subtle wrinkle in Ana's brow and the growing scowl on Marquez's lips. "Wait," she said softly. "If this girl is a reg, and this gets out...they'll give her the ingnas, won't they?"

"Probably, yes," Ana agreed. "Who knows what secrets Humbridge might have told her? This is even worse than a regular person being involved with a mundane."

"...Yeah."

They both looked at Marquez, but she didn't speak. She ran her fingers around the walking stick leaned against her chair and frowned at the carpet.

"Councilor," Cora began quietly, "maybe we should...find another angle? I found this proof, but...I don't want to be responsible for someone getting the ingnas. It's—it's too terrible." She gripped her ankles tight, unable to shake the memory of Thomas sitting at his kitchen table, the emptiness in his voice as he described the shell that used to be the woman he hoped to marry. "This woman seems...nice," Cora pressed. "A little spoiled and kept, maybe, but she was kind to a waiter who'd just dumped eggs all over her. She's not a criminal just because she's sleeping with a Councilor. We can't let this happen to her."

The beats of silence before Marquez looked up again were torture—but then the Councilor sighed.

"I agree," she said, and Cora's shoulders slumped with relief. "If it were up to me, the practice would be banned—but that's a difficult sell. Secrecy for our people *is* important, even if the Magistrate's methods of enforcing it have been questionable. For now, we need to focus on getting Humbridge to agree to vote for repealing the Order of Repression. We can do that without endangering this girl—we just have to let Humbridge believe we *would* endanger her, or it's an empty threat. But I can sell that," she said with a sly smile as she looked over at Cora. "This was good work, Ms. Daniels. And your desire for discretion when boldness would serve us better is admirable." Marquez pushed herself up from her seat with the help of her walking stick and nodded. "Let me take this matter from here. Thank you."

Cora glanced over at Ana, who was also smiling, and got to her feet. She knew when she was being dismissed. She thanked Marquez and almost skipped out of the room, unable to keep the beaming she felt inside from showing on her face. Marquez really was a good one.

Now—about that paperwork.

24

If anyone had tried to tell Elton a year ago that he would be standing in a courtyard full of people protesting the Magistrate, and that not only would he not be one of the one wearing an armband, but that he would also be standing next to Nathaniel Moore, he would have thought they were unmedicated. But here he was. And here Nathan was—almost completely unlike the man whose apartment Elton had walked into, ready to make the arrest of his life.

For the past three days, Nathan had stood in the center of the crowd, surrounded by people with signs and slogans who were ready to hang on his every word. He'd kept anyone from getting arrested, just as he promised he would. And, somehow—Thomas denied being the source—stories had begun to spread about him that were wholly different from the kind the Magistrate had been putting out for the last two hundred years. People knew about Adelina. They said her name like a martyr, and now, when Nathan arrived in the courtyard and the Chasers tightened their ranks, the other protestors closed in to protect him, too. He'd been adopted by the cause, it seemed.

One enthusiastic protestor had even painted a sign with the mark from the back of Nathan's neck on it—but when Nathan saw it, he tore it in two and told the boy not to be "a sycophantic idiot." At least the goodwill hadn't gone *completely* to his head.

Thomas was always busy at night. He'd taken over their host's guest room entirely the first night they'd arrived, leaving Nathan and Elton on the couch pullout. The floor in there was probably ruined now, knowing Thomas. Elton was never quite sure what his old roommate was *doing*, exactly, but he was almost always on the phone or shut in the guest room, looking gaunt and exhausted when he did periodically emerge. Thomas always seemed to know things before anyone else did, so whatever he was doing must have been useful.

Late one night, while Elton, Nathan, and Oliver were picking over the last of some takeout Mexican food, a loud, thumping knock shook the front door of the apartment. They all went still for a moment—an unexpected knock was not a good sign in the current Magistrate climate. Nathan and Elton moved into Oliver's bedroom with quick, quiet steps and pulled the door to so they could listen from around the corner. When Oliver opened the door and gave a friendly greeting, the voice at the door seemed to have no time for pleasantries.

"Where's Elton Willis?" the man asked.

Nathan looked up at the blond beside him with a curious purse of his lips, but Elton only frowned and leaned closer to the door.

"Uh," Oliver began uncertainly, "I don't know anybody by that name, sorry—"

"I know he's here. Don't make me ask again. You don't want me to have to ask again."

Elton's brow furrowed. Wait. He knew that voice. Before Oliver could stutter out another excuse that was likely to get him smacked, Elton pushed open the bedroom door and stepped into the living room.

In the doorway, a 40-something Chinese man in a black suit stood with his arms folded, a calm frown on his stubbled face. His dark eyes flicked over to Elton as he appeared, and he put a hand on Oliver's shoulder to move him out of the way so he could come inside. Elton did know this man.

"Keung dai lo," Elton said. "What are you—"

"Have you been contacted yet?"

"By who?"

"By whoever took Jo."

Elton's skin went cold. "What are you talking about?"

"I'll take that as a no." He glanced over his shoulder at Oliver, who

191

hastened to shut the door, then returned his attention to Elton. "Someone broke into Jo's apartment two days ago. She disappeared, but I've tracked her here. Since you're here too, I can only imagine someone took her to get to you."

"How the hell did you know where I was?"

He snorted. "You're underestimating me if you think I haven't known where you are every day for the last ten years. You aren't as subtle as you think you are." He paused as Nathan emerged from the bedroom, then gave the other man a purposeful look up and down. "This is him?"

"Uh—Keung dai lo, this is Nathaniel Moore. Nathan, this is Lai Shan Keung. An old friend of mine."

"Oh, and I just bet I can guess what sort of old friend," Nathan said with a laugh as he offered his hand. "Delighted."

Lai Shan ignored the gesture. "I thought he'd be taller."

"Well, my father was tall, but the milkman wasn't," Nathan chuckled.

"Keung dai lo, you said you know where Jo is?" Elton cut in, breaking the lidded stare his old friend had leveled on Nathan.

"I thought I'd check in with you first—see if there had been some kind of offer made. Do you know who would have done this?"

"I haven't made many friends this last year," Elton admitted. "But only one person has threatened to hurt Jo before, and he's already in a Magistrate jail."

"Um," Oliver interrupted, bending to scoop an unmarked white envelope from the floor where it had slid under the door. He held it out for the others to see, and Elton scowled. A Magistrate missive.

Nathan took it from Oliver's hand and opened it without hesitation, scanning the page before offering it to Elton. "Looks like whoever it is wants you to meet them tonight."

"And isn't afraid to use Magistrate methods to tell you," Lai Shan added.

"That means someone at the Magistrate knows where I am," Elton said with a wary glance toward Nathan. "So they know where you are. We'll need to move. We don't want Oliver in any more danger than he's already in." Their host didn't speak, but he did look a bit relieved.

"You're awfully calm knowing your ex-wife is being held captive somewhere, darling."

"They wouldn't bother to ask me to meet if they were going to kill her. And Jo can take care of herself." He looked up at Lai Shan. "You said you tracked her here?"

"I know where she is," he confirmed. "And it's not the address on this letter. It's *your* fault she's gotten involved in this, so let's go get her back before her stupid new gweilo boyfriend does something stupid."

"I'm coming as well, obviously," Nathan said.

Elton stared down at the paper in his hand. "If this is who I think it is, then I want to look him in the face." He glanced up at Nathan with a frown. "It has to be Hubbard."

"Then you go look him in the face, and we'll go get Jo," Lai Shan said, but Elton shook his head.

"This is my problem. You're right—she's involved because of me. I'm the one who needs to put an end to it." Elton picked up his suit jacket from where it had been laid over the arm of the couch, then slid the letter into his breast pocket along with his folio of spell papers. "I'll bring her back," he promised, one hand already on the door knob. He left the apartment without waiting for the others to voice the objections he knew were coming, though he heard Nathan's complaining as he shut the door behind him.

This was his responsibility.

The address the note gave led Elton to a construction site near the river, the uncovered metal frame of the new building slick from the evening's rain. What a cliche. Elton didn't try to walk quietly—he was expected, after all. A pair of men waiting by a stack of rebar met him before he got past the caution tape, and they stopped him from going further. He let them check his hands for a Chaser ring, and he didn't stop them from taking his folio or his phone from his pocket when they found them. Once they were satisfied, they led him back deeper into the site without a word.

Underneath one of the buildings in progress, a well-dressed man waited with his hands held behind his back, watching Elton approach through wire-rim glasses. He looked like he was in his sixties, maybe— dark hair with salt at his temples, slender, and a solemn frown on his lips, faintly visible in the dim light that reached them from the street. Another man stood just behind him, holding a large umbrella up to prevent the scattered rain droplets from falling on his superior.

"Mr. Willis," the man in the suit spoke up. He glanced at the men escorting Elton, and they moved to stand a few paces back. "I'm glad you came."

"I'm here for the woman you kidnapped, Magister," Elton said simply, but he couldn't help the venom in his voice as he forced out the man's title.

"Oh, let's not hold any pretension here. We both know you don't have a moral leg to stand on. I deserve recompense for the murder of my son—and I'm sure you would agree."

"Maybe I would if your son hadn't also been a murderer."

"Despite our differences of opinion, the facts of the matter are these—I have something you want. And you have something I want."

Elton frowned. "You're talking about a deal?"

"I know that Councilor Marquez has been working with Nathaniel Moore. I saw that girl that follows him around at the Magistrate Hall—Marquez isn't even trying to hide her. But I need solid proof that a Councilor is conspiring with a well-known anarchist. If you were to turn yourself in, testify against them, then Marquez will be removed from her office—and that is a vacancy I intend to fill. Being the one responsible for finally capturing Nathaniel Moore will all but guarantee my place. I will release your wife, of course, and I can make sure that your accommodations in the years to come are...less unpleasant than they should be."

A smolder of heat crept up the back of Elton's neck. He understood vengeance. Anger. Elton had killed this man's son—so he wanted Elton dead. But now that he saw the possibility of personal gain, the Magister was choosing to overlook his son's murder. Opportunistic serpent. "You expect me to turn Nathan in and go to prison so that you can *get a promotion?*"

"Honestly, it's all seemed to have worked out for the best," Hubbard went on with a small shrug. "I was furious with Nikita for failing to kill you both so many times, of course, but in hindsight, this is a far better opportunity than simple revenge. I'm sure you'll agree—if only due to your precarious situation, and that of your wife."

"You—*you* sent Korshunov after us?"

"And his failure is precisely the reason I don't intend to

underestimate your capabilities, Mr. Willis. You aren't an idiot. You must see how pointless all of this is. Cooperate with me, and I will see that your life is at least tolerable."

Elton grit his teeth, but he forced his hands to stay still at his sides. This man—who Elton only knew in the first place because he'd been covering up his son's murders of vulnerable women—had sent Korshunov to kill them. Had given a young Chaser leave to ignore the law for the sake of revenge. Every innocent person Korshunov had killed was because of Hubbard—or was it because of Elton?

No. This was all because of Hubbard. He'd been the one to put his own interests above his duty in the first place. Because of him, Korshunov had been set loose. Bystanders had been injured or killed. Cora had been scarred. Adelina had been brutally murdered. Even Korshunov himself had suffered—broken down, desperate, half insane. He was only Cora's age.

Now Jo was at risk. Nathan and Cora themselves had been in danger. Hubbard had put them in danger. And now he was asking Elton to agree to get off easy for his own crimes in exchange for turning Nathan in?

The burning indignation set in his chest by the suggestion startled him. Turn Nathan in—that's what he'd set out to do. What he'd devoted his career to. What he'd lost Jo for. It seemed...impossible now. Even if Hubbard had offered him freedom. A pardon. Impossible.

Elton lowered his gaze to the muddy ground. "A Magister is supposed to be a servant," he said. "Not a dictator. Not a judge and executioner." Nathan's gold bracelet was heavy around his wrist—they hadn't taken that. He stared across the darkness separating him from Hubbard and looked him in the eyes. "Your son deserved to die. So do you."

With a snapped word, the bracelet grew hot against his skin, and the three men surrounding them were crushed to the ground by a binding. Hubbard's eyes widened in a panic as the umbrella fell to the ground beside him, and he stepped back.

"You idiots," he growled, "I thought you searched him!"

Elton took his folio from the bound hand of one of the guards, slipped a paper free, and blew it from his hand. It split into strips as it fell, each one shooting along the mud toward a bare throat. He didn't need to hold the binding anymore.

Hubbard ran. He crossed the site in a slipping hurry, half skidding to a stop beside the car parked at the edge of the caution tape. He fumbled into the driver's seat and revved the engine, hauling the car away from the sidewalk. Elton stalked toward the fleeing car and held up a hand, throwing down an iridescent green barrier directly in front of it. The front of the car crumpled at the impact, the back wheels lifting from the road before slamming back down with a heavy crash. An abandoned hammer lay on top of one of the stacks of tarp-covered wood—Elton bent to pick it up on his way by. Smoke poured from the hood of the car as Elton approached, but the driver's side door still opened when he pulled the handle.

The air bag had kept Hubbard from too much damage, but he still looked dazed as he turned his head toward the open door. He started to speak—maybe a threat, or a plea, or a spell—but whatever it was didn't make it past his lips. This man wasn't a fighter. He'd spent a lifetime having other people do his dirty work. Elton snatched him by the front of his suit jacket and hauled him from the car, throwing him face first onto the asphalt and planting a foot on his throat to stop him turning fully over. It didn't take much pressure—only a single solid grind of Elton's heel—to collapse the Magister's windpipe and cut short any further attempts. Only strained gargling sounds came now.

Elton shifted the handle of the hammer in his hand as he took a single step back, looking down into Hubbard's frantic eyes.

"What were you thinking," Elton snarled, "sending a child after someone like me?"

The hammer hit Hubbard's temple first. After the third strike, the head broke bone, and Elton had to pull harder to jerk it free. The Magister's blood was hot as it splattered onto Elton's hands, and his body went still long before the last hit.

Finally, Elton let the hammer fall from his grip, and he dropped back into a sprawled seat on the road, hoping to steady his breath. His fingers were trembling even as they held his weight behind him. His head swam, and his heartbeat was deafening.

Elton sat up, wiped his bloody hands on the dark fabric of his pants, willed them to stop shaking. He didn't like this feeling. He'd killed people before—why did his pulse refuse to go down now?

He needed to leave.

Elton pushed to his feet and returned to the bodies of the guards, searching the man's pocket for his confiscated phone, then hurried away from the construction site on foot.

He was angry. He was *still* angry—that was why his hands trembled, why his legs felt weak, why he couldn't slow his breathing. He'd killed Hubbard in anger. This hadn't been planned—calm. Like the others.

Elton had never let anger take control of him like this before. Was this the inevitable next step? Kill enough people on purpose, and eventually you'll do it on instinct?

Was Nathan right to say no more?

Elton swore under his breath as he ducked into an alley to avoid passing under streetlights. How was it possible that Nathan had done a complete reversal in his life philosophy, and he had somehow been right about the way Elton should live his own life *both times*?

Almost the moment Elton had left the apartment, of course, Nathan and Lai Shan had exchanged a knowing look, and Nathan had thanked Oliver for his hospitality. Thomas promised to find them a new place to stay and relocate their things while the two more offensively-minded men were away, and to text Nathan the new address.

The poorly-lit warehouse where Jocelyn had been held was protected by a frankly insulting number of guards—they must have been counting on secrecy to keep her in their custody. But wherever Lai Shan got his information, it had clearly been accurate.

Nathan saw Elton's shadow in the way the man fought. Instead of paper talismans, he used one or two powders blown or tossed toward the unprepared guards, and the instant, twisting agony of their insides dropped them to the ground for him—but when he bent to slit their throats one by one, he had the same unhalting, methodical viciousness in his movements that Nathan had seen in his companion countless times over the past months.

He liked this man. And it didn't count towards Nathan's body count if Lai Shan was the one killing these Chasers, did it?

They found Jocelyn bound to a metal chair with agrimony rope and gagged with an oil-soaked cloth. Lai Shan cut her free with his knife, and she tossed the gag away with a snort. She was pretty—slender, with softly rounded cheeks and shoulder-length hair mostly fallen from its clip at the back of her head, and she wore a simple floral sundress and matching flats. She had a frown on her thick lips that gave such an impression of being irritatingly inconvenienced that Nathan liked her immensely straight away. The pair exchanged a few words in Cantonese as Lai Shan helped her to her feet, and the woman paused to spit some oil remnants onto the grungy floor before looking up at Nathan.

"You're him?"

"I've been known to be," he answered with a smile, and she raked her eyes down him like an appraiser.

"I thought you'd be taller."

Nathan sighed lightly. "A lot of that going around. A pleasure, regardless." He checked his phone and found a text waiting from Thomas, as promised. He moved quickly; Nathan had to give him that much. "Are you injured?"

"I'm fine. These idiots were all bark."

Nathan chuckled. Elton had let this woman get away?

Thomas had chosen them a very boring, very reasonably-priced extended stay hotel on the outskirts of the city. Nathan had one look at the beige-colored room and its low-pile carpet and took back any nice thoughts he'd had about Thomas that evening, but at least things were in order.

Elton was already slouching in one of the pleather lounge chairs, his arms draped across the arms and a cigarette loosely held in his fingers. Dried blood had caked into his clothes, and he stared blankly across at the empty chair opposite him. He immediately sunk forward and crushed the cigarette out on the sole of his shoe when they entered, tucking the ruined butt into his pocket as he stood. That's right—she had been the one to convince him to quit. That his first thought upon seeing her was to hide his indiscretion was adorable. He crossed the room in long, swift steps, but stopped short of coming within arm's reach of the woman who had once been his wife.

"Jo," he said, and Nathan fought the urge to put a hand over his own heart at the soft sentiment in the blond's voice. "Are you all right?"

"I'm fine," she snapped, feeling none of his hesitation about stepping close—but instead of the embrace he might have been hoping for, she shoved him in the chest. "No thanks to you! Didn't I tell you to be careful? Didn't I tell you not to do anything stupid? Killing a Magister's son counts as something *stupid*, you idiot! After everything you worked for, after everything you gave up to try and turn your life around, where are you? On the run again? I can't believe that you're thirty-five years old and you're *still*—hello, Thomas," she interrupted herself, glancing to the man in the bedroom doorway with a significantly softer tone.

"Hello, Jocelyn."

"—and you're *still* acting like some stupid, thug teenager!" she went on, undeterred. "What are you thinking?"

"Jo, I—"

"I don't even want to know what your answer is! What reason could there possibly be?" she cut him off, huffing out her next breath and crossing her arms to stare at him like he was a child.

"I adore this woman," Nathan said softly with a glance up at Lai Shan, and Jocelyn whirled on him in a fury.

"Don't even get me started on *you*! You're the real reason for all this!"

"Jo, please," Elton tried again, and when he took a step closer and reached out to place his hands on her arms, she deflated—but only a little. She still jutted out her chin as she looked up at him. "I'm sorry you got involved in all this. I'm just glad you're not hurt."

"And who did you hurt today, Elton?" she asked, uncrossing her arms to gesture at his stained clothes. "This Magister, he's dead now, isn't he? Just solve all your problems by putting them in a grave. I thought you'd grown out of this...violence," she finished, a bit strained now. "It was easier to forgive when you were just a stupid kid."

"You don't have to forgive me," he answered gently. "I don't expect you to forgive me for any of it."

"Good. I don't."

"Okay."

The couple stared at each other in silence for a few moments, and Nathan began to feel as if perhaps they ought to have some privacy, but Lai Shan cleared his throat loudly enough to break the tension in the room.

"I'm ready to get you home if you're ready to go, Jo," he said, but the woman hesitated.

"You shouldn't have anything else to worry about," Elton added. "I don't imagine Hubbard told anyone about any of this."

"Nothing to worry about except the friends and loved ones of the *other* people on your list of felonies," Jocelyn muttered bitterly. She shoved at Elton's chest again with the side of one fist, but he didn't move.

"Keung dai lo will take care of you," he said. "You should get home. I'm sure...what's his name is worried about you."

"Stop," she sighed, and he finally dropped his hands. She shook her head with her eyes on the floor a moment before looking back up at him. "Just...are you *really sure* you have to be involved in all this? I've heard about these protests, the trouble it's causing with the Magistrate, and with your record..."

"Jo," Elton interrupted gently, "you might not believe me, but I think...I think I finally get it. I did something tonight that I...never thought I'd do." He shifted his weight and looked so much like he wanted to hold her that Nathan's own heart grew a little tight. "I lost control. You'll probably say it should have happened years ago, but I feel...like I can do things differently now. Where I am now...I have the opportunity to do the good I set out to do when I joined the Magistrate in the first place. *Actual* good. Not just—lawful." He shot a sidelong glance at Thomas in the doorway, who was watching him with a faint, grim frown, then looked back into the woman's eyes. "Does that make any sense?"

Jocelyn gave a heavy, thoughtful sigh, and then she allowed her fingers to interlace with Elton's—just for a moment. "Just don't make me hear about you getting killed in some riot," she said.

"Promise."

She nodded, took a step back from him, and offered Thomas a brief wave goodbye before turning back toward the door. She paused, then glared up at Nathan, drawing close enough for him to smell the lingering sweat on her. "*You.* Are the one whose ass I'm going to kick if he gets killed."

"Understood," Nathan assured her. He offered her an unreturned smile and opened the suite door for her and her escort. He peered around the door to see if she would give Elton a longing look backward, but if she did, it was quick enough that Nathan missed it.

Once he shut the door, he moved to stand beside Elton and lightly nudged him with his elbow.

"She's a delight. I think I'm in love with her, myself." He tilted his head to look up at the blond. "Had you ever considered a threesome?"

"Nathan, please," Elton sighed, turning away from him to return to his chair by the window.

"Well, then it's no wonder your marriage deteriorated." Nathan crossed the room to fall into the chair opposite him, and he offered him a cigarette from his pack. Thomas shook his head silently and disappeared into the bedroom again as Elton accepted Nathan's light, and they both settled into their seats, smoke trailing toward the ceiling.

After a while of quiet, Nathan reached out one foot to gently prod the shoe of Elton's crossed leg.

"It's all going to turn out all right, you know," he said softly.

Elton took a long pull from his cigarette, eyes still looking out at the streetlights through the window, and he let it out in a slow breath before he nodded. "Yeah." He fidgeted with the cigarette in his fingers, turning it idly. "Thank you," he added after a moment. "For going to get her. You didn't have to."

"Of course. You don't have to ask for my help, Elton. You aren't a one-man show anymore. Neither of us are—for better or for worse."

Elton snorted softly, glancing sidelong at Nathan as he exhaled smoke. "I know."

25

"You're telling me I missed meeting Elton's ex-wife?" Cora said over the phone the next afternoon. "Man, office work is the pits."

"She wasn't in a very conversational mood," Thomas answered. Nathan and Elton had already left for the day's protest, so he had his phone laid on the dining table in their new suite, Cora's voice coming through the speaker so that he could listen to her while he ground herbs in a large mortar and pestle.

"Still! I would have liked to lay eyes on her, you know?"

"You'd like her. She really laid into him."

"He deserves it. But even so...stupid of Hubbard to poke the snake like that. It's all anyone can talk about this morning. I told Marquez what really happened, of course, but she's keeping quiet. I don't know whether that's better, or if everyone should know a Magister kidnapped a woman for the sake of revenge. There's going to be a big investigation, still."

"Someone will talk, and the truth will come out. Someone underpaid and overworked." Thomas poured a small slosh from a vial of oil into the mortar, then returned to his grinding. "Someone always talks."

"I know that voice. That's your 'I know something' voice. What do you know?"

Thomas snorted faintly. "I know you don't organize a kidnapping from the other side of the country, across a border, without involving a few people outside of your close circle. You can tell Marquez someone should be in contact with her soon."

"God, you're like some sort of sexy information broker," she said with a laugh.

"Please," Thomas muttered. He shifted in his chair and turned his grip on the pestle to help slow the tiring of his arm. He let a brief pause go by before he spoke again. "I hear you're getting along well with Mr. Brooks."

"Oh, shut up. Eli's great; he's knowledgeable, and passionate, and idealistic. He's really throwing his whole life into making a difference. I like him a lot. But you're sorely mistaken if you think that *optimism* is a trait I look for in a romantic partner, Mr. Proctor."

Thomas frowned into his bowl a moment, then tapped the paste from his pestle and laid it aside. She saw right through him—just like always. "I'm sure you and Marquez will have a lot to do very soon, regardless of how this afternoon goes. It won't look good for anyone at the Magistrate when it gets out that a Magister was using Chasers like his own personal PMCs, either."

"No, I guess not," Cora agreed. She sighed audibly into the phone. "I just want this wait to be over. How long does it take to vote?"

"There are a lot of Magisters," Thomas pointed out.

"It's stupid that this is even an issue. Marquez said she thinks we have the votes to get the Order of Repression repealed, but...fuck, I wish they'd vote faster."

"Even if it does pass, it seems like a bit of a hollow victory. It's not progress; it's just a return to the previous, slightly less restrictive status quo."

"There's that bitter realism that gets me going," she teased, and Thomas lifted his stone mortar to scoop the thick paste he'd made into a jar.

"Fasting," he said simply, causing a quiet laugh from the other end of the line.

"Sorry. Have you heard from Anne? How's Herman doing?"

"He's living his best life, I'm sure. He gets along with her other cat, apparently."

"That's good. I just—" She was cut off by a loud thump, and someone yelled something Thomas couldn't make out. A moment later, Cora's voice came through again, sounding as if she was holding the phone too close to her face. "It's back! The vote's back! It passed! It's repealed!"

Her laughter brought a faint smile to Thomas's face. It would be something, at least.

Word spread like wildfire across the crowded courtyard of the Magistrate Hall—the Order of Repression repealed. Brooks had barreled his way through the crowd to Nathan to tell him, leaving cheering and laughing protestors in his wake. Nathan smiled at the young man's beaming face. A victory—a small one, but meaningful—would reinvigorate the spirit of the people gathered here. Even Elton had a faint smile on his face.

"This isn't enough," Brooks said, loud enough for the people around him to hear, "but it's a start. When we all speak together, they have to listen. They will listen. And things will change."

Nathan gave the boy's shoulder an encouraging pat and shared a brief glance with Elton. He didn't plan to move on yet. The Chasers were still sometimes pushy, and Nathan wanted to be there to push back. Elton had been a great help himself, breaking bindings Nathan missed and throwing down his own barriers to cut off advancing Chasers. Nathan had chatted and made friends with the people passing out bottled water and snacks, and especially with the ones who stood by to patch up any minor injuries—as Nathan was usually the one sustaining them. He missed Cora. But she had seemed satisfied with her work so far when they talked on the phone, and Nathan was proud that she'd had a hand in the repeal of this order, so he was determined to do his part as well. He *could* be useful without doing any murders—it was just more difficult.

"Cora said she wanted to come down," Brooks said, "but with her still trying not to have any official ties, you know—"

His next words were cut short by a scream from the other side of the courtyard. The crowd shifted, and the screams multiplied like an echo of the first as the crowd shifted in sudden alarm.

Nathan pushed without hesitation through the bodies washing toward him away from the sounds of panic. Something was on the ground—something black and skittering like an animal, flowing in numbers across the concrete. They moved too quickly for Nathan to get a good look at them, but they seemed to have a surplus of legs, and they soon began to dart upward—burying sharp ends into the flesh of those too slow to move away. More than one person fell to the ground, and the others around them were hesitant to draw close enough to help. These things—he could feel their master prickling his skin.

Nathan followed the path the creatures had left, and there at the broad stairs of the Magistrate Hall, they poured from an opening in the concrete like ants pouring from a mound. And standing over them was their source. Korshunov. Even at this distance, Nathan could see his pale eyes locked onto him, unwavering even as fleeing protestors rushed between them. He looked bloodless and gaunt, wearing clothes that didn't fit him and already breathing heavily. How the hell had he gotten here?

"Elton," Nathan called, reaching back for the blond without taking his eyes from the young Chaser, "you need to get these people out of here."

"I don't think getting them to leave is going to be a problem," Elton answered over the rush of panicked shouts around them.

"Get Brooks home. And find Cora. Now." Nathan's frown deepened as he watched Korshunov across the courtyard, steadily waiting.

"I'm not just leaving you here," Elton protested.

"Something's wrong with him. I can smell it. Take care of them—I have him."

Elton started to speak up again, but he was drowned out by the noise of the crowd as Nathan moved forward. Korshunov lifted his hands, and at the faintest push outward, a blast of pressure flung the people still close to him from the ground. A few of them caught themselves, but most went skidding across the concrete, crushing underneath them the small black bodies of the creatures covering the courtyard like a living carpet. They hissed and chittered at Nathan's feet, but their purpose seemed to be to clear the space between Korshunov and himself of anyone who might interfere.

"Missed me already?" Nathan called. He needed to distract him—contain him—at least until the bulk of the people got out of the area. His bracelet warmed as he tried to lift the boy from his feet, but he was stuck fast to the ground; Nathan's spell didn't even sway him. What had

205

happened to this boy?

Korshunov's head dipped back, and his eyes rolled upward to white as a terrible shriek filled the air. Far above them, Nathan heard a thundering flap, and over the top of the Magistrate Hall, another spirit appeared—it had the shape of a bird, but it was the size of a bus. Its body glowed orange like embers, and the tips of its feathers crackled with every movement, dropping cinder over the steps of the Magistrate Hall.

To his side, Nathan caught a glimpse of Elton, snatching one of the standing Chasers by the front of his shirt and snapping commands to him and his paralyzed comrades.

"You think this barrier matters more than those people? Do your goddamn job, and help get them out of here!"

Nathan kept his attention on Korshunov's newest pet—which was fast swooping toward him and the people still falling over each other in their hurry to flee without being cut open by the monsters at their feet. Its cry was painful and almost deafening, but more concerning were its fiery talons, now stretching toward Nathan at the speed of a truck. He dug in his heels, locked his eyes on the falcon's shrieking face, and let out the air in his lungs. Just before the creature reached him, he breathed in, throat burning from the heat of the air around him, but the bird faltered—the flames at its wings failing and leaving blackened feather tips as the air left the space around them. Nathan still had to duck, but the spirit scraped to the ground behind him instead of colliding with him, a mess of singed feathers and rage. It even caught some of the insect-like creatures alight with its embers, sending thin, hissing cries into the air as they burned away to ash.

The protestors were thinning, at least—Elton and the Chasers seemed to be blocking them from the creepy crawlies on the ground while they retreated. Elton maintained a moving barrier at the rear of the crowd, separating them from Nathan and Korshunov with a translucent green wall. Good.

Nathan glanced around him as the creatures began to swarm toward him instead. The falcon was righting itself—he'd only have a moment. But it would be enough. He spread his fingers at his sides, scanning the expanse of the rippling insects one last time, then lifted his hands and dropped them, washing a stream of his own fire from his hands in a broad, expanding circle around him. The spirits gave satisfying screams as they crinkled away, clearing the courtyard except for the ashes debris they left—but they hadn't stopped clambering from the gap near Korshunov's feet, either. He needed to stop their master.

He dropped low enough to slap his palm against the cement, creating his own crack in the ground that zigzagged toward Korshunov and his pets. The boy finally moved as the break reached him, spilling his skittering spirits into the newly-made chasm. He shot forward faster than Nathan could see, stopping inches from his face as the heat from the falcon's renewed flames began to lick at Nathan's back.

Korshunov's skin was visibly clammy, and a faint tremble was in his limbs as he stared at Nathan with narrowed eyes—the one milky and glazed-over white. At his chest, where his ill-fitting shirt was only half buttoned, an angry red line in his skin had been stapled shut, from his collarbone down beyond where Nathan could see. The faint marks where he'd stitched groundings into himself were still visible, as well— not even healed. This boy was barely held-together parts. How was he doing magic like this?

Nathan was suddenly knocked backward by a quick motion of the Chaser's hand, and before he could catch himself, he was snatched by one of the bird's massive talons, crushing his shoulder in a burning grip that dug sharp points into his stomach and back. He felt familiar tingling at the backs of his eyes, but he fought the rise of black in his gut.

No. Not this time. I have him.

Kalfu would kill this boy. But Nathan had made a promise.

He fought to breathe in the hot air, and his hands burned where he tried to pull at the falcon's claws, but he managed to force out a spell that sparked from one of the stones on his necklace. Large chunks of earth and cement cracked free of the ground, raising themselves into the air before crashing back together at the spirit's head. They crushed into a solid mass, sending the bird writhing and shrieking as it fell onto its back, blinded and panicked. It bashed its head against the ground in an attempt to break loose, wings flailing and spreading hot cinders into the air.

Korshunov knocked Nathan back again, the force so focused that his head jerked as he stumbled, and he tasted blood. He spat out a binding that Korshunov had to shake off but was almost immediately pushed again, falling back and bracing himself to hit the ground—but instead he hit flesh, and something caught him under the armpits. He glanced upward and found Elton looking down at him, and he smirked, licking blood from his lips as the blond shoved him upright to steady footing.

Korshunov shattered the barrier Elton had put up a moment before, and he burst the stone prison around the falcon's head into rubble with a flick of his wrist, freeing it to rush toward them again. Elton dropped another barrier around it, so close its wings battered the inside surface, and Nathan turned on Korshunov. With a burning beneath the skin of his arms, he reached forward, the slipping sensation flowing from his hands until he jerked them backward. Korshunov stumbled now, lashed by the unseen cords hauling him toward the ground by his wrists. Elton grunted behind Nathan, and his barrier broke again as he was forced to his knees by the appearance of a flock of sharp, fluttering sprites that ran thin wire in a tight cross-hatch over his body. The bird cried out, the furious beat of its wings blowing smoke and hot ash over them.

This was getting dicey. Korshunov was fighting his grip, Elton was now bleeding from the tight lines in his skin, and the falcon was fast approaching. Nathan's skin was burned; he was losing blood. He needed to end this.

The spirit at his back singed the fabric of his shirt as it drew close, but if he turned to face it, he would lose his grip on Korshunov.

Before he had to choose, a clear voice echoed through the courtyard from the hall steps. Cora's voice. In an instant, the sprites holding Elton scattered, disappearing into powder in the air, and the falcon reared, giving one final, piercing call before it flapped its massive wings and launched itself into the sky.

"No," Korshunov growled, his head whipping around to the girl running toward them. "No!"

Elton was on his feet again, and he threw a pair of paper talismans toward the Chaser, one fastening itself over his mouth to seal it shut and the other breaking into two to wrap around his arms and help drag him to the ground. Nathan held him fast, and Korshunov fell to his knees at their combined pull. He thrashed against them, rough screams of rage tearing from his throat even through the muffling of the talisman. Cora put up her own orb of a barrier around him, stifling the noise, but he still pulled and jerked against his bindings so furiously that blood began to seep through the white sleeves of his shirt and pool into a stain that spread from the stapled-together flesh beneath his buttons. The three of them stood still and wary a few moments, until Korshunov seemed to wilt—whether from pure exhaustion or resignation, Nathan couldn't tell, but the boy slowly doubled over so his forehead touched the ground, his whole body trembling with each hiccupping breath.

He suddenly seemed very small.

As the Chasers returned to the square, they took Korshunov without question. One of them put him to sleep before he was freed from his bindings, and he was carried away from the courtyard in a rush.

"Are you guys okay?" Cora asked, moving closer to touch both of them on the arm as if to check they were solid. "I heard the commotion, and Marquez didn't want me to come out, but when I saw it was Korshunov—" She stopped and sighed. "Are you okay?"

"Fine; fine," Nathan promised her, though he definitely had burns on a good portion of his body. He glanced up the hall steps to watch Korshunov's handlers until they disappeared through the doors with him. They'd turned him in to Ray personally back in New Orleans. And now he'd shown up here, with power clearly beyond the capability of his body? Someone was going to have a lot to answer for.

Behind him, a woman cleared her throat. When Nathan turned to look, a handful of other Chasers stood by, each one of them looking weary and stained.

"People are going to come pouring out of that building in about ten more seconds," she said with a quick glance toward the Magistrate Hall. "It's probably better if you three aren't here when...people that aren't us show up."

Nathan hesitated. He recognized the faces frowning at him; these Chasers had been at the protests as often as he had—probably longer. He'd stared down more than one of them more than once, but they had shown more restraint than he'd expected. Perhaps these ones weren't so bad, after all.

"He was a Chaser, too," Elton said, tilting his head back toward the hall. "Take notes. And be better."

He tapped Nathan on the arm to urge him away, so Nathan followed, helped to hurry along by Cora's hand grasping tight onto his.

26

Nathan slept for almost a solid three days straight. Elton wasn't much better. Cora had been tired, herself, but she didn't have the luxury of a days-long nap. So she'd made Thomas promise to patch Nathan and Elton up properly, kissed him briefly goodbye, and returned to the Magistrate Hall to get back to work.

It turned out an all-out magic battle in the street caused a lot of paperwork. The protests had died down, for now, but there was a lot— *a lot*—of yelling at the next Magistrate sitting. They'd come up with some explanation they thought the regs would buy, and that evening, Cora had seen news reports on T.V. about a gas leak downtown and many people reporting mass hallucinations. It sounded sketchy as hell to her, but there were people out there who still thought the government didn't have aliens at Area 51, so she guessed some people would believe anything.

The Council had put Korshunov under absolute lockdown after what he'd done, and he had apparently talked to them—whether that had been entirely voluntary or not, Cora didn't ask. Hubbard's involvement was exposed, his reputation ruined. For all that mattered, now that he was dead. At least they would have the chance to fill his spot with someone better.

Korshunov himself had been charged with too many crimes to list.

He'd even been connected to a string of missing witches in the Boston area. Most of them were assumed dead, now, since they'd found the remains of a few victims in dumpsters on the outskirts of the city. Why he'd done it was anyone's guess. There was talk of having him hanged.

At the meeting, the Council had only told the Magisters that Hubbard and a few others had been involved in "despicable human experiments," but in private, Marquez had given Cora the details with a somber frown on her face.

"When they took that boy to the hospital," the Councilor said with her hands around a cup of coffee, "they found that he'd had his entire chest cut open only days before. It's a miracle he was able to get out of bed at all, let alone make it to the hall on his own and do the sort of magic he did. He'd had things...inserted into his chest cavity. Groundings, but—also other things. *Parts* of other people. Apparently he volunteered. The Chasers found them in the facility Hubbard and the others have been maintaining in Ontario. They were still alive. If you could call it that. On life support. It seems they had been trying to find a way to use *people* as a grounding, or as some sort of...amplifier, or..." She trailed off, shaking her head. "Monstrous."

"Jesus," Cora breathed. She folded her hands in her lap and leaned back in her chair; the smell of her coffee turned her stomach now. "Did they...you know, get that stuff...*out* of him?"

"He's recovering, I'm told. But he won't be leaving a Magistrate facility for the rest of his life. However long that may be."

"We turned him in to the Magistrate in New Orleans," Cora said, a furrow in her brow. "How did Hubbard get hold of him again? The Magister in New Orleans knew what he'd done."

"The paperwork was filed for a transfer to his home office in Ottawa. And Hubbard was a senior Magister; it's likely he simply told the official in New Orleans what was happening, and there was nothing to be done."

"Great."

"There is one other thing that I thought you and our mutual friend should know," Marquez went on, waiting until Cora looked up at her. "One of Korshunov's eyes has also been altered. By a spell. They think he's able to use it to see Nathaniel Moore somehow. Some manner of divination, or tracking. There are specialists attempting to work out how to undo it, but there have also been suggestions that someone capable of knowing where Nathaniel Moore is at any given time is a resource worth holding onto. The Council is still deliberating, but it's moot unless the spell can be undone in the first place."

Cora grimaced and hugged her own elbows tight against her sides.

"I'm against keeping it, of course," Marquez assured her, a little more softly. "Even aside from the gruesomeness of such a spell, if we open the door to surveilling individual citizens, I hate to think where it would lead."

"Well, that's something," Cora murmured. She rubbed her thumbs over her arms and took a deep breath that hunched her shoulders. "They...aren't really going to hang him, are they?"

"You don't want them to?"

She frowned. "Part of me does. He's done terrible things. But at the same time...what kind of person can do those things to themselves? He's obviously...unwell. And Hubbard was using him. So I feel...kind of sorry for him, too. Nathan even decided not to kill him—twice. And he's got more cause than most people to want him punished. I think...I think that the Magistrate ought to show that it can *help* people like Korshunov. And maybe next time, they can help them *before* they do the kinds of things Korshunov did, instead of weaponizing them."

Marquez watched her in silence for a few beats, and a faint smile touched her lips. "I wholly agree, Ms. Daniels."

That evening, Cora sat cross-legged on the bed in her hotel room, staring down at her phone with her cheeks mushed between her fists. This was a call she had to make—but also one she was afraid to make. Finally, she reached down with one hesitant hand, unlocked her phone, and tapped Thomas's name in her recent calls.

"Hey," she said a little too loudly when he answered. "Are Nathan and Elton up?"

"At the moment. Do you need something?"

"I just...will you guys come meet me? All three of you? I feel like...I want to have a drink. With everyone."

Thomas paused. "Is everything all right?"

"Yeah. Yeah, yeah. Just. Will you come? I know you're fasting, but I'll...buy you a seltzer, or something."

"Of course. I'll tell them."

"There's a place around the corner from my hotel. I'll text you the address, and meet you in an hour?"

"Sure. See you then."

"Okay. See you then." Cora hung up the phone, then dropped it back onto the bed with a slow, puffing exhale. Okay.

Cora was the first to arrive at the bar, so she found an empty booth and sat facing the door, barely taking her eyes off of it until she saw Nathan appear. She lifted up from her seat to wave him and the others over, and once they all had drinks in front of them—Thomas settling for only a water—she reached her hands across the table and laid them flat, pressing her fingertips into the lacquered surface as if it would help stabilize her.

"Here it comes, darling," Nathan said, tilting his head toward the blond beside him, "the 'I suppose you're all wondering why I've gathered you here.'"

"What?" Cora said, snapped out of her tension. "Shut up. This is serious."

"Sorry, my love—sorry. I'll put on my serious face for you." But he didn't even try to hide his smile as he took a sip from his drink.

"Is something going on, Cora?" Elton asked, as usual, doing a much better job of looking serious.

She took a deep breath, then did her best to summarize everything that had happened at the Magistrate Hall over the last few days—what Marquez knew about Korshunov, how she and others expected a rage of backlash from the community once word got out that the Magistrate was apparently so inept it was not only incapable of stopping its own people from committing war crimes, but it was simply unaware of them to begin with. She told them that Marquez, and now Councilors Young and Martin, were beginning a push for more regulations, more supervision, accountability, transparency. More training for Chasers. Changes that would make a real difference. Despite everything that had happened, there was a lot of good news to share.

When she'd finished, she paused, looking around the table at the three men listening intently to her. The next part would be harder to get out.

"All that to say, that...Marquez has offered me a job. A real one. Me and Eli, actually. Not—the same job, but like—you know. Jobs, plural. And I think...I want to take it. She says she can handle fixing my record for school, and I can do this as my required service until that's up, so..." She trailed off, glancing between their faces, but her gaze settled uncertainly on Nathan. "So I think I'm going to stay here."

Nathan watched her quietly for a few beats, then set down his glass and reached out to lay his hand over hers. "You'll be incredible, my love."

"But I don't want to never see you again," she said in a rush, her cheeks warming as she realized how pathetic it sounded.

"Cora," he scolded. "I'm offended at the insinuation. You think that something as bureaucratic as a Magistrate job could keep me away from you?" Nathan glanced over at Elton and leaned over until his shoulder rested against the larger man's. "What do you think, darling? Are you interested in a bit of under-the-table work for a young, aspiring Magister?"

"It couldn't hurt to have another friend on the inside," Elton agreed, and his faint smile finally relaxed her shoulders into a slump.

"Don't think I won't put you both to work," she said with a grin.

"I intend to remain at your service until the very end of my days, Cora." Nathan lifted his glass again and tinked it against hers. "You'll be on the Council yourself in no time."

"Maybe let's not go that far," Cora said with a laugh, but she matched Nathan's smile as she took a drink of her beer.

Nathan drained his glass, then looked into it with a heavy sigh. "Darling, would you look at that. Come and get another with me, hm?" He pulled the blond by his sleeve when he frowned, but when he tilted his lifted eyebrows across the table toward Thomas, Elton seemed to understand, and they both scooted out of the booth.

Cora mouthed a quick "thank you" to Nathan, and he winked over his shoulder at her as they made their way to the bar.

Thomas had his elbows on the table, hands loosely cupped around his glass and eyes on the surface of the water as if he expected a dinosaur to ripple it any moment. Cora hesitated a moment, then nudged his elbow with hers.

"Did you know," she began when he looked up at her, "that there are usually, like, eight or ten direct flights from Philadelphia to Boston every single day?"

"I did not," he answered evenly, but she saw the uncertainty in his eyes.

"Well I do. I also know that it's less than a six hour drive." She shrugged. "Or, you know, there's probably real estate up for grabs in a big city like this. Commercial rentals, you know. I heard there's a lot of new age type shopping in South Philly, but not many places to get really good stuff witches need, you know?"

"Cora—"

"There are lots of options," she interrupted him. "That's all I'm saying."

"I had...assumed that once you were out of the house, and things were reasonably back to normal, that our—time together," he said carefully, not quite meeting her eyes, "would be...a pleasant footnote."

"A footnote? Christ, Thomas, sweep a girl off her feet."

"I just meant—"

"Is that what you want this to be? A pleasant footnote?"

"No," he said immediately, then frowned as though he was embarrassed by the swiftness of his own answer. "No," he tried again. "But especially if you're going to be taking a job with the Magistrate, you'll have so much work to do here—important work—and I don't want you to have to be tied to—"

"Someone like me," she finished along with him, smiling at the pouty scowl he turned on her. "Give it a rest. Even people who work for the Magistrate get days off, and I want to spend mine making bread in a shitty colonial kitchen, okay? Or would you rather I just leave it on the doorstep so you don't have to look at me?"

Thomas smiled then, just a little, and shook his head. "I would miss your terrible singing."

"Terr—you're terrible," she laughed, tugging him a little closer by his sleeve. "Kissing isn't against the fasting rules, is it?"

"Not so long as it doesn't cause me any impure thoughts."

"Hm, better not, then," she murmured, but she smiled and pressed a long kiss to his lips anyway.

"Disgusting!" Nathan's loud voice interrupted them, jolting Thomas away from her as he and Elton returned to their places. "*Mister* Proctor,

I did hope you might be able to show some *decorum* in public, but it seems I've placed the bar rather too high."

"You had an extra shot while you were up there, didn't you?" Cora teased, but Nathan only lifted his refilled glass of liquor.

"Irrelevant." He glanced around the table at the others, nodding toward them until they lifted their own glasses as well. Elton didn't even seem that reluctant to humor him. "There's much left to be done to make the prospect of being governed bearable, but for now, here's to taking steps. To seeing the world in all its tainted glory and loving it still."

Cora laced her fingers with Thomas's under the table, and she smiled across the table at Nathan and Elton over their clinking glasses. Everything was only going to get better from here.

27

Nikita opened his eyes, but his body wouldn't move. He squinted against the harsh fluorescent light above him, unable to focus on any details of the stark room. He was restrained—the straps of the hospital bed had been pulled snug at his wrists, ankles, and across his middle—but even if they hadn't, his muscles were too dull and heavy to lift. They must have given him something.

His head hurt. He tried to shift, tried to call out. Even breathing was difficult—something was around his neck. He couldn't tilt his head enough to see it, but the weight of the metal gave it away. A dampening collar.

A flash hit him of Moore, sitting on a plush chair with a bowl of noodles in his lap, laughing at something Nikita couldn't hear. He was still there. Still free. Still laughing. Still.

Whatever had been put into Nikita's body pressed him down into the bed and drooped his eyes. He didn't have the strength.

The next time he flinched and blinked himself awake, two men were standing over him—one in a lab coat, one in a suit. He didn't even get the chance to try to speak. When his gaze met the eyes of the man in the suit, everything went black.

The students at the academy lurked in clusters, faceless whispers hissing in his ears as he walked by. They knew he didn't belong. They laughed at him, turned their backs on him, sneered at him and looked down on him. His grandmother's voice was in his ear, demanding he be better than he was and all the while knowing he never would.

He was a child, hunkered in the corner of a drafty apartment. His grandmother's venomous rage seemed to shake the room, but no matter where he hid, her gnarled, grasping hands reached for him, clawing at the wood floor by his feet or scratching into the faded wallpaper of the corner. He wanted to scream, but he didn't dare. Her fingernails scraped his skin til it bled, but he couldn't make himself small enough. He spent an eternity under the bed, arms covering his head to muffle his whimpering sobs. It would be worse if she heard them.

Nikita woke in a cold sweat. Someone helped him turn his head so he didn't choke on his own vomit as it spilled into a waiting bowl. His whole body ached. When he'd thrown up everything inside him, they left him in sweat-soaked blankets to fall into a dreamless sleep that felt like a blessing.

A flickering sound in the room made him flinch. The light in the room never changed, so he had no idea if an hour had passed, or a week. The bulbs above him were still too bright for him to get a good sense of his surroundings beyond the beeping machine at his side, but the figure that stood near the foot of his bed was clear to him. Moore. Nikita didn't even have enough fight in him to pull against his restraints.

"I heard how you found me," Moore said, soft and calm in the droning buzz of the room. He took a step closer, tilting his head as he leaned to get a better look at Nikita's blind side. "It sounds like impressive magic. And such a cost—you're nothing if not determined, little bird."

Nikita exhaled as evenly as he could manage, teeth clenched tight and fingers digging weakly into the hard bed.

"They're trying to sort out what to do about it," Moore went on. "How to undo what you did. But I think I know the simplest way. Can you guess?"

"You think," Nikita said, the dry rasp of his own voice foreign to him, "that I want to stay like this? To watch you...every day? While I rot in this room?"

"Oh," Moore said with sadistic delight in his voice, "now when you put it that way, perhaps I ought to let you keep it." He leaned against the bed and drew his fingertips lightly over Nikita's cheek. He paused with his thumb pressing into the boy's cheekbone. "But no. I think better to sever our tender connection now."

"Just take it," Nikita hissed, unable to keep his breath from hitching.

Moore bent down close to Nikita's ear and dropped his voice to a whisper. "This will be the last time you see me, little bird. And you ought to hope it's the last time I see you."

His palm flattened over Nikita's milky eye, and in an instant, a searing pain blew straight through to the back of his skull. He couldn't help the scream that tore out of him as his limbs jerked reflexively against their straps. By the time his brain recovered enough for him to open his remaining eye, he was alone again. A soft, pathetic hiccup fell from his throat as his body sank more heavily into the bed. He was done.

Finally done.

EPILOGUE

Cora placed the lid back on the cauldron hung over the fire, straightening herself with a soft grunt. She was getting too old for this. It was an inconvenient tradition, cooking directly in the broad fireplace, but at least it helped keep the house warm while the snow was falling outside. She'd had a pair of trusted contractors come in years ago to fix up the innards of the old colonial—plumbing, wiring, things like that—but the living space was kept exactly the same. Except for the new fridge. She'd decided that was an acceptable update and left the root cellar for things like pickled vegetables and jams.

The familiar floorboards creaked under her feet as she made her way across to the study with her warm mug of tea in both hands. The house was pleasantly quiet now that Evan and his family had left—Cora liked his kids, but tweens could be so noisy they rattled the foundations. Still, it was nice to sometimes have an excuse to air out a couple of the guest rooms.

Cora had met Evan almost forty years ago, when Nathan and Elton had tracked him down in San Jose. He was a reg, but he'd been told stories by his grandmother about his grandfather the witch—Evan had apparently always put it down to an excuse the old woman gave for why she'd been run out on. Little did he know that it was simply down to Nathan's personality flaws.

They got along well very quickly, once he'd adjusted to the surprise of meeting Nathan himself. Now that he was married and had children of his own, he occasionally came by for a long weekend holiday. Nathan kept in touch with him, too, but he hadn't joined them for this particular visit. It had been a few months since she'd heard from Nathan and Elton at all, actually. But that wasn't that unusual.

Now that Cora was nearing sixty, they were both positively ancient—as she reminded them frequently. She had been settled into her work for some time now, so she required very little in the way of "under-the-table" favors from them these days. She'd been made the Magister of Yuma County, Arizona almost fifteen years ago, and most of her work had been community-building and statute changes. She'd spent decades communicating with Eli in Philadelphia, coordinating proposals and planning arguments. By now, she was happy to take lots of long vacations up to Salem and let her younger someday-replacement learn the ropes in her absence.

Things really were better now. Reforms had been put into place all across North America that made it more possible for people to go to the Magistrate for help, not just punishment. Cora hadn't done it alone, of course, but in her time, enough newer, younger people had taken office that real change could be made. She was proud of the progress they'd made.

Even Korshunov—whom she had requested updates on now and then—had been put into a hospital where he could be treated like a human being and helped to sort through the absolute mess his mind must have been. He'd died of health complications a few years ago, she was told, but before that, he'd even been allowed to remove his dampening collar during the day. The nurse had told Cora that he would often sit in the facility's small garden, summoning tiny water sprites and allowing them to rest in his palm. He never talked much, and he certainly never communicated with Cora directly. But she told herself that he'd done as well as could be expected, in the end.

She took her regular seat on the pillowed sofa by the bookshelf and blew on her tea before taking a sip.

The quiet wasn't always nice.

On the shelf across from the couch, a small stand drew her eye. Thomas's wand—his *key of the work*, she thought with a smile—sat perched on a pair of short wooden prongs, where it had been for the last twenty years, untouched except for the occasional dusting.

He'd been very calm in the days and weeks before his death. As the appointed day drew closer, Cora had begun to press him for potential options, loopholes, workarounds—anything. He wouldn't hear of it. He had a deal, he said. Bathin had kept up his end. He'd helped and served him countless times over the previous thirty years. It was time for Thomas to pay him. So, he focused on getting his affairs in order.

When the day came, Cora had laid curled under his arm, determined to stay awake until the last moment. But she'd dozed off while he softly stroked her hair, and when she'd woken up, he was gone.

Nathan and Elton had come the week before, and they helped her place him in his reserved space in the family crypt. They'd stayed for days afterward, as well, until she'd assured them that she was just fine and only wanted to return to work. It had only been partly a lie.

Thomas had left her the house, since he had no other family, and she hadn't considered selling it, of course—this was where he was. It was where Adelina was. It would probably be where Cora stayed, too, when that time came. That suited her just fine.

She had finished her tea and was just about to go check on the cauldron bubbling tonight's stew in the kitchen when her phone blipped sharply on the coffee table. She checked the screen and smiled to see a message from Nathan, but her brow furrowed into a frown of confusion as she scanned the text.

Do you remember that guy you asked us to look at, who they caught for human trafficking in Ohio?

Cora typed back, *What about him?*

The message barely showed sent when a heavy thump sounded from outside the porch. Cora hesitated, then set her phone down and walked to the front door. She jumped a little at the solid knock that followed, but she reached for the knob and pulled the door open when she reached it.

An unconscious man—at least, she hoped he was only unconscious—tumbled across her threshold in a heap. When she raised her eyes, she saw two familiar men she hadn't seen in decades. Nathan had his forearm leaned against the doorframe near his head, tilting a bright smile at her. For a moment, she thought she was back in that crappy hotel room in Arizona, being barged in on by a man far too young to be who she thought he was. Elton stood next to him, hands in his pockets, also looking much more strapping and youthful than the last time she'd seen him. She looked between them once more with a hand pressed to her heart.

"Oh, you didn't," she whispered.

Nathan stepped over the collapsed body and into the house. "Happy birthday, my love."

She moved back on instinct as Elton dragged the poor man fully inside and shut the door behind him. "It's not my birthday yet."

"Soon enough; soon enough. And it's a big one, isn't it? You're all set to retire, aren't you?"

"Yes," she agreed warily.

"Don't you want to fully enjoy it?"

"Nathan, there's no way—Elton, you let him talk *you* into this?"

The blond gave a small, helpless shrug and nodded down at the body. "They were going to hang him anyway. And you know how long people stay on death row. All the appeals. Years and years. Wasted," he added with a faint lift of his eyebrows.

Nathan circled around behind her and paused to touch her thick braid of grey-streaked hair. "Let your replacement take the reins now. You've earned yourself a long retirement. Let's have some fun—the three of us."

She hesitated, holding her hands tightly to her stomach in an attempt to keep the fluttering there from showing on her face. "Nathan, I..."

He laid gentle hands on her shoulders and leaned down close to her, his murmur warm against her cheek. "Come along, my love. Now repeat after me."

ABOUT THE AUTHOR

T.S. likes to write about what makes people tick, whether that's deeply-rooted emotional issues, childhood trauma, or just plain hedonism. She tells stories about real people who live in less-real worlds full of werewolves, witches, demons, and the occasional alien.

Born in the South, T.S. started writing young and now writes while working as a Paralegal. In her down time, she plays video games, watches true crime documentaries, and spends time with her husband, daughter, and two cats.

Made in the USA
Middletown, DE
26 January 2023

21907278R10139